CHAPTER 1

I hate today.

Which doesn't bode well, since it's only eight thirty in the morning.

This is par for the course with my life right now, since the past three weeks haven't particularly been my favorite either. Before that—which feels like ages ago—I was feeling like I was on the right path. Like everything I had planned for myself was happening. And I actually remember thinking, "Life can't get any better." Clearly, I jinxed myself.

Because my life is not on track. Not even close.

Lately, every morning I wake up with hopes that this will be the day when things will look up for me. The day my life will take a turn for the better and I'll get myself back on track. Apparently, today is not that day.

Right now, I'm sitting in an air-conditioned office, holding a piece of paper in my hands, staring at the words in front of me and trying to make sense of it all. The top of the paper, in bold lettering, says, "CT Anderson Bank," and underneath it, "Holly Murphy—Supervisor Assessment."

Under that are a whole bunch of words I can't believe I'm reading. Words like "too controlling" and "micro-managing" and "not a team player." It's all there, in Times New Roman, eleven-point type. Coincidentally, these are some of the words Nathan — my ex-fiancé — used when he called off our wedding nearly three weeks ago. He even used the words "not a team player" — whatever that's supposed to mean. And this was all only a little over two months before we were to marry.

Way to kick me when I'm down, Life.

"Holly?" My boss, Marie, asks, and I look up to find concerned eyes peering at me across a modern, pale-colored wooden desk. Marie's A-line blond bob barely moves as she tilts her head in my direction. She clears her throat. "I know it's difficult," she says, her eyes moving down to the piece of paper I'm grasping.

My eyes follow suit. "Right," I say in response. I could think of some other words to describe the situation besides *difficult*. Some very *colorful* words.

"I know this is not what you need to hear right now after . . . uh . . . everything," she says. "The timing sucks."

She's got her pity eyes on again. I've gotten this look a lot lately — the past three weeks, to be precise. Not just from Marie, but from everyone. My friends, my dad, my coworkers, my cake designer, my venue manager, my photographer. The pity from the last two only went so far, though. Not far enough to give me my deposit back, those jerkfaces.

I let out a big breath, blowing the air out so hard that my lips make an involuntary raspberry noise, like a horse.

just A name

BECKY MONSON

Just a Name
Copyright © 2018 Becky Monson V2
Cover Art by Angela Talley Smith

OTHER BOOKS BY BECKY

To Robin, Molly, Brenda, and Melanie. My Florida gals. Thanks for all the writing material. Dinners with you are some of my favorite times ever.

JUST A NAME

"Listen," says Marie as she picks up her copy of the report. "The assessment did say you were . . . um," she looks down, scanning it, ". . . organized. So that's good, right?" She looks up from the paper with a bright smile, as if this is supposed to lift my spirits.

"Sure," I say blankly. I believe Nathan said the same thing when he broke up with me.

I'm an evil overlord with a side of organized. Go, me.

The truth is, I'm blindsided by this. I don't see these things about myself. Not the controlling, micromanaging, not-a-team-player part, at least. I never thought I was a perfect manager, but I thought I was doing pretty well. Sure, I sometimes have to nudge my small team of five, like when I have to get on Sara and Sarah (or "the Sarahs" as I call them) for taking too many breaks. But how is that micromanaging or controlling? That's just doing my job.

I never thought I was the perfect girlfriend either, but I was blindsided with Nathan, too. I thought we had a good thing going there. Very symbiotic.

Marie clears her throat and sets the paper down and then plants her elbows on the desk, resting her chin on intertwining fingers. She sighs, a huge audible sigh. "Holly, I'm not saying the manager position won't be yours."

My shoulders drop. There's another kick in the gut. This is what I've been working toward, what I've wanted all along since starting at CT Anderson Bank. A chance to be on the executive team — to run the entire call center instead of the small group I currently manage, the team that apparently hates me.

Mike, the current manager of the call center, told Marie he's planning on leaving sometime this summer. Marie shared this bit of info with me right before Nathan called off the wedding. Back when my life was on track. The good old days.

"I'm confident the executive team will want you in there once Mike officially leaves," Marie continues, probably after seeing my look of despair.

"But," I hold up the supervisor assessment by the corner, because it's the super-huge *but* in the room.

"But," she repeats with a nod to the paper, "I think you can do better."

I close my eyes. The feeling of tears pooling behind them makes my nose tingle.

That's the real problem here. I don't even know what I'm doing wrong.

Blinking back the tears and opening my eyes, I place the stupid paper in my lap. Reaching up, I wrap a tendril of my thick red hair around my index finger and tug lightly, a habit of mine ever since I can remember.

"I understand," I say after a few beats of silence.

"Do you?" she asks.

"No, not really."

She laughs in an ironic way. "Holly, I think you need to relax. You need to let go of the reins a little. Give your team some wiggle room. It's like what I have to do with my teenagers. I can't keep hovering over them, like one of those helicopter parents. I have to let them get out there and figure things out for themselves."

"I don't hover," I say, sounding appalled, abandoning the hair tugging. Marie's eyes move from mine to the paper in my hands, which claims that I do, in fact, hover.

We sit there for a moment, silence surrounding us except for the soft hum of the air conditioner and Marie tapping her fingers on her desk. The drumming noise bounces around in my head. *Drum, drum, drum. Holly's a control freak. Drum, drum, drum. Everyone hates me.*

Marie's eyes roam over my face. "When's the last time you took a vacation?"

"Huh?" I ask, caught off guard by the question.

"A vacation," she says. "When was the last one?"

"Um . . ." I trail off, trying to think of the last time I went out of town. "I think Nathan and I went to Miami for a weekend a couple months ago."

I'm just throwing this out there. I can't remember the last time we went down there together. When we first started dating, we took little weekend getaways to Miami often since flights from Orlando to Miami are cheap and Nathan's folks live there. But then life got busier, and then there was a wedding to plan . . . and we kept finding reasons not to go.

"I don't mean a weekend thing—I mean actual time off from work," she says.

"I did have that stomach bug last year," I offer.

"That doesn't count. I mean actual vacation time," she says, accentuating the last three words.

"Well, I was going to be taking a *big* vacation, but . . ." I let out a high-pitched, uncomfortable laugh.

"Right . . ." she trails off, obviously at a loss for words

here. My canceled wedding and subsequent canceled honeymoon are an awkward topic for pretty much everyone. She pushes her laptop to the side. "Why don't you take a vacation during that time anyway? Give yourself a chance to unwind. Take a break from everything. You already have the time off."

The thing is, this is the same advice I've been given by nearly everyone already. Including Nathan. He told me I could have the plane tickets for our honeymoon to London and Paris—like that was some consolation prize or something. Like his ticket with the name Nathan Jones on it would be of any use to me now. Didn't he realize you can't change the name? I thought about telling him and letting him have the ticket so he could at least cash it in. But I didn't. I do feel mildly guilty about that.

"I don't know, Marie. I think it would be better for me to stay here. I'm not sure I should be alone during that time. I need . . . I need things to be normal." I fidget with the cuff of my button-down shirt.

"I understand. I do," she says, with a few quick nods of her head. I love this about Marie. She's always been a bit mama-bird toward me since she became my boss. I latch onto it, because I didn't have much of a mom for most of my life.

She leans back in her seat, propping her chin on her steepled fingers. "I read an article the other day," she says. "It was in the *Harvard Business Journal* and it was about how Americans don't take enough vacations."

"Okay," I say, drawing out the word.

"Yes." She dips her chin once. "Did you know that working all the time and never taking any vacation can affect your work life? It's actually been proven it can hinder productivity."

"I did not know that," I say, wondering where she's going with this.

"I'll forward you the article and I want you to read it. And I want you to take some time off. Doctor's orders," she says, even though she's not remotely a doctor.

"But, Marie," I say, my voice taking on a somewhat defensive tone, "shouldn't I worry about fixing this first?" I motion toward the paper now in my lap.

She shakes her head. "It's not just about that. It's about you taking care of yourself. Plus, I think if you take some time for you and step away from it," she points at the assessment, "you'll be able to figure things out—maybe see things with a clearer vision."

"I don't think—"

"Holly," she holds up a hand to stop my protest. "You never took any time off after . . . um . . . everything," she says, gingerly referring to my canceled wedding. "And as your boss, and someone who is genuinely concerned about you, I think you need this. You need a vacation. You need to *live* a little."

I sigh deeply. "Well, I suppose I could take a few days off and get things sorted around my condo."

Not that I have anything to sort there. I did all that already. I thought it would be therapeutic to get rid of everything that was Nathan's—purging him from my life. I kept the couch we bought for the condo we were going to live in after the wedding. I kept the condo too. Mostly because neither of those fit into the box I brought to Nathan, and also, despite the memories both will invoke, I want them. Even if the mortgage on the condo—a high-rise in downtown Orlando within walking distance from work—is going to pinch a little.

"No," Marie says, her voice stern. "You need to take a vacation—a real one. Go somewhere fun. Why don't you get a group of friends together and do one of those last minute deals? You could go next week, even." I look up to see Marie's eyes twinkling at me with all the possibilities.

I feel the blood drain out my face. Next week? "I don't think I could get something planned that fast."

"Then don't make plans," she says. "Find a location and get a plane ticket. And probably a hotel. The rest will fall into place."

I just realized this woman, as supportive as she's been to me, doesn't know me at all. I don't fly by the seat of my pants. I like plans. I like making them in advance and following them. I couldn't just hop on a plane and go somewhere. I'm not impulsive. I'm not a ride-or-die kind of girl. I don't want to ride *or* die.

"I'm not sure I could swing it," I say.

"Well, make it happen," she says with a quick nod. "I want a vacation request on my desk. I'll give you a week."

"A week?" I echo, incredulity in my tone.

"Yes. I'm telling you this as your boss and your friend."

"But my team—"

JUST A NAME

"I have full confidence you'll figure it all out," she cuts me off, a determined look on her face.

I want to say something, anything that will get her off this path, but I know that look. Once Marie is set on something, she can't be talked down. It's best if I just let it lie for now.

Marie dismisses me, and I give her a meager smile—it's all I can muster under the circumstances—and then say goodbye as I do the walk of shame back to my office. It's not really an official walk of shame, per se, because no one besides Marie knows what just happened. My team took the assessment separately and were asked not to talk about it. They don't even know about the meeting this morning. But it feels like a walk of shame to me.

I enter my office and shut the door behind me. I look around the space, the one I worked so hard to earn after being in a cubicle for so long. I like the simplicity of it all—not a lot of color, just clean and pristine, how I like it. I plop down in my gray ergonomic chair and roll myself up to my desk. Then I move my pen holder slightly to the left of my phone because it looked off. Then I move it back again, and that looks off too. Then I consider throwing the thing across the room because everything in my life feels askew right now.

I sit back and close my eyes. Through the thin walls of my office, I can hear faint sounds of chatter and the clicking of fingers typing on keyboards. I hear this every day, but today it feels … different.

This is not how this day was supposed to go. Instead of

coming in this morning and finding out everything is going well with my team and I'm on track for the manager position, I find out my team hates me, the manager position is up in the air, and my boss is now hellbent on me taking a vacation so I can "clear my head" and "figure things out."

This will not do. What needs to be fixed here is my team. I can't exactly fix how they think of me when I'm off at some resort, sitting on the beach and drinking a margarita, can I? No, I need to be here showing them I do know how to manage them, and I'm not all the things they think about me. And anyway, I don't even like margaritas.

I need to buy some time. Some time to get my team situation fixed, and then … then after that I can go on a vacation or whatever. But how do I fix this?

When I was younger, my dad would always say, "You can't climb the mountain just by sitting and staring at the base." Of course, he also used to say, "People will disappoint you, but pizza is forever."

I sit up straight in my seat. I may have been able to scrub Nathan out of my life, but I can't exactly do that with my team—not if I want this promotion. I'm not going to sit back. I'm going to climb that mountain.

And maybe get some pizza.

CHAPTER 2

"Holly?" a deep voice says from behind me as I wait for my order at the Lava Java, a quaint coffee shop across the street from my office building.

Oh, please not now. Not now. Not. Now.

What's next? A rainstorm? Actually, that's highly likely with the smell of rain in the air, the rumble of thunder in the distance, and the ominous clouds I saw as I walked over here. Typical springtime in Orlando.

I turn around and find Logan Palmer standing there in dark jeans, a fitted black T-shirt, and flip-flops. Or, in other words, his standard outfit. The T-shirt color can vary from day to day, but that's about it. His light-brown hair is disheveled, and the beginnings of stubble appear around his jaw.

"Logan," I say, feeling like a big chunk of ice just landed in my belly.

So far this morning, I've found out my team hates me—and I could miss out on one of the biggest opportunities of my career because of it—and my boss wants me to run away on some crazy trip before I can even fix it.

And now? Now I run into Nathan's best friend, roommate, and business partner, who has never liked me, and I'm quite sure is one of the reasons things ended like they did. The way Nathan broke it off reeked of Logan, actually.

"How . . . are you?" he asks, his fingers extending and then clenching into fists at his sides. Even with my average height and three-inch heels he has to peer down at me, his sea-blue eyes searching my face as he does. He looks . . . nervous.

Nervous is not a word I would use for Logan Palmer. Standoffish, brooding, apathetic, and dismissive, sure. Also, maybe some more colorful words . . . like a particular one referring to a donkey. But definitely not nervous. It's probably because this is the first time we've seen each other since Nathan and I broke up, and he's not sure how to act toward me. To be honest, I'm feeling a little nervous myself, but that's not an uncommon feeling for me to have around Logan.

This Logan standing in front of me now, with all the hand fidgeting and eye blinking, is not at all what I was expecting when I saw him again. I had hoped to *never* see him again after Nathan and I broke up because I figured when I did, he'd have some sort of crap-eating grin on his face. Or some kind of smug look, since Logan isn't one to smile all that much. He never said aloud how much he hated Nathan and me together, but he didn't have to. No, he made that pretty obvious with all the glares and eye rolls.

"I'm good," I finally answer him, keeping my words to a

minimum. This is a lie, of course. He's the cherry on top of my day-from-hell sundae.

"That's good," he says, now tapping a hand on his thigh. A grumbling and fizzing sound erupts from the espresso machine only a few feet away from us, and not long after, the scent of freshly brewed coffee grounds wafts our way.

"And you?" I ask, although I don't really care. What I need to do is keep searching my phone for articles on how to make my employees like me. Which was what I was doing before Mr. Stick-Up-His-Butt interrupted me.

So far, all the articles I've found require too much work, so that's why I'm settling for the next best thing to help me win my team's affections: bribery. That's why I'm at the Lava Java—a place I haven't graced with my presence in three weeks—to get coffee and scones for my team.

"I'm doing good," Logan says, still tapping his hand on his leg. "Just working," he adds, giving a quick nod over at a booth in the corner of the coffee shop.

"Right," I say.

And that would be the reason I haven't been to the Lava Java—a place I used to frequent nearly every day before Nathan and I broke up. Because Logan works here. Well, he doesn't work-work here, he's just taken up residence here, working from his laptop in the corner booth that's basically been permanently reserved for him. I'm pretty sure there are imprints of his backside in the fake leather seat.

In the beginning it was him and Nathan working here because their apartment—which is only a quarter of a mile away—was "stifling their creativity," or something. Eventually Nathan found his creativity back at the apartment, and Logan stayed here. He's on a first name basis with the staff and has a running tab. Nathan also had a tab—and I'm still on it. I did feel a bit guilty when the barista who took my order automatically charged it to him. But only a bit. I'll fix it next time I come in.

"I . . . haven't seen you in a while," Logan says.

"Well . . . you know," I say, not needing to finish that sentence.

"Yeah," he says. He reaches up and scratches the back of his neck.

I'm quite baffled by the Logan standing in front of me. He's so . . . not like *him*. Of course, it's not like we have had the most in-depth conversations for me to understand who he is. Most of what I know about Logan is from things Nathan has told me. Or things I garnered myself from the few actual conversations we've had.

"So . . . I . . . uh," he starts.

I pull my chin down, my head slightly tilted. "Logan," I say in a reproachful tone, cutting him off.

"Yeah?"

I purse my lips together, briefly. "We don't have to do this," I say, the words practically vomiting out of my mouth. I'm going to give the guy a break. An out, really. He doesn't need to feel obligated to talk to me. We don't need to salvage anything between us because there's no point. He's never liked me. Even with the whole both being raised by our dads thing, we couldn't find common ground. I tried and tried to get him to like me, since he's Nathan's best friend and I'm Nathan's fiancée. *Was.* I *was* Nathan's fiancée. I've been in the habit of calling myself that for so long, it's hard to stop.

"We don't have to do what?" he asks, his brows pulling inward.

"I—" I stop myself because I thought he would get where I was going since Logan's a pretty smart guy. He's developed a few genius apps, after all. Lucrative ones. But maybe those kinds of smarts don't translate well into emotional intelligence.

"Order ready for Holly!" a woman with dark brown dreadlocks yells out from the pickup counter.

"We don't have to do what?" Logan repeats, his tone tense, his stance more rigid.

I shake my head. It's only 9:30 in the morning and it already feels like the longest day of my life. Do I really want to get into this now?

"Never mind. Don't worry about it," I say, deciding I *don't* want to get into this right now. Maybe I'll just go back to not coming to this particular coffee shop and settle for the craptastic coffee they offer in the break room. I wouldn't even be here right now if it weren't for the bribing.

I take the few steps to the counter and grab the bag of scones and the container holding the drinks.

"Do you, uh . . . need help?" Logan asks, eyeing me as I try to balance everything.

"No, I'm good." I probably do need help, but I don't want it from Logan.

I offer him a goodbye over my shoulder and then head

toward the door, hoping against hope that I don't drop anything.

"Holly," a higher-pitched voice sing-songs my name as I walk down the hall toward the break room. All I wanted was a cup of coffee—I didn't have enough hands to grab myself one at the Lava Java, and I'm not going back there. Only one stinking cup of coffee. Is that too much to ask?

I let out a sigh as I stop in my tracks. I had hoped to avoid her today, but as I know all too well, Tiffany Brantley cannot be avoided. She's like a rash that won't go away.

Tiffany runs the fraud resolutions team and I run the complaint resolutions team—both of which are two small branches of the large customer service center that's currently being run by Mike Caldwell. *Mike*, who is planning on leaving this summer, and whose position I thought was in the bag until three hours ago.

I'm not even supposed to know about the job, but Marie told me in confidence because she knew how hard I've been working toward it. But now that's all up in the air, and I've got very little time to sort it all out. Especially since, at some point, Tiffany will find out about the job and she'll be all over it. Like a rash.

She approaches me and as usual she's in an impeccably tailored pantsuit—dark gray today—and not one bleached-blond hair out of place.

"Hello there, Holly," Tiffany says, bright-eyed and full

of spunk. I dig my fingernails into my palm, concentrating all my annoyance into them.

"What can I do for you, Tiffany?" I ask blandly. I want to get my coffee and then go back to my office where I can continue figuring out how to fix everything with my team. The bribery was well received, but I need to do more.

"I was wondering if your team is done with their report?" she asks, a condescending smile on her lips.

"Report?"

"Yes, my team needs the PFC report from your team. We can't do ours without yours," she says, again in her singsong voice. Gosh, I want to slap her. Right across her perfectly made-up face.

It takes me only a second to recall what she's talking about. The Possible Fraudulent Case Report, or PFC, was just established last week and Tiffany's team relies on my team for the initial reporting.

The fact that she's asking me for it means it's late.

I will not freak out.

"Oh, right," I say, willing myself to be cool and calm. "I'm sure it's done. Probably got lost in the shuffle or something. I'll check on it." My caffeine trip now abandoned, I head toward the large office where my team sits.

Now's my chance. I know we talked about this in our Friday meeting, so it might have been forgotten over the weekend. No big deal, honest oversight. Could happen to anyone.

I'm repeating this in my head because now is my opportunity to walk into my team's office and show them I can be cool about this. Normally I would have marched in there and given them the what-for — kindly, of course. But not today. Today I'll be calm and collected and my aura will ooze patience and understanding. I don't need to go on a vacation to have a fresh start with my team; we can start right now. I will just tell them kindly that they need to get the report done today and I will not freak out.

I will not freak out. I will not *freak out.*

"Hey, team," I say as I walk into the office where my team of five sits. The Sarahs — Sara, and Sarah — Avery, Jim, and Brad.

The room is fairly large and separated by cubicles. It has the typical fluorescent lighting most office buildings provide, but CT Anderson Bank saw fit to paint the walls in a bright shade of yellow. Like that might help them remember what color the sun is since they rarely get to see it working here. It smells of paper, over-worked desktop computer fans, and a hint of Axe body spray. That would be Jim's doing.

Brad is just getting off a call, which means I have my entire team's attention.

"So, hey," I begin. "I just talked to Tiffany, and she's looking for the PFC report that was due earlier today."

They're all looking at me blankly.

"You know, the Possible Fraudulent Case report? The one her team needs so they can do their report? We talked about it in the team meeting on Friday?"

Crickets.

Breathe in, Holly. Just breathe. You are cool. You are calm.

You're freaking collected.

"Oh!" Sara-without-an-h says, standing up from her chair. She twirls some of her blond-highlighted hair around her pointer finger.

"Yes?" I feel somewhat elated that at least one person remembered.

"Oh, wait," she says, and sits down, her chair making a puffing sound as she does. "Never mind."

"Um . . . okay, anyone else?" I ask, looking around the room at a bunch of vacant eyes.

"Is it, like, that report with the complaint cases that could be fraudulent?" Avery asks in her monotone voice as she stares up at me, her dark straight hair framing her face, her dark brown eyes full of irritation. She glares at me through her dark-rimmed glasses. This is her normal look. I can probably count how many times I've seen a genuine smile from Avery on one hand. Now that I think of it, I don't think I've ever seen her smile genuinely.

"Yes!" I say, a little over-excited. "That's right, Avery." I beam at her and she recoils back in response, her nose wrinkling like she's smelled something stinky.

Her response isn't all that unexpected since I've never beamed at anyone in this office, or anyone ever. I laugh awkwardly, wanting to be done here.

Think about the promotion, I tell myself. *You can do this.*

"So, can you guys get it done?" I ask, scanning the room.

"Yeah," Brad says, not even looking up from his computer. His hair is wild and his bangs are long and practically cover his eyes and I so badly want to clip them back with a bobby pin or something — or at least introduce him to some gel. Like me, he's a ginger and reminds me a lot of Ron from *Harry Potter*, but without the British accent that would help his awkwardness. "Can you just remind us what it is . . . uh . . . exactly?" he asks.

I pause, my eyes searching their faces. Surely they can't all have forgotten. I mean, I know it was on Friday, and they probably had Friday-brain. But I'm sure we talked about it.

Okay, Holly, this is an opportunity. The gods of job-promoting are shining down on you. Even though I know we've discussed this, I can use this to show my team that it's all good.

It's allllllll gooooooood.

I take a deep breath, then explain it to them once again.

"Any questions?" I ask after I've finished.

"Um, yeah," Jim, says from his cubicle. He's wearing his normal outfit of ratty jeans and a polo. He pushes his glasses up on his nose. "Could you repeat the last part? I think I missed it."

"Which part?"

"That one part, about the complaint stats . . . or something."

"So, *all* the parts," I say slowly.

He nods, as do the Sarahs. Brad has still not looked up from his computer, and the only person who looks like they understood anything is Avery. I start to breathe a little heavier, many emotions filling my belly as I stare at my team. Frustration being the top of that list of emotions. Murderous being the second.

Okay, calm down, Holly. I need to think of what I would

usually do right now, and do the opposite. *Deep, deep breath.*

What I normally would do is tell them how to do the report once again. This time I would probably use a more stern and frustrated tone. I see now that this might have been construed as hovering . . . or possibly micromanaging.

So therefore, I will not do any of that.

"Okay, so I think we're good here?" I say, knowing by their blank stares that we are *so* not good here. But I've explained the process twice, so they can figure it out. This is me not hovering.

"Wait, you're just going to leave?" Brad asks, his eyebrows knitted together.

"I ... have full faith in you," I say, not intending for that to come out as robot-like as it did.

I give them my best you've-got-this smile, and then I leave their office, shutting the door and feeling quite proud of myself.

Maybe this whole fixing my relationship with my team will be faster than I thought.

CHAPTER 3

"What the *H* is he doing here?" Quinn, my best friend of fourteen years, asks after following my gaze from our table to the entrance of Hester's, where, waiting by the hostess stand, are Nathan, my ex-fiancé, and Logan, who I've now seen twice in one day.

What the *H*, indeed.

I'd just been telling my friends about my not-so-great day and now it looks like my evening isn't going to be much better. I was about to ask my friends for advice about work before those two buttheads waltzed in. Of all the restaurants in Central Florida …

Every Monday night since I started working at my big girl job, I've met up with my friends for dinner at Hester's, a quaint restaurant within walking distance from the office, and also not far from my condo. Quinn, Bree, and Alex are here, but Thomas is late. As usual.

Not so long ago, Nathan and Logan used to be a fixture in our weekly meet-up, but they haven't been here on a Monday night since the breakup. At least, until tonight.

"Do you want me to punch him? I'll punch him, Hols. Just say the word," says Alex, who works at the bank with me. He's got his game face on, his bright blue eyes wide like he's ready for a throw-down.

"It's okay," I say. Although picturing muscly Alex take down lithe Nathan does make me a little happy.

It's a fairly crowded night at Hester's, and Nathan and Logan have yet to see us. Or they have and are pretending like they haven't. Either option works for me.

"Look at him," Bree says with a head bob toward the hostess stand. The martini in her hand almost looks ridiculous with her messy blond bun, cutoff jean shorts, and white tee. But in an odd way, it works for Bree. "Who does he think he is, coming into our territory?" She squints over at the hostess stand.

"Our territory?" I huff a laugh out my nose. "Yeah, you guys, this isn't *West Side Story*. Nathan can go where he wants." Let's be honest, I'm actually feeling a little territorial right now.

This isn't the first time I've seen Nathan since he called off our wedding. About a week after he ended things, I decided that maybe we could try being friends. I didn't want to lose him altogether, after all. He'd been such a big part of my life for so long. So we had coffee one day to discuss our friend-ness and it didn't go so well. Nathan was all gung-ho about the friend thing. I, on the other hand, after seeing his stupid face, felt the need to pour coffee on his head. I didn't, of course. I threw a muffin at him. It didn't have quite the effect I was going for. In hindsight, I may have rushed the whole friend thing.

Even now, two weeks post muffingate, seeing him standing at the front of Hester's waiting for a table, I'm not sure I want to be friends with him.

"This is a bunch of *S*," Quinn says, a whining tone in her voice. "Hester's is *our* place."

Quinn has recently taken a vow of non-swearing after a slip of the tongue nearly got her fired from her midday news reporting job. Said slip of the tongue also made her quasi-famous on the internet, but that's another story. So, because she's not really keen on losing her job, she's taken to cussing with initial letters and has required that we all do the same. Thomas is the only one who won't get on board.

"Last I looked, Hester's is a public place," I say, trying a hand at being impartial. "Anyone can come here." It's actually a very stereotypical place for late-twenty-somethings to hang out, with its kitschy décor, subpar food, and throwback turn-of-the-century music. And until three weeks ago, Nathan and Logan were able to hang out here on Mondays without any protest from my friends. Funny how a breakup can affect so many areas of your life.

"Yeah, but couldn't you have negotiated rights in the divorce?" Quinn asks, batting her dark blue eyes at me. She twists in her chair, tugging on the neck of the black knit dress she's wearing.

"There was no divorce, because there was no marriage. Thank you very much," I say reaching up and aligning my knife and fork next to my now empty wine glass. Quinn gives me an apologetic expression.

I glance over as Nathan looks my way and our eyes lock. Not in a romantic way. Just more of a what-the-hell-are-you-doing-here way. Or maybe that's what I'm trying to convey. Nathan, in his causal business attire and disheveled dark curly hair, appears as if he's both pleased and surprised to see me. Pleased because Nathan always carries a pleasant look on his face. He's the picture of cool, calm, and collected. Always the salesman, since that's what he does for the company he and Logan own. His look of surprise means he didn't expect me to be out tonight. I'm suddenly glad I am. No, I'm not crying on my couch and watching sappy movies while I eat ice cream. None of that ever happened. Well, the ice cream did. And of course I cried. But there were no sappy movies.

I see him whisper something to Logan, and then they both start walking toward our table. I could have sworn my face did not seem very welcoming, but Nathan was never good at reading my facial expressions.

"Crap, you guys, I made eye contact," I say in a stage whisper as Nathan and Logan navigate their way through the restaurant and toward the round table we're occupying.

"Why would you do that?" Quinn asks, her whole face scrunched up. She looks me up and down as if she's wondering if she knows me at all — even though she knows me better than anyone else. Maybe even better than the man who's walking toward us.

"Hey," Nathan says as he and Logan approach the table. Nathan rubs his hands together — something he's always done. And it signifies nothing, I've realized. He does it when he's happy, sad, anxious, or just whenever. Standing next to him, Logan pulls his phone out of his pocket and starts navigating around it one-handed with his thumb. I'm guessing he finds this awkward as well.

"Hello," I say, sounding ridiculously formal, like how you'd greet someone you don't really know. Like your manicurist. Or your OB/GYN. I wish that were the case — I'd love to be visiting my gynecologist instead of being here in this moment. But this is not an acquaintance; this is Nathan, and I know Nathan. I know everything about him. I know he's most ticklish on the back of his neck, just below his hairline. I know that, for breakfast, he likes his eggs over easy and his toast barely browned and slathered in butter. I know he has a constellation of moles on his back that look oddly like the Big Dipper. Besides his mom, I'm probably the only person in the world who could identify his body if ever there were a need. Which is mostly a morbid thought. Mostly.

Too controlling. Is that what he sees when he looks at me? Does he feel anything? Does he miss me? Is he relieved that we're no longer together? There's no way to tell because he just looks like Nathan. Easygoing as ever.

"Alex, Quinn, Bree," Nathan says, his head doing a quick bob as he acknowledges my friends.

They mutter replies back. I'm pretty sure Alex calls him a douchebag under his breath. Nathan doesn't notice.

"Holly," Logan says, giving me a quick lift of the corner of his mouth — or, his signature smile. Which isn't even a smile at all.

"Logan," I reply.

We stare at each other for a weird moment.

"Hi, Logan," Quinn pipes in, breaking the stare, her long eyelashes bat a few extra times as she peers up at him.

Once upon a time, Quinn had a thing for Logan. Maybe she still does. Logan's a pretty good looking guy, when his personality doesn't mess it up. Okay, fine. He's a really good looking guy. I can acknowledge that, even though he has never been anything but cold and aloof around me. Except for earlier today when he was awkward and weird. Currently he's all back into that smelling-a-fart expression he usually has around me and my friends.

Nathan and I tried to set up Logan and Quinn once, but the chemistry just wasn't there. At least on Logan's part. Which is ridiculous, since Quinn is stunning. Soft curves and a face not easily forgotten. Of course, even Quinn doesn't appreciate her own looks. She's constantly complaining about being too fat, which she's absolutely not. But she does work in an industry where she's being unceasingly scrutinized. At least that's one thing I can appreciate about my job at CT Anderson Bank. No one to scrutinize how I appear, because it's not part of my job. My management skills, however . . .

"What brings you to *our* corner of the world?" Bree asks, emphasizing the *our* in a very territorial way. I imagine the tables being pushed to the side as we do a dance off to see who this place really belongs to.

"Just grabbing a bite," Nathan says, rubbing his hands together again.

"You couldn't find another place in all Orlando?" Bree asks, her fingers daintily holding her martini glass even though it's now empty.

Nathan squints. "I didn't really think about it," he says and then gestures with his head toward Logan. "Logan planned it."

Of course this was Logan's idea. Of course. That makes me feel better, knowing it wasn't Nathan's idea to come here.

"We can go somewhere else if it bothers you," Nathan says, his sincere eyes focusing on me.

"No," I say as my friends reply with okays and yeses.

"You guys," I say, in a very chastising tone as I look around at my friends. My eyes move to the man standing in front of us. The man I was supposed to marry. "Nathan, it's fine," I tell him.

I'm totally being the bigger person here. Go, me.

The hostess calls out Nathan's name, notifying him that there's a table ready for him, the timing perfect. I had a feeling, as I watched Alex's face, that he was considering a throw-down right here in the middle of Hester's. He's quite protective of me . . . of all of us, really.

"Well, it was good to see you all," Nathan says. Logan grunts a goodbye.

"Don't they make a lovely couple?" Alex asks after they walk away, and Bree snickers.

I watch as they walk over to their table and sit down and then stand back up only seconds later as Logan waves over at the entrance to the busy restaurant. My eyes travel to where he's waving and I see a tall brunette and a shorter blonde wave back and then saunter over to the table. The tall brunette with bright red lipstick and a slinky tank that's tucked into a very skin-tight pencil skirt takes the seat next to Logan and the blonde, who's wearing a very short red sleeveless sheath dress, sits by Nathan. I can't hear what they're saying, the restaurant is much too loud, but their gestures convey that there are introductions happening as they all shake hands and nod at one another.

"Holy S," Quinn says, "is Nathan on a date?"

I had, of course, just thought those same words in my head, however I didn't use any initials in my thoughts. Only full curse words for me. Because this does seem like some sort of date. I had expected Nathan to move on fairly quickly; he was never one to be alone—a bit of a serial monogamist—but it had only been three weeks. Three freaking weeks.

It appears to be a blind date since it seems like they're all meeting for the first time. But for Nathan to even agree to any kind of date now . . . did I mean anything to him? At all? I should have told him yes when he offered to leave.

"Hols, don't jump to conclusions," Quinn says, probably in response to the look on my face. "It could be a business meeting."

"Yeah," Bree says. "A business meeting in the evening, with Sluts-R-Us. Makes perfect sense." Sarcasm duly noted.

"I never liked him," Alex says, leaning back in his chair, his head shaking. This is the lie all my friends have told me, even though up until less than a month ago that was definitely not the case.

Well, this has been fun.

"What are you doing?" Quinn asks as she sees me trying to get the attention of our server.

"I'm leaving," I say, waving my hand around.

"You can't leave, Hols," Bree says. "If you do, he wins."

"This isn't a game," I say.

"What did I miss?" Thomas asks, slightly breathless as he takes a seat. Everyone says their hellos, except for me, of course. I'm still trying to leave.

"Nathan and Logan showed up," Quinn says to Thomas, and then does a little head bob over toward where they're sitting.

"Well, would you look at that," Thomas says not even discreetly gawking. He takes in a quick breath. "OMG, is Nathan on a date?"

Subtlety is not Thomas's strong suit. Maybe it's the lawyer in him. Or the a-hole. I love Thomas but I can only take him in small doses, and I've had a lot of those small doses recently since our parents are dating each other. That's right, my dad is dating Thomas's mom. There are many reasons why this is not awesome.

"We don't know that it's a date," Quinn snaps, with a quick eyebrow raise, trying to nonverbally get Thomas to shut it. They have a way of talking in only facial expressions, those two.

"Well, it sure looks like it," Thomas says, not even noticing Quinn's facial clues. His tie is askew and the top of his shirt unbuttoned, but his blondish hair is gelled into place so well not even a hurricane could budge it.

"And I'm leaving," I say, still trying to get the attention of the server.

"You can't leave. I just got here," Thomas pouts. "Besides, I owe you a drink," he says with a double eyebrow raise.

"You do?" I question him dubiously. This reeks of something stinky. Thomas never buys drinks for anyone. Even when we're taking turns buying rounds, he never offers or he waits until the end of the night when everyone is leaving and says how drinks are on him next time since he never got around to it this time. Bit of an evil genius, that one.

"Yes, I owe you a drink because you guessed correctly on Mugshot Monday," he says, a large grin on his face.

"I did?" I ask, my brows pulled downward.

Every Monday, for probably the last five years, Thomas sends an e-mail to a handful of us with three mugshots he finds online, and we're to guess the crime. Aptly titled: Mugshot Mondays. I haven't played for a while because I'd started to feel bad for people who were being unknowingly subjected to our fun, even though real names were never revealed (nothing a Google search couldn't remedy, though). Especially since there's a mugshot of my own mother floating around out there. Not that any of my friends know anything about that.

But today, I felt like playing. Maybe because I wanted to see that there are other people out there having just as crappy a time as I am. Or worse.

And I won. Even before when I played it religiously, I

never ever won. Somehow this feels like a silver lining to my drab evening. The tiniest, teeniest, silver lining known to man, but I'll take it.

"Hey," Bree says, her upper lip curling up on one side, very Elvis-like. "Since when have you been buying drinks for the winners? I got it right last week and all I got from you was an e-mail with a picture of a cat that said 'you done good, beeeeeyotch.'"

"Yes, well, I changed the rules, just today. From now on, anyone that gets Mugshot Mondays correct gets a drink on me." He slaps his hands on his thighs and I have a sinking suspicion this rule will change next week.

"Well, I've already had my two drinks for the night," I say with a nod to the empty wine glass in front of me. "So I'll have to take a rain check."

"Hols, look around you," Thomas says. "Your ex-fiancé has shown up tonight and is now sitting at another table on what appears to be a date—ouch!" he says, reaching down to rub the leg that I'm quite sure Quinn just kicked. He recovers quickly. "You deserve a drink. You need to get that stick out of your butt and live a little—ouch! Stop that!" He reaches down to rub his leg again. Quinn has very long legs. Quite useful in situations such as this.

"I have a stick up my butt," I say, my tone even.

"Well, sure," Thomas says, scooting his chair back a bit so Quinn can't reach him. "With all the planning, and the rules, and everything having to be in the right place," he says, motioning toward my wine glass and then to the fact that I'm currently aligning my fork and knife together.

"So I'm controlling, then," I say, abandoning the utensils.

"Yes—ouch!—I mean, no," he says, rubbing his leg again. He underestimated the length of Quinn's legs and scoots his chair away even farther.

I sigh, slumping down in my chair. "I'm boring," I say.

"No," Thomas scoffs, and the others join in, chorusing no's around me. "You need to lighten up a bit. Live a little," he says.

"Oh yeah, Hols," Bree says. "That's a good idea. Go to work hungover. Maybe your team will like you more."

"What?" I scrunch my face up at her.

"What team? What did I miss?" Thomas asks, his eyes darting around the table as he searches for answers.

"Holly is having trouble with her team at work. They don't . . . love her," Quinn says gingerly.

"They hate me," I say. Although I'm hopeful my less hovering approach from today is making them have second thoughts about me.

"Oh," Thomas scoffs. "Boring."

"That's not helpful," Quinn says.

"You want helpful? Then here's my advice. Hols—"

"Don't even say she should sleep with them," Quinn cuts him off.

"I wasn't going to say that," Thomas protests, looking appalled. "I was going to say that Holly here just needs to start passing out the compliments."

"Huh?" I ask, not following.

"It's easy to get people to like you, just compliment

them," he says, peering at me as if I've got no brain. "Everyone loves to be praised. They'll eat that crap up and they'll all be your lackeys in no time. Like, take Alex here." Thomas gestures at Alex, who's sitting across the table from him. "I like the shirt you're wearing today, Alex," he says.

Alex looks down at the light blue button-up and rubs a hand down the front of it. "Thanks," he says. His lips pull up into a pleasant smile.

"See?" Thomas says turning to me, a smug smile on his face. "It works. And like with this example, you don't even have to be honest, either."

"Hey," Alex protests.

I squint at Thomas, not sure I'm buying any of this. "And this works," I say, skepticism in my tone. It all seems a bit patronizing.

"Of course it does," he says. Then he raises his eyebrows and points a finger at me. "But if it doesn't, then you should most definitely sleep with them."

"You're disgusting," Quinn says, and we all nod our head in agreement.

CHAPTER 4

I wake up early the next morning, too many thoughts swirling around in my brain. My job, the promotion, my team, my boss, vacations I don't want to take, and then there was last night.

I had tried so hard to keep my eyes only on my friends as we chatted at Hester's, and not on whatever was happening at Logan and Nathan's table. But they couldn't be stopped—like they were moving on their own accord and my brain wasn't even involved. Almost like a car wreck you can't look away from. But it wasn't a car wreck—not at all. And gauging by the blond woman's hand as it crept up Nathan's arm throughout the night and the almost hypnotic way he was staring at her, it was the very opposite of a car wreck. It looked a lot like a beginning. Like a brand new shiny car. And I was the old dumpy used car sitting in the corner with my friends.

But the sad truth is, I gave Nathan two years—*two years* of my life—and it only took him three weeks to move on. I told Quinn this last night and she said I was jumping to conclusions too fast and also that I sounded like I was writing lyrics to a country song. I tend to wax poetic when I'm tipsy.

I decide since I'm awake, I might as well start my morning and get into work early. I do all my normal morning things—go for a quick run, shower, get ready, and then find myself on my way to work an hour before my normal start time. This feels good—there's a gentle breeze, the downtown Orlando streets are quieter, and I feel kind of like I have the world to myself. But then I quickly realize I'm not quite so alone when I'm propositioned by a homeless guy as I pass the train tracks.

Another perk of being this early is I can grab a cup of coffee at the Lava Java and Logan won't be there yet. Maybe I'll do this more often. I feel like I'm already off to a better start today.

Nope. I spoke to soon. My happy balloon pops as I enter the small coffee shop and see the booth where Logan normally sits, and there he is in jeans and a navy blue T-shirt.

S-word.

And to make matters worse, he sees me. We make eye contact. My stupid, stupid eyes lock with his, and now I can't even turn around and leave. Because that would be weird, and I can't have anything getting back to Nathan like that. Not that I'm even sure it would. I can't see Logan telling Nathan he saw me at the coffee shop today and I was acting weird. In my experience, men don't talk about that stuff. Well, Thomas might. But he's a beast of his own.

Even so, I need to play it cool. I'll just nod my head at Logan, acknowledge that I see him, grab my coffee, and go.

Easy peasy. Only not so easy, because Logan stands up and walks toward me. Well, that plan's foiled.

"Holly," Logan says as he approaches me. His hands are doing that twitchy thing again, and as if he realizes this, he puts them in his pockets and then takes a stance that seems a tad forced.

"Logan," I say, only this is the first word I've spoken since I woke up this morning and it comes out scratchy and sultry sounding. I clear my throat and say his name again in my normal voice.

"Holly," he says back.

"Logan," I say again.

"Holly."

Do I say his name again? Why are we even saying each other's names?

I don't say anything, so we stand there in what seems like a face-off. Only Logan's lips are pulled up ever so slightly so I don't think he thinks we're in a face-off. And really, what would we be facing off about? Is this about last night?

"Why were you at Hester's last night?" my mouth asks before I can stop it. I feel my eyes go wide with shock. Why would I even ask that? I don't want to talk about it, not with Logan. And what about my whole inner monologue about not wanting anything to get back to Nathan? Surely *this* will get back to him.

Logan doesn't even flinch. "We were getting dinner," he says, his hands still stuffed in his pockets as if he doesn't trust them to move freely.

"Right," I say, feeling stupid.

"If you're asking why we were with those women . . ." he trails off, brows raised as he searches my face.

"No," I say a little too quickly, shaking my head to add emphasis. "I wasn't asking that." I laugh awkwardly.

This is not going well.

"It was a business dinner," he says flatly.

"Um, okay," I say, disbelief in my tone. I add an eye roll for emphasis.

"I'm telling you the truth," he says. "They're from AppLee."

"AppLee?"

"Yeah, AppLee. Kind of a big deal, actually. They want to purchase Digits."

"Oh," I say, my mind doing double time, putting pieces into place like a puzzle. AppLee is a large smart phone app-building company that Nathan and Logan have been trying to sell their accounting app to. It's what they've been working for. AppLee is a *really* big deal.

But the women they were with? Surely they don't work for AppLee—they didn't even look like they came from work. Even as I think this, though, my mind wanders back to what they were wearing—the short red sheath dress and the silky tank with the pencil skirt . . . if you slapped a suit coat on each of those outfits, you'd have work attire. Even the short red dress—heaven knows Tiffany's worn similar dresses to work.

Could it have been a business meeting? But what about flirty-mcflirtyson who was all up in Nathan's space? Maybe

I read into that too?

Logan takes a hand out of his pocket and runs it through his hair.

"Um . . . so how did it go?" My mind is running all over the place and I need time to sort it out, so for now I decide that I'm just going to go with this whole business meeting thing. Plus, Logan is a lot of things, but a liar is not one of them. I've only known him to be honest. Too honest, sometimes.

He scans the room with his eyes before settling them back on me. "Good. I think."

"That's good," I say.

"Yeah . . ." He pauses, searching the room again as if eye contact is too hard. "As long as Nathan doesn't screw it up," he says. Something briefly crosses his face, like he didn't mean to tell me what he just did, but it passes quickly.

"What do you mean?"

"I . . . I mean, it's nothing. It's fine. I think it went well," he says.

"Well, good then." I'm half curious why he's saying Nathan could screw this deal up—Nathan, who could sell condoms to a nun. I think if anyone could screw it up it would be the socially awkward man standing in front of me.

"Yeah," he says, nodding his head. Both hands now back in his pockets.

We both stand there, not looking anywhere but at each other. I start chewing on the side of my bottom lip wondering how I can be done here. I glance over at the counter and see the woman with the dreads behind the counter waiting for me. Seeing my escape, I quickly take the few steps to get to the counter and then place my order—which they put on Nathan's tab, and I'm too flustered to fix it. Next time.

I turn back around to find Logan still there. I half expected him to go back to his booth. Or maybe I'd hoped.

Right, so I'm just going to say it.

"Listen, Logan," I say. "We don't have to do this."

"Have to do what?"

Oh, sweet déjà vu. Do I really have to spell this out?

"We don't have to continue *this*," I gesture between him and me.

"What exactly is *this*?" he says, pulling a hand out of his pocket and mimicking my gesture.

"Logan," I say tilting my head to the side in irritation. What is he not getting here? "I mean, you and I don't have to continue this—whatever we have—now that Nathan and I are done."

There's not a word to describe it—what Logan and I are, or rather, were. We were never friends, just forced to get along because of Nathan. Not for lack of me trying, though. I *so* wanted Logan to like me. I've never experienced that before, wanting someone to like me. I've never wanted to work on it—either someone likes me or they don't. I think it was only because Logan is Nathan's best friend; I wanted to work on it so we could be one big, happy family. It feels slightly relieving that I don't have to work on this anymore. I can go back to not caring who likes me. Well, except for my team. I *need* them to like me. Crap.

"Why wouldn't we?" he asks, eyeing me with confusion.

"I mean . . . look, Logan, I know you never liked me, so I don't want you to feel like when you see me, you have to talk to me." There, I've said it.

"Who says I don't like you?" Logan asks, confusion on his face mixed with something like . . . hurt, maybe? I'm not sure.

The barista calls out my name and I move over to the pickup counter and grab my coffee.

I hold my coffee up to show him I got what I came here for. "Well, I'll see you around, Logan."

He huffs through his nose, his brows knit together. "Holly, who says I don't like you?"

I sigh. He's not going to let this go as easily as I thought he would. "No one, really," I say. "It's just, you know, pretty obvious."

"I—" he cuts off, running a hand through his hair. "How?"

"How?"

"Yes. How is it obvious?"

I laugh a fake, almost witchy sounding laugh. Where did that come from? I freaking cackled. "Where do I begin?" I ask.

"Give me an example," he says, folding his arms.

"Let's see, you barely acknowledged me when we first met. You'd get pissy whenever I came over to the apartment. You were a total jerk at my engagement party. Do I need to go on?"

Logan briefly stares down at his flip-flop-adorned feet. I

do give him some credit here, because he does look ashamed. His eyes move back to me.

"I just wanted for us all to get along." I don't even know why I'm saying this. It's futile. I don't want Nathan back, and I don't need Logan's friendship. Not anymore.

"Holly," he takes a step closer to me and gently wraps a hand around my upper arm. It feels so foreign, yet doesn't at the same time. I don't think Logan has ever touched me. Not on purpose at least. His hand is warm against my skin, and my arm prickles instantly from the touch.

"Don't," I say, shaking off his arm. "It's fine. You don't need to apologize—"

"I wasn't going to," he says, cutting me off.

"Oh," I say, looking down at the drink in my hand. This is not how I thought this would go.

"I like you just fine," he says, his hand opening and closing as if touching me was a very trying task.

Right. What any person loves to hear: *I like you just fine.*

"Okay, fine. Then you just didn't like Nathan and me together," I say.

He doesn't say anything, and that's my answer.

"Well, at any rate," I take in a big breath, "you're off the hook now." I give him a forced smile.

He still has nothing to say, so I take that as my cue to leave. There goes my great start to the day.

And it's only getting worse.

"Knock, knock!" a voice says from outside my door.

Oh, yay. Tiffany. I'd sell my soul to anyone who could magically zap me out of my office, I swear it. Just tell me where to sign, Satan. I'm yours for the taking.

"Knock, knock!" she says again.

"Come in," I finally say.

"Hi, Holly," she says as she walks in my office. Her hair is up in one of those updos I can never get my hair to do and she's wearing a pant suit that looks like she just picked it up from the cleaners. I've only been at work for an hour and my striped button-down blouse and navy blue pencil skirt appears as if I've been rolling around on my floor.

Well, I got propositioned by a bum today, so in your face, Tiffany.

"Oh, hey, Tiffany," I say and then turn my focus back to my computer screen.

She takes a seat in one of the chairs in front of my desk, lays a small stack of papers in front of her, and then clears her throat. I take a deep breath and glance over at her.

"What can I help you with?" I ask, my tone dry. I can't fake it today.

"So," she starts, a patronizing smile on her face. "We got the PFC report from your team—"

"You did?" I say, cutting her off, sounding utterly surprised—because I am *utterly* surprised.

"Yes," she says. "Your team sent it over last night."

My heart warms. My new approach is working. I can't help but feel a little burst of pride for my team. My little lovely team. It's going to be easy to shower them with praise and compliments today.

"Yes, but the report they sent was all wrong," she says, tapping the small stack of papers in front of her.

And just like that, my burst of pride is trampled. Stamped on, jumped on, and beaten with a bat for good measure.

She slides the report over to me using her index finger. "Can you see that this gets fixed?"

I pick up the paper-clipped packet and briefly scan the front page.

"You know," she says, and I look up to see her fake smile, "a little proper training with your team might be needed." She bats her eyes like she's being so helpful. Helpful like a big *B*-word. "I could help you, you know."

Oh, she could help, could she? Give me a freaking break. I'll allow that to happen as soon as our current president stops doing his comb-over. So, *never.*

Anyway, Tiffany's team is easier than mine. And I'd know because we were both on that team once upon a time. That's where we both started at CT Anderson Bank — the fraud resolutions team. Then Marie made us both supervisors and stuck me with the island of misfit toys. I mean, Jim is for sure the choo-choo with square wheels.

I plaster my own fake smile on my face and say, "Thank you for the offer, but I think we're doing just fine."

She gives me a smile like she doesn't believe me. Without a goodbye, she stands up and saunters out of my office, her shoes making soft padding sounds as she leaves.

I put my forehead on my desk. Time to go talk to my

team. I can't even use Thomas's advice and start passing out compliments. *Hey everyone, you sucked at the PFC report, but Jim, that ratty old polo you're wearing really suits you.*

Nope, it's back to the bribery.

CHAPTER 5

Marie will not let this vacation thing go.

This morning at work I logged in to find a bunch of emails from my boss, all about last-minute vacation deals, all of them to the beach. She's not moving on like I'd hoped. And why did they all have to be on the beach? I'm not a huge fan, honestly. I'm like part of the one percent, or maybe I'm the *only* percent that doesn't like it. I hate sand everywhere, and that sticky feeling from the salt water . . . also the beach was my mom's most favorite place. And it reminds me of her, which I also don't love. I wonder how much she's missing the beach now that's she spent the last three years in an orange jumpsuit locked inside a building.

I did finally read the article Marie wanted me to read— the one from *The Harvard Business Review* about vacations. Okay, it was interesting. I'll give her that. But it still seems so counterintuitive. Why would time away make me a better boss? No, I need to fix everything here first before I can do any of that.

I decided to do a search of my own to show her vacations

don't work; it's a well-known fact that you can always find something on the internet — some fact or research — to back up your claim.

I typed in "reasons why you shouldn't take a vacation from work," and over three hundred million — *three hundred million* — search results came up. But every one of them was *in favor* of a vacation. Well, I obviously didn't look up every result, but I got to page twenty before I gave up my plight.

Since Marie is not letting this go and the internet has failed me, I called Quinn and asked her for help. Quinn is my person. She's my go-to for pretty much everything. If anyone will know what to do, it's her. I need her to help me think of ways I can get my team to like me and I need to figure this out fast. Finding ways to buy me some time with my boss would be helpful as well.

Quinn Pearson has been my best friend since the first day of middle school. We were both new — which is the worst possible time to move schools, as anyone who's been to middle school can attest to. Quinn's family had moved from Boston and my dad had taken a job in Orlando, so we had to leave Charlotte, North Carolina. It was only him and me since my mom had decided being a wife and mom was not for her, so she peaced-out just before my twelfth birthday.

Quinn and I were both in the midst of our ugly phases — me with my massive curly red hair and freckles — and Quinn being nearly as tall as the teachers. We were destined to be besties after meeting in the lunch line and bonding over the fact that we were both new at the school and had both been insulted within the first hour of being there. Someone had called her *Amazon woman* — which was rather apropos, honestly — and I was asked by a kid with a very disproportionate head-to-body ratio (it was like a grapefruit on a chopstick) if *the carpet matched the drapes*. I didn't even know what that meant until Quinn explained it to me.

We were basically inseparable from then on out. We went to the same high school, during which I figured out how to tame my crazy hair and tone down my freckles with makeup, and Quinn's height no longer mattered as the boys caught up to her. After graduation we attended the University of Florida, where we became obnoxious Gators fans and did all the stupid college stuff girls who are trying to figure themselves out do. Well, Quinn did that. I was more the conservative type. It was during our sophomore year that we met Bree.

"Hey," Quinn says, slightly breathless as she takes a seat across from me ten minutes after she was supposed to be here, which is actually not bad for her.

"Hey," I return the greeting. I don't even bother to make a comment about her tardiness because it's wasted breath.

"Okay," she slaps her hands on the table. "I know exactly what you need to do."

Yep, that's Quinn — getting right down to business. She's not big on small talk. Plus, we've known each other for more than half our lives, so we don't have a need to talk about the weather or other useless topics of conversation.

And she's got her crazy eyes on. Quinn's crazy eyes are usually accompanied by some harebrained idea. Sometimes they're good ideas — like the time she decided she was going to start doing furniture restoration, which she still does and is amazing at. Other times — like the time in college when she decided she could learn how to wax eyebrows by watching tutorials on YouTube and then promptly took half my eyebrow off, was not one of her better ones.

"Let's hear it," I say.

She bounces around in her chair. "Okay, do you remember that woman in New York who did that nationwide search for a guy with the same name as her ex-boyfriend to go on that trip to China with her?"

My eyes travel up to the ugly tiled ceiling and fluorescent lighting of our favorite pizzeria as I try to recall the story. I'm also trying to figure out what this has to do with anything.

"It was about two years ago. It was all over the news," Quinn says, now tapping her fingers on the table excitedly.

"Oh, right," I say as I recall the story. I remember reading about it and thinking it was so clever and hoping they would fall in love, but the guy she went with had a girlfriend.

Quinn's eyebrows move up and down and she nods her head rapidly. I'm not sure what's she getting at.

"I can't go to China," I say to her.

"Not China, silly." She rolls her eyes, slapping the table again with her hands.

"I'm not following."

She lets out a loud breath, still giving me the how-are-you-not-getting-this eyes.

"Hols, you have two tickets to London and Paris."

"Yes, and one of those tickets can't be used."

"Exactly," she says, her eyebrows still dancing up and down.

"Quinn, I need you to help me with my team. Not a vacation. And besides, I already told you I don't want to go by myself." I don't even know why I must defend myself on this. Who wants to go on their honeymoon alone?

She huffs a breath out of her nose. "Well I'd go with you, but you know I can't."

"Right," I say with an eye roll. "You have Fat Camp."

"Shhhhhh," she says, her eyes scanning the area around us to make sure no one heard. There's no one within hearing distance.

"Can't you just go another time?"

"You know I can't."

Quinn is going to some mind/body/spirit retreat that she got on the waiting list for last year and finally got a spot, and it happens to be when I would have been on my honeymoon. It's something to do with finding a healthy relationship with food, hence the "fat camp" reference.

"Holly," Quinn says, slapping the table twice as she says my name. "You have two tickets for a trip that's probably already been painstakingly planned." She eyes me knowingly.

I shrug. It was pretty close to being all planned. I ditched the effort when it was no longer necessary.

"So, let's find you another Nathan Jones to go with you," she says, her mouth forming a huge smile.

JUST A NAME

I sit there for a second before I truly realize what she's saying.

"And before you say anything," she holds out a hand, "I already looked it up on Facebook and there are like, a gajillion Nathan Joneses out there. It will be super easy to find someone. Plus," she pauses for emphasis, "your bestie happens to have the means to help you do the search. I mean, it's kind of kismet if you think about it."

I'm at a loss for words right now and I start blinking rapidly. What was I just thinking about Quinn knowing what I should do?

"Quinn," I say, feeling disappointed that this was not what I asked her to help me with, and realizing my best friend of over fourteen years doesn't know me at all. "You can't be serious."

"I know," she holds out a hand as she reads the expression on my face. "I know this isn't what you asked me to help you with, and I know it's not something Holly Murphy does, but think about it, Hols, this is just what you need to do."

"In what world would I ever need to do this?" I ask, totally dumbfounded.

She looks at me, her face becoming serious. "This is the perfect way to get your boss off your back. You have an option sitting here, right in your lap. And plus, with everything that happened with Nathan . . . I just think maybe doing something different—and yes, a bit crazy—might shake things up a bit. You need to, you know . . . *live* a little."

Why does everyone keep saying that?

"How is going on a trip with someone I don't know *living* a little? What if he ends up being a psychotic killer or something? Then I wouldn't be living at all. I'd be dead."

Quinn stares at me, slowly shaking her head from side to side. "Give me a little credit. We'd vet all the contestants at the station. Background checks and all."

"Contestants? Like a game show?" I say, horrified, and louder than I intended.

"No," she says, emphatically. But then her eyes drop down to the table, her mouth doing that twisty thing again. "Well, I guess . . . sort of."

"Yeah, that's a big *H* no from me."

"Ah, thank you for saying *H*," she says, tilting her head to the side and giving me a smile of approval.

I shake my head and chuckle at my best friend. My ridiculous, off-her-rocker best friend. She's come up with a lot of crazy plans in the past, but this one has to be the craziest.

"What am I gonna do with you?" I ask, actually wondering.

She takes a deep breath. "Fine. Don't do it for you. Do it for me."

Ah, and the truth comes out.

"I'm hanging by a thread at work," she says, her eyes downcast, her lips pulled into a frown. She looks back up at me. "I need to bring in ratings. I need to do something to get Jerry off my back."

Jerry would be Quinn's producer for the midday news.

Things haven't been as great for her at work since her f-bomb went viral. I think I may have helped it go viral. Not by sharing, but by watching it repeatedly. In my defense, I didn't know each time I watched counted as a view. Last I looked, she was over ten million views.

"I wish I could help you, Quinn," I say, trying to infuse as much sympathy as I can into my voice. I *am* sympathetic to what she's going through, especially now that my own career could be hanging by a proverbial thread.

"You know, you do owe me . . ." she trails off with a smirk.

I smack my hand over my mouth, "Are you serious?"

"I told you someday I'd find a way for you to pay me back," she sing-songs.

One time in college I'd decided it would be a smart idea to take a road trip from Gainesville up to Charlotte to find my mother. I had found her name online and then made a plan to go search for her. I made it all the way to Columbia, South Carolina, and then my car broke down. Like, not-fixable broke down. I couldn't call my dad because it would have broken his heart to know I'd gone looking for my mom after all she put us through, so I called Quinn. She dropped everything and drove up to Columbia, picked me up, and even took me all the way to Charlotte, only to find out that no one by the name of Melanie Murphy lived at the house I had found online.

Driving all the way up there and then being my support when I was so disappointed was the kindest thing anyone had ever done for me, and when I told her that on the drive home, she had smiled and said, "Oh, don't you worry. Someday you'll pay me back."

"You know I love you for that. And I do owe you, but I think going on a trip with a complete stranger for ten days is kinda bigger," I say.

"Hollllllyyyyyyyy," she whines my name. Then she gives me the puppy dog eyes—the ones that have never worked in the history of our friendship, ever.

"It's gonna be a hard pass from me," I say, wishing there was something else I could do to help her.

She leans down and puts her forehead on the small two-person dining table we're sitting at. "I knew it was a long shot," she says.

"You get points for trying," I say.

"Points aren't going to help me keep my job," she says.

"You are ridiculously talented. They'd be idiots to get rid of you."

"If only I could make this stupid video go away."

"It'll die down at some point; they always do," I say, briefly reaching across the table and putting my hand over hers.

"Will you at least think about it?" she asks, her head tilted to the side.

"I could tell you yes, but I think we both know I won't."

"Fine," she says, frowning.

"Come on," I say getting up from my seat. "Let's fix our problems temporarily with pizza."

"Sounds like a plan."

CHAPTER 6

Quinn may have been useless and I still need to figure out what I can do to get Marie off my back, but as far as my team goes, I think the bribery might be working.

I'm sitting at my desk the next morning staring at the PFC report that my team did last night, and it's all correct. They did it. And I didn't have to do any prodding. Well, not my normal amount of prodding.

I'm feeling much better about everything today. Much better than I did last night when Quinn presented me with her ridiculous idea.

But now I have to do something I've been putting off, something that may pop my current bubble of joy. I need to open my Carrie Parker planner.

I'd normally be excited to do this because I'm pretty much obsessed with planners. I've carried one with me since the sixth grade. Since my mom left. Which I'm sure has all kinds of psychological connotations I don't want to think about.

This particular planner—the one I've been putting off

opening—was going to be the planner I used for the next eighteen months. I special ordered it so I could use it to finalize wedding plans and then begin my married life to Nathan. The irony is, it was those very wedding plans that ended up being the demise of our relationship.

It started out okay. I mean the engagement itself was kind of a mess because Nathan didn't plan anything, but I was mostly all right with that. One night after we'd been dating for nearly a year and a half, we'd gone to dinner and then went back to Nathan's and Logan's apartment. Like any typical night at their place, when we got there Logan was on the couch watching TV, and we joined him. So there we were, sitting on the couch, Logan on one side, and me cozied up to Nathan on the other side. We were watching college football and during a commercial break, Nathan turned to me and said, "So should we do this marriage thing or what?" I asked him if this was a proposal and he said, "Yeah," and the next day we went ring shopping. No getting on one knee, no talking to my dad beforehand. No planning of any kind, really.

In hindsight, this should have been a red flag, right? But I didn't think too much about it at the time, or at least I would put it out of my mind when thoughts of *this was not how you imagined it* would creep into my head. Besides, Nathan had so many good qualities, like the fact that he worked hard and was successful because of it, and he had a good heart. What he lacked in organization and planning I made up for. Opposites attract and all that.

Once I had a ring on my finger, it was decided that I

could do all the wedding stuff because Nathan knew I "liked that sort of thing" and it "wasn't his thing." It was actually quite perfect. I would plan and make everything perfect, like I enjoyed doing, and he could just show up and say vows.

And that worked. Until it didn't. I think Logan may have said something to him — it was the only reasonable explanation I could wrap my brain around with Nathan's total about-face — because suddenly, out of the blue and just under four months away from the wedding, he wanted to be part of the planning. I was on board until he wanted to change things. And by things, I mean *everything*. Plans I had spent so much time making.

I wanted a more classic wedding, with a sit-down dinner and a live band; Nathan decided he wanted a DJ and to eat buffet style. He wanted it to be "less stuffy." He even wanted me to change my dress — the dress I had already spent a ridiculous amount of money on and had already gone in for alterations. He thought we could wear something less formal. There was even a mention of him wearing . . . jeans. I believe I shuddered.

I finally asked him why he picked then to start wanting to be involved after so many things had already been planned. That's when the fighting really started. Words were said that were hard to take back. And then one chilly evening in March, he came over to my apartment and said he couldn't do it anymore. And that was it. It was over. The beautiful June wedding — with all the bright spring colors and all the hours of work and planning — was off.

I try hard not to think about all the money that was lost. The deposits for the venue and the photographer were the most expensive, and we got neither of those back, but we were able to get everything else. My dad was so great about it. He's always great about stuff like that, and anyway he's not hurting for money. I'm sure it had to pinch, but he simply put his arms around me and said all the things a good dad should say, like "you're better than him," and "you deserve more," and "I never liked him." The last bit was a total lie. My dad loved Nathan, I'm pretty sure he still does. I mean, he stopped golfing with him once we broke up, but that was only out of loyalty to me.

So now I'm staring at the box holding the planner that will never be used for my wedding or my life with Nathan. And although I'm feeling better about all that—this part still might hurt.

I grab scissors and carefully open the box. Pulling the tissue-paper-covered planner out, I set it on my desk and stare at it. I decide pulling the Band-Aid off fast is my best approach, so I rip open the small, round, gold sticker that's holding the tissue together, and there it is.

I let out a sigh because it's beautiful. It's *beautiful*. The floral cover is stunning. I run my fingers down it, feeling the texture of the hardback glossy cover until I get to the gold embossed name in the bottom right-hand corner.

Holly Jones. Not Holly Murphy, but my married name. Or what was to *be* my married name. In bright, shiny gold.

So now what to do with my precious Carrie Parker planner? I have some options, of course. I could try to send it back, but it was a special order and I vaguely remember having your name printed on it invalidates all return policies. At the time I ordered it, I didn't care about the return policy, because why would I? There was no impending breakup when I placed the order.

What I kind of want to do right now is throw this planner across the room. But I can't. Even with what all this planner represents, I can't even bring myself to disrespect it in such a way. I suppose I could *gently* place it in the trashcan, but then what purpose would that serve? Some freegan would probably find it and re-purpose it as a coaster. No, thank you.

I stare at it sitting on my desk and wonder how something that thrills me to my core could now be so ruined.

Seeing my name on this cover reminds me of a time when it was easy—because most of the time, it *was* easy with Nathan. I mourn the excitement of it all. Taking steps in the direction my life was supposed to go.

I pull out a sharpie and begin drawing hearts over the Jones part of my name to try to cover it up. But then I realize Nathan's last name doesn't deserve hearts, not from me at least, so then I try to change it to a row of crossbones and skulls. I've never been praised for my artistic skills, because I have none, so now it looks like blobs. Blobs across the last name I'll never have. Actually, blobs are quite fitting.

Maybe I need to abandon planners altogether. Maybe that's how I can try to be less controlling, less rigid. I could throw caution to the wind and let my day go how it will go. This thought immediately makes me develop a large knot in the pit of my stomach. It feels too much like something my mom would do—her fly-by-the-seat-of-her-pants attitude toward life. And I definitely don't want to be like that.

"Hi, Dad," I say as I enter the small Mexican restaurant where we've been meeting every third Friday for the past couple of years. We started this tradition because we were both so busy that it was the best way to make time for each other. It was my idea, of course. I didn't get my planning and organizational skills from my dad. Or my mom. I still sometimes wonder if I were adopted.

We only have one rule on our night out—no one else can come. It's always just the two of us, no matter what. Oh, and I guess another rule: there must always be chips and salsa. Hence the Mexican restaurant choice. When my mom first left and my dad and I were trying to get our footing, chips and salsa were our go-to snack . . . and sometimes meal. It's become a sort of tradition between us. We're also chips and salsa snobs—none of that out-of-the-jar stuff for us.

It's strange that last time we had dinner I was still engaged to Nathan. Funny how things can change in a month. And last time we were here we talked a lot about wedding plans—well, I talked a lot about the plans and my dad listened. Things were getting sticky between Nathan and me at that time.

"Hey, darlin'," Dad says with just a hint of a Southern

drawl when he sees me. It used to be thicker when we lived in North Carolina.

I give him a peck on the cheek and then take a seat in the booth across from him. A large bowl of tortilla chips and smaller bowl of fresh salsa sit on the table between us. My mouth waters at the sight.

"What's new?" I ask as I get settled, shifting around in my seat until I'm comfortable. The fake leather of the booth feels cool underneath my cotton pencil skirt and from somewhere behind me I can hear a mariachi band playing and singing.

"Well," he chuckles to himself. "A lot, actually."

"Really," I say, stopping as I was about to get a tortilla chip.

For the past two years, since we've been meeting here regularly, when I've asked my dad "what's new" his response every time has been "same old, same old." My heart sinks a little. He's got a smile on his face, which to everyone else would mean everything is fine—but my dad always has a smile on his face. That's usually how people describe James Murphy—the guy who's always smiling.

But I know his smiles. He's got a lot of different ones. He's got a happy smile, of course. But he also has a sad smile. I saw a lot of that when I was younger. He also has a different smile for when he's tired, bored, pensive, and an extra special one for when he's just . . . let one. Which is one of my least favorite smiles—especially when we're stuck in a small space. Like a car or an elevator. It's a very toothy grin.

Today's smile seems . . . nervous. It's kind of wobbly, and I can't say I've ever seen this side of him. My dad is relaxed, loosely wound. A lot like Nathan, actually. Which, I'm sure, is one of those Freudian things that drew me to Nathan that I'd prefer not to acknowledge. Ever.

Because I'm not a relaxed, loosely wound person, I suddenly feel jittery and flustered. The din of the restaurant is not helping.

"Is everything okay?" I ask.

"Yeah," he says, bobbing his head. "Sure, darlin'. Everything's good . . . great even."

"Then why the smile?" I point at his face.

He reaches up and touches his lips. "What do ya mean?" He pulls his brow inward, confused at my line of thinking.

"You seem . . . I don't know . . . like, kinda nervous? Maybe?"

He takes a big breath, exhaling loudly. Loud enough that I can hear him over the noise of the restaurant. He reaches across the table and puts a hand over mine, his hazel green eyes—the ones that match mine—searching my face. My mind immediately starts moving. He's dying. He's got some deadly disease. Or maybe something not so deadly but still scary. Like diabetes. Or maybe he's found a lump somewhere. There are so many terrible possibilities. My heart starts racing, blood pumping quickly through my veins.

"Right," he nods a few times, his eyes downcast.

"So what is it? Just tell me. Oh my gosh, you have cancer?" I say, with a strangled voice. This also comes out quite a bit louder than I intend and right as the mariachi band finishes their song, so the occupants of the surrounding tables all turn to gape at us.

"No," he says, waving the notion off with his hand. "No, no. I don't have cancer." He says this loud enough so all of the now concerned onlookers can hear this and go back to what they were doing. Which they do.

"Then what is it?" I clear my throat.

"Well," he lets out another breath.

"Dad, just say it," I say, frustrated. He knows I dislike it when people stretch things out.

"Okay, I'm getting married."

"What?"

"I've asked Miranda to marry me."

"What?" I ask, so confused. Miranda? Thomas's mom? But … they've only been dating since the new year. Less than five months.

"And she said yes."

"What?"

He angles his head to the side, his smile now full of frustration. "Are you really asking 'what' or can you not hear me?"

I stare at him for a few seconds. "I . . . I . . ." I can't seem to get a word out. I'm having an internal struggle of — well, one, having this thrown at me with no warning or anything. I didn't even know he and Miranda were that serious. And two, I'm his daughter — his *only* daughter — and I feel taken aback that I'm just finding this out. Right now.

"I know," my dad says, dipping his chin one time. "You

don't like having things thrown at you, and believe me, I wanted to tell you. But then there was everything with Nathan . . ." he trails off, not needing to finish that sentence.

Right. So my dad — the great man he is — wanted to tell me everything that was going on in his life, but since it was in direct opposition to what was happening in mine, he didn't.

I blink rapidly, trying to get my bearings. This is not how I should be reacting. I realize this. I should be jumping for joy and excited for him. Because I am . . . mostly excited for him.

I take in a deep breath. "It's . . . great, Dad," I say, trying to sound upbeat, but really I sound like I've got some constipation issues.

His posture loosens, he sits back against the booth, his shoulders falling.

"Is it?" he asks.

"Sure," I say, still sounding unsteady. "I'm . . . I was just a little surprised, that's all."

"I get that," he says with a quick nod. "And like I said, I wanted to tell you."

"It's okay, Dad," I say, holding a hand out to stop him from going on.

His lips pull up into a happier smile. "So what do you think?"

"Of you and Miranda . . . getting married?" I look down at the table, wondering what I really *do* think.

I like Miranda. She's funny, and kind. And I think she and my dad are great together, even if they haven't dated that long. I . . . well, part of me wonders how all of this will affect me. Which is selfish, I know. But for years now I've been the only woman in my dad's life, apart from a few dates here and there. I guess I feel a little nervous about it.

My dad reaches over again, putting a hand on top of my nervously twitching one. "You know you'll always be my little girl."

I look up to find him studying me tentatively. I give him a reassuring smile. He really does know me so well.

"Of course," I say, shaking my head. It makes me wonder if he felt how I'm feeling now when I told him I was marrying Nathan. Like he wouldn't always be the center of my world.

"So, when?" I ask.

"When?"

"Yes, when is the wedding?"

"Oh," he stares down at his hands. "Well, that's the other thing I wanted to talk to you about."

"Oh?"

"Yeah . . ." He's got the nervous smile on again.

"Spit it out, Dad," I say, now with a nervous smile of my own.

"Well, you know I'm not getting any younger."

"So?" That's not a topic I like to think about. He's only in his early fifties, so it's easy right now to forget someday he's going to get older. Old enough to leave me.

"I don't want to wait too long."

"Okay?"

He reaches up and scratches his jaw. "I was thinking," he

lets out a breath, "I was thinking since we can't get the deposit back on the venue and the photographer that—"

"You want to get married on my wedding day—or," I shake my head, "what was supposed to be my wedding day?"

"Yes and no. I called and they still have the place available for both Friday and Saturday. So maybe we'd do it on Friday."

Right. Friday we were using the facility for the rehearsal.

I sit there for a second, staring at the chips and salsa, my brain a whirl of thoughts.

"It was a dumb idea," he says, shaking his head. "Just forget it."

"No." I hold out a hand to stop him. "It's a practical idea. I mean, it seems like a logical answer. You want to get married, there happens to be a venue you've paid the deposit for."

We sit there in silence, well, as silent as we can in this ridiculously loud restaurant. Why do we come here again?

The whole thing seems unconventional, but also makes sense. My dad wants to marry Miranda right away. He's already paid the deposit for the venue. I'm not sure what bothers me more—him wanting to marry and start his life with Miranda as soon as he can, or him using the venue that was supposed to be for my wedding.

Okay, maybe both things bother me equally.

I can feel my dad's eyes on me and I know he's giving me the space to think—like he always does. He knows I just need a few minutes to work things out in my brain. Nathan could never figure that out. He always thought my silence was me shutting him out, but I was only trying to figure things out before I verbalized them.

"Yeah," I finally say. "Sure, I'd be okay with that." And that's the realization I come to. My dad's happiness is what's most important to me and should come first. No matter what.

"You sure, darlin'?" He leans his elbows on the table, his serious face on. It's rare to see him looking this earnest. I'm one of the few people privy to his non-smiling face.

"Yes, I'm sure," I say and his smile creeps back onto his face, at first tentative, but then it grows into a full James Murphy smile. My heart warms a bit at the sight. His happiness really is most important to me.

"So what's the plan? What do you need me to help with?" I pull my Carrie Parker planner out of my purse. I couldn't bring myself to waste it.

"That's my girl, always planning," he says.

"Well, you don't have much time," I say, tapping an imaginary watch on my wrist.

"I'm not worried about all that right now. We'll figure it out," he says, dismissing the words with a wave of his hand.

"Right," I say, remembering that unlike me, my dad doesn't have to know all the things right away. He's fine to just make a decision and then let things happen how they will. I, on the other hand, made Nathan sit down and plan things the same night he proposed.

I put the planner back in my bag. Mostly because I don't

want to stare at the ruined front cover with my scribbled-out name. Or my dad to see it and ask me.

"Plus, Miranda will want to take care of most of it. Besides, now that — thanks to you — we have a venue and a photographer, that makes things a whole lot easier."

So they are also using the photographer — the other vendor we couldn't get the deposit back from. That's . . . awesome.

I reach over and grab a chip and dip it into the salsa. I'm not so hungry since I'm still trying to reconcile all of this. But my brain is functioning enough to know I need to start acting normal — or at least try to — so my dad can see I'm okay with it. And I *am* okay with it. Mostly.

"Are you sure you're okay?" he asks, reaching over and grabbing a chip and dipping it into the salsa. The chip I grabbed is still in my hand, having never made its way to my mouth.

Then I realize something that has me pulling the chip away again and my eyes bugging out of my head.

"We're going to be related to Thomas," I say, sounding panicked.

My dad chuckles. "Yep, we will be."

"Oh, gosh. I don't even know *what* to think about that."

"Well, you always wanted a sibling."

"Not him," I say, adding a bit of a whine for emphasis. I love Thomas, I really do. But at an arm's length. This union between our parents will have him all up in my space. We'll be at a wrist length in no time. I just know him.

"How about we not think about that right now," he says,

trying to placate me.

I allow it, only because it feels better to push that aside for now.

I glance up to see my dad's face contort and then change into a very toothy grin.

"Dad!" I close my eyes, pulling my head back as I scrunch my face. "Not in public."

"Sorry, darlin'. Couldn't be helped," he says, his smile now very self-satisfactory.

CHAPTER 7

Because Quinn failed me, I reached out to Bree over the weekend to see if she had any ideas to help me with my work situation. Her idea was to invite me to a yoga class. She said it would "clear my mind" and "help me balance my chakras" or something.

I was feeling a bit desperate, so yesterday I went to a class with her. I don't think any chakras were balanced. Instead, I found myself twisted into so many pretzel shapes and contortions that I wondered if my body would ever go back to normal again. I somehow made it through the class, but it didn't do much for my work predicament.

I can't chalk it up as a complete fail, though, since I'm currently using the breathing techniques to help me get through my Monday morning meeting with my team.

"So tell me again, why do we have to do it this way?" Sara-without-an-h asks . . . again.

Deep breath in through your nose, slowly out through your mouth.

"Because," I say after my deep breath, "this is how they

want it to be done." I point up at the ceiling where, directly above us one floor up, the executive offices are.

"God?" Sara asks.

Do not roll your eyes. Do. Not. Deep breath. Deep breath. Remember the breathing.

"The executive team," I say. The people in charge, the big kahunas, my superiors.

"But they can't expect us to always stay on script," Avery says in her monotone voice, her dark, perfectly sculpted eyebrows furrowed.

"Actually, they can and they do," I say, trying not to clip every freaking word with frustration.

Thirty minutes of this. Thirty minutes, and it's as if my words are just bouncing off their heads. Like tiny rubber balls. *Bounce, bounce, bounce.* I was told by the team lead for quality assurance that there's been some quality control issues with my team and I need to talk to them about sticking with the script. Thank goodness Marie is at an offsite business meeting for most of this week. I don't need her finding this out.

"The thing is," Brad says, "the customers don't have a script." His ginger bangs are hanging over his eyes again. Doesn't that annoy him?

"Right," I say.

"So it's kind of hard for us to stay on the script if they aren't," he says, and the others start nodding their heads in agreement.

Inhale, exhale. I am one with the universe. Or whatever.

After a very long breath, I muster up any strength I have

left and say, "Yes, I understand that. But as you can see," I point to the script that's in front of me, the script that's in front of everyone in this room, "there are ways to bring them back to the script."

"Maybe we should do some role-playing," Jim offers. Jim with the glasses and the greasy hair and the disorderly clothing. And the Axe body spray. It's extra-strong today and not helping my headache.

"Great idea," I say and smile at Jim, my cheek muscles aching. Look at me being all complimentary and awesome-boss-like. I will not point out that I offered this idea up earlier and was shot down. *Namaste.*

We do this for another half hour. And unbelievably, I feel like there might be a breakthrough happening. Like my team and I are actually working together, and they're understanding what I need them to do. And the excitement I'm having at this sliver of possibility makes me feel like I might be able to do this. I can run a team and keep my feelings in check. Maybe yoga helped after all.

Twenty minutes later, though, I'm lying on the floor of my office with my legs up against the wall in some pose I learned in yoga, trying to calm myself.

After I left my team, I went back to my office and listened in on three calls. Brad did fine, he stayed on script and had a pleasant tone to his voice (this has been a problem in the past). Jim sounded very robot-like, but he got the job done. We will, however, need to address the robot tones . . . again. Sarah-with-an-h, though . . . her caller got a little flirty. This is not out of the norm around here; we've all been flirted with over the phone. But as we've been trained, we're supposed to keep the client on task. Sarah did not keep the client on task. In her defense, he was a little hard to get back on track. Not in her defense, she kept giggling like an idiotic fourteen-year-old.

My first instinct was to march into their office and tell Sarah all the things she did wrong. In a yelling tone. But then I thought about the promotion and the breathing I had learned and decided I needed to check myself before I wrecked myself, as Ice-T so poignantly rapped. Hence my current position. And yes, I'm wearing a skirt. I was able to pull it over my thighs . . . mostly.

How can I stay on my well-thought-out life plan when everyone is doing everything to ruin it? Perhaps I did it all wrong. Perhaps you're just supposed to sail through life, seeing where the wind takes you. But that's how my mom lived, and I saw what it did to her. No. This is a blip, that's all. A big, freaking, annoying blip. Well, you know what? I'm mentally giving you the middle finger, you stupid blip.

Inhale, exhale. Inhale, exhale.

"Holly," a voice from behind me says, startling me from my thoughts. I'm at the Lava Java because I'm ... well, I'm avoiding. I couldn't take another minute in my stifling office. And also all the deep breathing made me light headed and I needed some air. So, I grabbed my wallet and walked over here. My wallet wasn't necessary since I'm still on

Nathan's tab. Which I'll fix next time, I swear.

"Logan," I say as I turn around. I can't hide my irritation. I had hoped this time maybe he wouldn't be here, or maybe he'd be back to his old ways of ignoring me. But no such luck. I mean, he does "like me just fine," after all. We're pretty much besties.

"How are you?" Logan asks, putting his hands in his pockets.

"I'm . . ." I let out a big breath. My standard answer is usually a quick "good" to this question. But I'm not good. Not right now. But this is Logan and there's like a hundred-million percent chance he won't care anyway, so what the heck. "Not great, actually," I say.

"Really?" A look of real concern crosses his face, which both surprises and confuses me.

"Yep," I say.

"Nathan?" he asks, pulling his eyebrows in even farther.

"What?" I shake my head. "No, I . . ." I stall because it dawns on me that my current problems, or at least the ones that have been on my mind the most, have nothing to do with Nathan or the canceled wedding. It all has to do with work. If I'm honest with myself, I've thought of him and the breakup less and less, lately. Huh. That's interesting.

A male voice from behind the service counter calls my name. I take the few steps needed to get to the counter and pick up my coffee, all the while pondering how little I've been thinking about Nathan and our broken engagement. I don't even feel that ping of sadness run through me like I used to.

"So then why?" Logan asks, pulling me out of my thoughts.

I give him a one-shoulder shrug, holding on to my fresh coffee with both hands. "It's just work stuff."

He rocks back on the heels of his flip-flops, his hands still in his pockets. "Do you . . . uh . . . want to talk about it?"

"With you?" The words pop out of my mouth so quickly I have no time to think them through or at least filter my tone so I don't sound so surprised.

"Yeah." The corner of his mouth lifts slightly — the beginnings of a smile. I've never gotten a full smile from Logan. I've seen it from a distance before. It's a pretty dazzling smile, if I'm being honest. I mean, if there wasn't such a jerk behind it, it would be dazzling.

"No . . . that's . . . okay," I say, moving my head back and forth as I fumble through my words.

The other corner of his mouth lifts up now. "I'm a good listener."

Was that what he was doing all that time before when he stared at me like I was a complete buffoon? Listening? I don't think I believe him.

"Come on," he says, with a head nod in the direction of his normal booth. "Step into my office."

I snort-laugh at this because it catches me so off guard. Did Logan Stand-Off-Ish Palmer make a joke?

He doesn't respond. Instead, he puts a hand on my lower back and guides me toward the booth. The touch of his hand has me feeling all kinds of uncomfortable. The last time I was here, he touched my arm, and now he's touching my back. It's confusing, and odd, and so freaking weird.

We take seats across from each other and I set my coffee in front of me. I feel strange and jittery. I'm in a situation I've never been before—and never imagined I'd ever be in—and, well, I'm not quite sure what do to with myself.

"So what's going on?" Logan asks, intertwining his fingers and placing his hands on the table—poised and ready to listen.

I swallow and then mimic his hands, intertwining my fingers and settling them on the table. "Well," I start and then stop myself.

He stares at me, waiting on my words. Should I get out of this? I could stand up and walk away. I let out a breath. And then for some reason, I tell him. I just start talking. I tell him about the promotion, the whole vacation thing, and my team.

When I'm finished, I sit back in my seat. It feels good to dump all this out. No new clarity on my part, more of a refreshing feeling. I don't do this very often. Quinn is pretty much the one and only recipient of my thought-dumps. I can tell her anything and she won't judge me. And if she does, she'll just tell me: "I'm judging you so hard right now." But letting it all out to Logan feels different from telling Quinn. He's listening to me in a way that makes it seem like he's present. Like he's not trying to interject anything or only listening to respond.

"I see," he finally says after staring at me for a few beats.

I eye him dubiously. "Do you?"

The corner of his mouth lifts slightly again. "Do you

want my opinion?"

I take in a quick breath. He's asking me and not just offering it? That's not normal. At least not in my experience.

"Um . . . sure," I say feeling quite curious that Logan has an opinion and it has to do with me.

"You need to take a vacation."

"Wow, profound," I say sarcastically and a bit disappointed. I had—for a brief second—wondered if Logan might have the answer. Like maybe he had all this profound information and he just never offered it until asked. What a bummer.

His lips pull up again, the echo of a smile. "Sometimes it's the hard answer," he says, his eyes moving down to the table between us. "Although, I never thought taking a vacation would be the hard answer."

"Hmph," I mutter through closed lips.

"But," he looks up, his eyes meeting mine, "that's kind of your thing."

"My 'thing'?"

"Making the easy stuff harder," he says.

"What? That's ridiculous."

"Is it?"

"Yes—yeah. I don't do that."

His lips pull out into an even line, that normal facial expression of his. He sits back in his seat and studies me.

I shake my head, feeling so very odd. Like the first day of school when you were a kid. Almost out-of-body. "Logan, you have no idea what my 'thing' is."

"Sure I do," he says, a smug expression on his face.

"Oh, I get it," I dip my chin to my chest. "You're one of those guys who thinks they have women pegged."

He shakes his head in slow and small movements, his eyes on me. "I've never claimed to understand women."

"But you think you know me?"

"Well, we've been around each other quite a bit."

"Yeah, but it's not like you've had any real conversations with me."

He shrugs one shoulder. "It doesn't matter if we've had long conversations; I've been around you enough to see."

"I don't believe you."

"Okay, well, let me ask you this. When's the last time you did something spontaneous?"

"Well . . . I . . ." I stop so I can think for a second. "I came here on a whim," I say after a few seconds, feeling quite smug by my answer. Because I did come here without thinking about it. Mostly to avoid work.

"Here?" He scrunches his forehead.

"Yeah. Here."

"Ooo," he shakes his hands, palms facing me, "how daring."

"Shut up," I say, half-irritated, half-laughing. Logan made a joke and is now teasing me? He chuckles too, through a closed-mouth smile. His laugh is low and guttural and his whole body moves as he does it. My insides twist and turn in strange ways seeing him like this.

"How about something bigger," he says.

I struggle to come up with an answer, and I really want to come up with one—to prove him wrong. I know there's one, I have one. I just need some time.

"Well . . . I can't think of anything right now," I say.

His lips curl up smugly and I feel a sudden burst of irritation. This whole situation is ridiculous. Talking to Logan, opening up to him . . . him acting like he knows me at all. Which he doesn't. The whole thing is silly. And stupid. And annoying.

I go to stand, scooting out of the booth, which is never as easy as scooting back a chair and standing up. There's maneuvering and probably some awkward facial features and noises as the skin on my leg moves along the fake leather seat. I finally get myself out of the booth and grab my coffee.

"Well, thanks for your thoughts," I say, making sure that through my tone, it's very obvious I'm not thankful, nor has anything he said been helpful. Because I'm not. And it hasn't.

"Anytime," he says with a lift of his chin.

With that, I turn around and leave.

"Knock, knock!" a sing-song voice says from outside my office door, paired with a couple of light knocks.

I should have left for the day rather than coming back here after the Lava Java.

"Come in," I say wishing I had some sort of trap door I could disappear through.

"Holly," Tiffany says, a smile on her face. Today she's wearing a royal blue dress that hugs her curves perfectly.

"I just popped in to see how today went," she says, standing in the doorway. She probably wants me to invite her in to take a seat, but I don't.

"Today?" I ask, even though I know exactly what she's talking about.

"Yes, your team training?" She comes in and takes a seat anyway. She sits with her butt perched on the edge of the chair, as if ready to spring off at any minute. Oh, if only she would.

"Oh, yes," I bat a hand around in the air. "It went great," I lie.

"Oh, good," she says. "It's so hard to manage these kids, am I right?" She laughs a super annoying laugh. And kids? I think Brad is like five years older than me.

"Sure," I say, only capable of mustering up half of a fake smile.

"Of course, when you train them right, they just do their job. Like my team," she says, echoing my fake smile and adding a patronizing tone to her voice.

I see Tiffany has decided not to spar and go straight for the gut-punch. I'd say the B-word is quite fitting right now. I can't say it out loud, but I shall say it repeatedly in my head.

"Do you have anything else for me, Tiffany?" *Or are you here to rub your amazing training skills in my face? B-word. B-word, B-word, B-word.*

"Actually, yes," she says with an expression on her face that tells me this is the real reason she's in my office and I find I want to be anywhere but here. Like on a beach, even.

"Do tell," I say blandly.

She leans forward and splays her hands on my desk. "I have it on good authority," she says low and quietly, "that Mike is leaving in July." I go rigid in my seat, but keep my facial expressions in check.

"Really?" I say, trying to feign non-interest. I'm trying to figure out how she could have this bit of info. Marie said no one else but she knew about Mike leaving and about the job opening. I was told to keep it to myself until further notice. And now Tiffany knows and has a date, even. July? That's like three months away. So soon.

"How do you know this?" I ask, not able to help myself.

"Oh, silly Holly," she says with a cackle of delight. "I can't tell you that." She shakes her head, her face full of condescension. "Anyway, I just wanted to warn you."

"Warn me?"

"Yes," she says.

I tilt my head, looking at her through squinty eyes. "Why would I need a warning?"

She squints back. "Well, because clearly the job will go to either you or me."

"You don't know that," I say. "They could hire from outside." I'm just saying this. Marie has already told me they were planning on hiring internally.

"True," she nods in agreement. She peers over her shoulder again, and then back to me when she feels confident no one is listening, "But I have it on good authority that it's going to be an inside promotion."

"Interesting," I say, leaning back in my chair as I feign

nonchalance. Inside I'm still trying to figure out how she would know. Did Marie tell her? No, there's no way it was Marie.

"I also wanted to warn you about something else," she says, her voice lowering even further, the corner of her lip twitching upward. "My source has told me that I'm the front-runner."

This time I'm not able to hold back any facial expressions. My jaw drops in reflex, my mouth forming an O. And upon my reaction, her lip twitch transforms into an unmistakable smirk.

She thinks she's the front-runner? She . . . her . . . Tiffany . . . the front runner for Mike's job. Well now, isn't that *interesting*. I kind of want to say I have it on *real* authority that the job is mine . . . if I can get my team to stop being such stupid freaking babies. I can't tell her this since I was told in confidence by Marie, but, oh, how I wish I could rub it in her smug face. Pretty sure that would fix my chakras.

"Now, Holly, don't you go worrying about all that," she says, a sudden lightness to her tone, fakeness oozing from every pore. "I'm sure you still have a chance. But, you know, I wanted to give you a heads-up so you don't get too excited about the idea."

Oh, Tiffany. So helpful. So B-word-y.

"That is so kind of you, Tiffany," I say, mustering up my best mocking tone.

"Well, what are friends for?" she says.

Oh, Tiffany. Tiffany, Tiffany, Tiffany. We aren't friends and we never will be, is what I want to say.

JUST A NAME

"Well, I sure do appreciate it," is what I really say. But I make sure it's oozing with extra-thick patronizing tones.

With that, she excuses herself from my office and is off as quickly as her tinkling Manolo Blahniks can take her.

I slouch back in my chair, letting out a deep breath. This definitely changes things. Just like that, I have a deadline *and* competition.

There's no way I'm taking a vacation now.

CHAPTER 8

"I leave you both alone for thirty seconds to find you molesting a cabinet?" Thomas asks, dramatically moving his hands around.

It's Wednesday evening and Quinn invited Thomas and me to go antique shopping with her because she likes to have me there for a second opinion, and she makes Thomas come so he can help us load whatever she buys into her car.

Currently we're in an antique shop in downtown Winter Park, and Quinn and I both have our hands on a light gray antique curio cabinet, feeling the fine detail and design that's on the doors.

"Shut up, Thomas," Quinn says.

"What do you want to do with it?" I ask.

"Fix it up. Sand down some parts. Paint it sky blue," she says. We both continue touching the molding on the front.

"It's hideous," Thomas declares.

"I think I'm going to buy it," Quinn says, and Thomas's body sags in displeasure. He doesn't just do the neck and shoulder sag, but rather a whole-body effort.

"I think it's gorgeous," I say.

"This old thing?" Thomas says, holding his hand in the direction of the cabinet. With its worn paint and sagging left door, it will need some help, but the potential is there. "Oh right, I forgot you like this kind of crap," he says to Quinn.

Quinn doesn't just like antiques, it's her only hobby. And she's fantastically talented at it. She can find some of the ugliest pieces and change them into something incredible. She even has her own online store, which is rapidly growing in popularity. *Quinn Creates* is what she calls it, and the items she puts up sell within days. Hours, sometimes.

"Nothing a little Quinn lovin' can't fix," she says in response to Thomas, a smirk on her face.

"That's what all the guys are saying," Thomas says, earning a slap on the arm from Quinn and an eye roll from me.

"I think it's a great piece," I say.

"It's a piece all right," says Thomas.

"Why do we even bring you?" I ask.

"Well, obviously you need something pretty to look at," he says, circling his face with his index finger. "I mean, look around you. Even the people who shop at these places are hideous." He nods his head toward an elderly lady wearing what appears to be a house coat standing a few feet away from us, perusing through a basket of old door knobs.

"You're disgusting," Quinn says, when she sees who he's referring to.

"Are you buying this piece of junk or not?" he asks. "I'm starving."

After studying it for a bit more, she declares it worthy of her Quinn-ness and purchases it. We then decide to walk down the street to the Green Grill to get some dinner, the damp, warm evening air making my skin and clothes feel sticky during the short jaunt.

The restaurant — all organic — is packed tonight, which is strange for a Wednesday. But we put our name in and take a seat on one of the benches they have in the waiting area.

Thomas and Quinn are bickering about something when the door to the restaurant opens, wafting in the humid air, and I hear a laugh.

I don't even need to see a face, I'd recognize his laugh anywhere. Nathan. Of all the restaurants in all Central Florida . . .

Nathan walks in all bright-eyed, his hair tousled like it always is. Hanging onto his arm as he enters is the blond girl from that night at Hester's. The night Logan said was just a business dinner. *Allegedly.* But there's nothing businesslike about the scene before me. Once they come in through the door, Nathan wraps an arm around the blondie's shoulders and she snuggles into him, resting her head on him. He leans his head down and says something that must have been funny because she lets out a high-pitched laugh.

They waltz up to the host stand, an aura of happiness surrounding them. After a few words to the host, Nathan looks to his left and there I am. Sitting with Quinn and Thomas, who have stopped fighting to take in the scene I'm seeing.

"Holly," Nathan says as he walks toward us, a big smile on his face.

"Nathan," I say, giving him my best cheesy grin. The fakest one I can muster.

"And Quinn and Thomas. Good to see you," he says, acknowledging my friends. "This is Christine," he says, giving one nod to the girl he's still got his arm around.

I can't even muster up a hello, so I smile thinly. I was supposed to be marrying this man in a little over a month. Our lives were to be intertwined permanently. Now he's standing here, his arm around another woman. It's all so . . . weird. And I feel like I should feel at least a little heartbroken at the sight, but I don't. Not at all. Awkward, yes. Heartbroken, not so much.

"And how did you two lovebirds meet?" Thomas asks. Which ups the awkward level to a fever pitch. Thomas is good at this. It's one of his many skills—making things even more uncomfortable than they already are.

"Uh," Nathan says, now appearing a little sheepish. The situation must have just dawned on him fully. He's often a little slow on the uptake. Especially in social situations.

"Through work," Christine answers for him. "My company wants to buy Nathan's latest app."

Well, at least now I know Logan was telling the truth about that.

She peers up at Nathan after she says this, a look of pride in her face, and smiles. He smiles back. She reminds me of a garden fairy with her wispy blond hair and her cute button nose. She's also several inches shorter than Nathan.

And she's dressed in skinny jeans and a tight cotton tank. Much more dressed down than the last time I saw her and also very different from how I dress. I don't do cotton tanks. Unless I'm running. Nathan used to get on me about that, saying I always had to dress up for everything. But I'm not a jeans and T-shirt kind of girl.

The host calls out Quinn's name and we say quick good-byes and I throw out a "nice to meet you" even though it wasn't all that nice.

We take our seats at a round table far off in the corner and I throw out a quick wish that Nathan and the pixie will be seated far away. But since the Universe or karma or whatever seems to have left me and has most likely grabbed a soda and some popcorn and taken a comfortable seat to see how this life of mine is going to play out, my hopes are low.

The server arrives and we order drinks and an appetizer to share.

Thomas sits back in his chair dramatically. "All right, Hols. Let's talk about the elephant in the room."

"I'd rather not," I say.

"We need to talk about it."

"We don't," I say.

He lets out a deep sigh and then smacks his lips. "What are we going to do about our parents getting married?"

I let out a small snort as Quinn's eyes go wide with this bit of news.

I didn't know he knew. And I hadn't said anything because my dad had told me not to until Miranda had had a chance to talk to Thomas. I also know right away that Thomas doesn't know there's a date and a venue as well, because he would have led with that info. He wouldn't be able to hold himself back.

"What?" Quinn says, stunned by this info.

"It's true," Thomas says, his face moving to hers. "Holly and I are going to be," he gulps for emphasis, "siblings."

"Are you serious?" Quinn says loudly, slapping the table in front of her. The older couple at the table next to us turns to look.

"Keep it down," Thomas says to Quinn. "I've told you more than once, you have the voice of a banshee."

Quinn rolls her eyes.

"When did you find out?" I ask.

"Monday," he says flatly.

"Your parents are getting married," Quinn says, obviously having trouble wrapping her brain around this information.

"Yes," Thomas says. "Unless we can stop them."

"Why would we do that?" I ask. I'm not asking to ask—I really want to know why. Is there something Thomas knows that I don't?

"Well, for starters, they haven't dated that long."

I nod my head—that was my initial worry as well. It all started on New Year's Eve at a party that Thomas threw. I had invited my dad along because spending the night before the New Year together has always been a tradition. It was only about a half hour into the party that my dad and Miranda struck up a conversation, and that was the beginning of it all.

"And, I mean, well, you've seen my mom," he tilts his head toward me.

"What's that supposed to mean? My dad's a catch," I say, instantly annoyed that Thomas might think his mom is better than my dad. If anything, it's the opposite.

"Yeah, Hols's dad is a total babe," Quinn says, and I give her a face full of disgust. Quinn has always said my dad is handsome and then usually adds some sort of "if I weren't your best friend" clause. Which is gross on so many levels.

"But now my dreams of Mommy and Daddy ever getting back together are totally squashed," Thomas says.

"Thomas, your dad has been remarried for years. That dream was squashed long ago," Quinn says, her face full of confusion.

"Yes, but this is the final nail in that coffin," Thomas says, a notable whining tone to his voice. "And anyway, her last name will be Murphy."

"What's wrong with Murphy?" pipes in Quinn, and I nod my head agreeing with that question.

He smacks his lips again. "It's the whole double 'M' thing. Miranda Murphy."

"But she's Miranda Moore now," I say.

"I know, and how sad for her. She did a disservice to herself with that, and now she's doing it again. I just had higher hopes that if she remarried, she'd get a better monogram," he hangs his head wearily.

I want to say that "disservice" is the only reason he exists right now, but decide to let him have his moment. Plus, I know what this is really about as I spy Nathan and Christine being seated not too far from us. Thomas is very good at getting people to divert their attention. Deflecting. He's awesome at it. It's a talent, and probably why he's so good at the lawyer thing.

"Wow, Thomas," Quinn says. "I've heard a lot of stupid things out of your mouth, and this one probably ranks at the top."

Thomas gives her a one shoulder shrug and then gives me a wink. I smile and shake my head at him. For all the things he's not—couth, inhibited, thoughtful—he makes up for in other ways. Maybe this whole sibling thing won't be so bad.

We order our food after our appetizer comes out, the discussion centering around our normal topics. Relationships—which doesn't last long since none of us are in one—and work.

"Jerry still all up in your face?" Thomas asks Quinn after taking a long sip of some fruity drink he ordered.

She sighs. "Yeah, he's being such an *A*. I can't seem to do anything right and I don't know what else to do. That stupid video will haunt me forever."

I pull my lips in tight to keep myself from smiling. Poor Quinn. It doesn't help that I pulled up the video to watch today because I needed a pick-me-up at work after meeting with my team. As I see Thomas trying to keep himself from laughing as well, I wonder if he also watched it. What terrible friends we are.

"So you need to find something else that will grab his attention. Something to get his mind off it," Thomas says after a beat.

"Well, I had the perfect idea, but Holly screwed that up," she says.

I snort out my nose, and then add an eye roll for emphasis. "Sorry to disappoint you."

Thomas looks back and forth between us, trying to figure out what we're talking about. "What did I miss?"

Quinn takes a big, dramatic breath. "I thought Holly here should do a search for another Nathan Jones to go on her honeymoon with her," she says. "I could set it up with the station, make it a story. Jerry would eat that crap up."

"What?" Thomas looks flabbergasted. "You think Holly should find another Nathan Jones—a stranger Nathan Jones—to go on what was supposed to be her honeymoon? Like that weirdo lady from New York did?"

"Right?" I say, grateful he feels the same as me.

He turns his head to me. "Hols, how could you *not* do this?"

Oh, right. I should have known he'd side with Quinn. Silly me.

My eyes stare briefly at the ceiling before I respond. "Because," I finally say, "do I seem like the type of person who would do something like that?"

"That's exactly why you should do it," he says.

"That's exactly why I shouldn't do it," I retort.

"This is a win/win for everyone, though," Thomas says, and Quinn dips her chin, agreeing.

"It's a win for everyone but me," I say, feeling defensive.

In what world would this ever be a win for me?

"If you do it, Quinn will get gross Jerry off her back, you will take a vacation, which will get your boss off your back. Weren't you whining about that at Hester's on Monday night?"

"I didn't whine," I scoff. I'd been trying to get my friends to help me figure out what to do with my boss now that I know Tiffany is on the prowl for Mike's job.

"Yes, you did," he says, giving me his best condescending stare. "But also, this will be utterly entertaining for me, and you know I like to be entertained — and you, my dear," he slaps me lightly on the arm, "will get your revenge." He does a quick head nod to where Nathan and Christine are sitting. "It's actually a win-win-win-win," he says, as he counts off on his fingers.

I grunt. "What would I need revenge for?"

"Uh, bucko over there. Duh." He juts a thumb over his shoulder in Nathan's direction. Quinn nods her head in approval.

I gape at them both, my face scrunched up in annoyance. "You guys, that's . . . well, messed up. On many levels. I don't want revenge against Nathan. There's no revenge to be had. And besides, how would doing that even get revenge? More likely it would be more revenge against me when it all blows up in my face."

"It wouldn't," Quinn says.

"Yes. It would."

"Oh, Holly," Thomas says, a patronizing grin on his face. "My dear, sweet, naive Holly." He reaches over and pats me on the head.

"Stop it," I say, pushing his hand away.

He stops the patting but keeps the grin. "No matter if it blows up in your face, it would still be revenge on Nathan."

"How's that?" Quinn asks, placing her elbow on the table, her chin in her hand.

"Because it would be something Holly's never done before."

"Why are we talking about me like I'm not here?"

Thomas turns to me. "Wasn't that one of the things Nathan complained about?" He mimics Quinn, with his chin in his hand, elbow perched on the table. "Your lack of adventure, wasn't it?"

I sigh. That *was* one of Nathan's complaints. He was always wanting to do adventurous things with me. Like go zip lining or jump out of a plane. But there were too many variables for me. I'm not a living-on-the-edge kind of person, and I never will be. That was my mother's mantra—you only live once. YOLO. I think she coined the phrase. At least that was her mantra when she wasn't in bed. She spent a lot of time in that bed. Now she's spending all her time in a jail cell. See where adventure gets you?

"Yes, that was one of our issues," I say. Then I shake my head. "It doesn't matter, because I'm not doing it. And even if I did do it—which I'm not," I throw in, seeing Quinn's face morph into a hopeful expression, "I can't leave now. I have too much on the line."

"We forgot one other variable," Thomas says, his not-giving-up-face now on.

"And that is?"

"The whole thing might make Nathan insanely jealous and want you back."

I shake my head. Does Thomas even hear anything I say? "Even if that did happen, I wouldn't want him back."

"Yeah, good idea," Thomas says, sarcasm swimming in his tone. "He's not attractive or wealthy or anything."

"He's a total jerk," says Quinn, defending me with her tone. I know she's saying this for my benefit because that's not true either. No, Nathan was the whole deal. He just wasn't the right deal for me.

"You guys, I don't want Nathan back, or revenge, or to entertain you, Thomas. There's no way I'm going to do it," I say.

"Well, then, that's your funeral," Thomas says.

"Yes, because death is clearly the only other option," I say.

"Well, it might be my funeral," Quinn says.

"Sorry, Quinn," I say, reaching over and putting my hand on top of hers. "You know I'll help you any way I can. Just not this way."

She looks over and gives me a sad smile. "I might hold you to that."

CHAPTER 9

You know that saying "when life gives you lemons, make lemonade"? Well, right now life is giving me lemons. And I don't want to make lemonade with them. I want to squeeze the juice into someone's paper cut.

It's the next day and I've just finished meeting with the Sarahs regarding their break time . . . again. Their breaks are too long and too often. And this is not something only I've observed. Avery has also voiced her annoyance about it as well. Multiple times.

It *is* annoying. It was my second meeting with them regarding this—but unlike last time, I couldn't be all straightforward. I need them to like me, so this time I had to be more coddling. I don't like to coddle, it makes me feel all itchy and dirty.

The crazy part? Sarah-with-an-h said, in a snotty tone, "Why are you being so nice about this?" And the other Sara said, "Yeah, why aren't you, like, getting all mad?" They were actually annoyed that I wasn't getting mad, and then Sarah asked me why I was being so weird lately with all the treats I'd been bringing in and how I've been "like, all sweet around us and whatever." Those were her actual words.

So apparently my trying and putting in all this effort is bothering them.

I can't win.

The meeting ended okay, I think. I was able to bring it back around saying crap like, "We're all in this together." They seemed to come around and told me they would work on it. We'll see how long that lasts.

Now, Alex and I are heading to the Lava Java. I need a pick-me-up and recruited Alex to join me.

Alex started working for CT Anderson Bank about a year ago as a junior executive in the marketing department. I took him under my wing after he inadvertently sent the word *wieners* instead of *webinars* to a large portion of the company. Try as I might, I haven't yet been able to get some of the guys on the management team to stop referring to him as the Wiener Man. He's been a champ about dealing with it, because at this point the only other option would be to find another job.

Not long after wienergate, I asked him to hang out at Hester's with my friends because I had this grand notion of setting him up with Quinn. I thought Alex, with his kind heart and boy-next-door good looks, and Quinn with her striking blue eyes and quick wit, would make the most perfect babies. I apparently suck at matchmaking, because I soon found out that Alex—sweet, naive boy that he is—seemed to only have eyes for Bree, much to the disappointment of both Quinn and me. And dearest Bree—who truly has a flare for the wrong kind of guy— has never shown any interest. Not in that way, at least.

We walk across the street from the bank to the Lava Java. The air is thick with humidity and it attaches to my face, my skin, my clothes, and my hair as we walk.

"How is it so hot already?" Alex asks, his face contorted with annoyance. He bats his hands around to get a grouping of gnats out of our path as we walk. "It's not even May yet."

"You do know it's summer here pretty much all year, right?"

He gives me a half smile. Of course he knows that, having grown up on the beach near Ft. Myers. His parents still live there. Although Southern Florida has the sea breeze, which we don't get here in Central Florida.

A side benefit of having Alex with me at the Lava Java is he can be my bodyguard in case Logan is there. Well, I don't really need a bodyguard for Logan. I just think he won't bother to talk to me if I have Alex there.

Alex opens the door to the café, the smell of coffee wafting through, the blast of air-conditioning hitting my face as I walk inside. My eyes, without even asking me, travel to the booth where Logan usually sits, and to my surprise, he's not there. I look a little closer to make sure there's no computer there, or earphones. It's empty. Also, to my surprise, I don't get a feeling of elation like I expected. Instead, I feel like this day is topsy-turvy. My employees think I'm being too nice, and Logan isn't at the Lava Java. What is happening with this world?

"What are you staring at?" Alex asks, his eyes moving over to Logan's usual table.

"Nothing," I quickly say, moving my head over to the menu hanging on the wall behind the service counter, as if that's what I've been looking at all along.

Alex and I place our orders and then wait by the pickup counter, chatting about frivolous things. It feels nice to chat with Alex. No pretense. No expectations.

"Holly . . . Alex," I hear a deep voice say from behind us. Oh, yay.

We both turn around to find Logan standing there. Gray V-neck tee, hands in the pockets of his jeans. His lips are pulled into that same thin line.

Well, apparently having Alex didn't stop Logan from coming over here like I thought it would. Where did he come from, anyway? I know all his stuff wasn't at his normal table. And now I sound like a weird stalker.

"Logan," Alex says, holding out a hand to shake his. Logan complies. Alex is clearly a terrible bodyguard. Not that he knew he was one. "Good to see you, man. How you been?"

"Good," Logan says, both corners of his mouth lifting briefly — like, millisecond briefly.

"How's the app thing going?" Alex asks. Alex is one of those people who are good at making conversation. It makes me wonder if he even notices that talking to Logan is sort of like talking to a wall. A wall that only grunts out one word answers. Well, at least that's how it was for me up until last week, before he got all talk-y.

"Good," says The Wall.

Alex's phone rings in his pocket and he pulls it out. I catch a glimpse of the caller ID and see the name *Bree Donnells* before he turns the phone away from me.

"I've gotta take this," he says to Logan and me. "Be right back." He walks out of the coffee shop and stands outside the door.

I can't believe he ditched me like that. And for Bree? When is he ever going to figure out Bree's too blinded by her own stupidity to realize how great he is? I've tried to get her to see the light. We all have.

Logan gives me a small, closed-mouth smile when I turn back to him.

"I . . . uh . . . didn't think you were here," I say pointing over to his normal booth.

"Oh, yeah," he reaches up and scratches the back of his neck. "Someone was sitting there when I got here this morning. So I took the booth in the back." He lifts his chin in the direction of his make-shift office. The booth is situated so you wouldn't be able to see if someone was sitting there. "Were you looking for me?" His lips pull into a smirk.

"No," I say a little too emphatically. "I happened to look over in that area and, you know, just noticed."

"Right," he says, his lips pulling up on one side. A cocky almost-smile.

"And anyway, it's right over there, front and center. *You* had to actually look over this way to see me from that booth." I gesture with my hand over in the direction of his current seating arrangement.

"I could hear you," he says.

"What?"

"I could hear you talking," he says.

I put my hands on my waist, one leg out in front of me. "Are you stalking me?"

Now both of his lips pull up into a smile. A broader one than I've ever gotten. No teeth, though.

"It's only stalking if you're ugly," he quips.

I take in a quick breath, my jaw slackening. "You made a joke," I say.

"Yeah." He gives me a preposterous look.

"I didn't think you were capable of making jokes."

He scrunches up his face. "I make jokes."

"No, you don't," I retort.

"Yes, I do," he replies.

I hear my and Alex's names called from behind the pickup counter and I pick up our coffees. I look out the door to see Alex still standing outside talking on his phone.

"How's the vacation planning going?" Logan asks.

"Um," I twist my lips to the side, wondering what Alex and Bree could be talking about. "I'm sorry, what?" I say, turning back to Logan.

"The vacation?"

"Oh, that." I shrug a shoulder. "I can't do that. Not right now."

Not until the promotion is mine and Tiffany has to walk away with her tail between her legs. And maybe find a new place of employment. Ah, to dream.

My biggest conundrum now is how to convince Marie that I need more time—*a lot* more time before I can take any time off. I can't exactly tell her what Tiffany told me. No one is supposed to know. That would open up a whole can of worms I don't want to open. There's got to be a way I can get her to see.

"Well, it was good seeing you, Logan," I say holding up a coffee in his direction as a way of waving since I don't have any hands to make the gesture.

"See you," he says, seeming somewhat disappointed. At least, I think so. You never know with him. Probably not, because what would he have to be disappointed about? He puts his hands in his pockets, giving me a quick lift of his chin even though he actually has two empty hands. But waving might be too intimate for Logan.

"What was that all about?" I ask Alex, who's just hung up as I walk out. I hand him his coffee.

"Nothing," he says, taking the coffee from me. We start walking toward the crosswalk that will take us across the street to the bank.

"I saw Bree's name on your caller ID," I say as we walk.

"Oh," he says. "Yeah, she just wanted to talk."

"Do you do that often?"

"What, talk?" He looks at me, confusion on his face.

"Yeah," I say.

"Uh, yeah," he says. "We talk."

"That's good," I say.

"It is."

"That's all you're going to tell me, isn't it?" I ask.

"Yep." He gives me a wink. "Come on, let's get back to the grind."

With that, he grabs my forearm gently and guides me across the street.

I think Marie's disappointed with me.

When I got back from the Lava Java, there was a message on my computer from her telling me she's back from her offsite meetings and needed to meet with me right away. So I went straight to her office, and she did not seem happy to see me.

Also, the first words out of her mouth were, "I'm disappointed in you, Holly." So there's that.

My stomach twists and turns and I try to think of what the problem might be. Then it dawns on me. She must have found out that Tiffany knows about Mike's job and thinks I told her. Okay, I can fix this.

"I think I know why you're mad," I say tentatively.

"Well," she says, none-to-pleased, "you should know."

"Yes," I say, weaving my fingers together and placing my hands in my lap. "Let me first tell you I had no idea. I mean, I don't know how she knows. I—"

"Wait," Marie says, stopping me from continuing. Which is good. I tend to run-off when I'm nervous. "What are you talking about?"

I scrunch my face. What if I'm wrong and this is not what she's mad about? "Well, what do you think I'm talking about?"

She eyes me wearily. "I haven't a clue."

Okay, so maybe I'm wrong. That was a close one. "Then what are you disappointed about?"

She lets out a breath. "Because, Holly. You are not taking this vacation thing seriously."

"Oh," I say. "Well —"

She cuts me off with a hand. "I gave you a week to get me a vacation request and it's been ten days and the only thing you've done is put it off."

I reach up and wrap some hair around my finger, my eyes downcast. "I *have* been working on it," I say. I look up to find her glaring at me, her head pitched to the side, her eyes full of disbelief.

"Have you? Because, honestly, it's a vacation. I'm not asking you to become a black belt in karate."

I take a deep breath and sit up confidently. I'm just going to be straight with Marie. I need to tell her that fixing things with my team is what I need to do first, and then I can go. What I can't tell her is I also need to be here to make sure Tiffany doesn't dig her talons into Mike's old job. So really, I need to put off a vacation until after I've secured the promotion.

But before I can say anything, Marie has pulled her laptop over, clicked on a few buttons and turns the screen around for me to see.

"See that number there?" She points to the highlighted number near the bottom of the screen.

"Yes," I say, not sure what it means.

"Those are your accrued days off since you've started working. Sixty-five days."

"Okay," I say.

"See the number under that? Those are the days you have yet to take off."

I nibble on my bottom lip. Sixty-two days. I have only taken three personal days off since I started working here. In my defense, we do get a lot of holidays off since this is a bank and all. But I'm not sure I should throw that out there right now.

"Sixty-two days," Marie says, flabbergasted.

"Marie," I start, trying to come up with my on-the-spot defense.

"Do you know what I see when I look at you?" Marie says, holding a hand out to stop me from going any further. "I see someone who is working too hard, someone who has put work ahead of life. And I understand you're a hard worker, and I like that about you—but people who work this much will break. I've seen it happen too many times."

I mentally scoff at that. That wouldn't happen to me.

She sighs. "Mike's job, the one you've been working toward—do you know why he's leaving? He can't take the stress of it anymore. He's tired of trying to juggle it all." She looks me in the eyes. "I need to see you taking care of yourself so I know you'll be able to handle all the responsibility. And three days off in the past five years? That's not you taking care of you."

"I—" I start but then stop, as she shakes her head at me. What can I even say to that?

She breathes out a heavy breath. "Just go, Holly." She bats a hand at me toward the door of her office. I've never seen her this mad.

I can't leave it like this. I need to fix this. But what can I do?

"Well, I do have something planned," I say, the words spilling out of my mouth as I realize I do have an option. The worst option ever.

"You do?" Her face brightens up at this.

"Yes," I say. Then I lick my lips to stall for a second. "I just . . . wasn't sure how to tell you."

She scrunches her forehead. "Why's that?"

"I'm not sure it falls under what you're wanting me to do," I say and lick my lips again. They feel suddenly very dry, as does my throat.

"Tell me," she says.

"Well, my friend Quinn approached me for a news feature, to go on my honeymoon, but with someone with the same name as my fiancé."

"Huh?" Marie questions, confusion on her face.

I take a steadying breath. "Quinn—my friend—does the midday news for channel four, and she pitched an idea where I do a nationwide search for someone with the same name as Nathan to go on my honeymoon trip with me. You can't change the name on a ticket, see, so it would have to be someone with his exact name."

"Didn't that woman in New York do the same thing a while back?" she asks, her eyes getting brighter.

"Yes," I say, feeling sickly butterflies gathering in my

stomach.

"I followed that story and I was disappointed when they didn't fall in love."

"Right," I say, now feeling like I might throw up the butterflies.

"And your friend Quinn can help you do the same thing?"

"Yeah, she's already pitched it to the station and they love the idea." This is a lie—I have no idea if Quinn's even told Jerry about it. Although, knowing Quinn . . . it's possible.

"And you're going to do it?" She squints at me through her square-rimmed glasses.

I take a big breath, "I was considering it . . ."

Marie stares at me for a minute, as if she's taking in all I've just said. Then the corners of her mouth pull up until they've formed a huge smile and she chuckles to herself.

"Well," she says, "I have to say, Holly, this is a big surprise."

"Yes," I say, feeling unsteady and not really believing what I've just said. This is a big surprise for all of us. "Of course, I'm not sure how this will look for the bank, so obviously I'm willing to . . . uh . . . not do it because of all that." I circle my hands around in front of me.

"Oh, no," Marie says, shaking her head. "You have to do it."

"I do?" The nausea is now a real thing. I might puke. Right here on Marie's gray carpet.

"Yes, of course," she says, her eyes bright with excitement. "I honestly didn't think you'd have something like this in you." She leans forward, her elbow on the desk, her cheek perched on her fist.

I want to yell "I DON'T HAVE IT IN ME!" and then run from the room screaming, but instead I grab the sides of my chair, steadying myself, holding me to my seat.

"But this," she chuckles to herself. "What an adventure." She looks to the side, her face full of wonderment.

"Yeah," is all I can muster. Then I look up, making one last-ditch effort before I think I'll have to excuse myself to hurl. "I mean, this could look bad for the company, having their employee do something like this. All over the news and," I swallow loudly, "all . . . uh . . . that."

She bats the words away with her hand. "Oh, I'm not worried about that. You know how to be discreet. And who knows, maybe this will be good advertising for the bank. One of our own doing something so crazy, so adventurous, so fun. No, I think this is just what you need. I have to say, I was disappointed before, but now ... now I'm really proud of you, Holly."

She's using all my trigger words . . . crazy . . . adventurous. I'm none of those things. Those were my mom's things.

Oh, all the cuss words ever invented. What have I done?

CHAPTER 10

I am freaking out. No, wait. I am freaking the *freak* out.

After meeting with Marie, I had no choice but to call Quinn and tell her I'd do the trip. She was ridiculously excited, as I would have expected. She told me she owed me her firstborn, which I told her I didn't want. Then she got all annoyed that I wouldn't want her firstborn, especially because Chris Hemsworth was going to be the father. She was going to name the baby Thor, and how could I not want baby Thor?

Obviously, the conversation took a weird turn.

We did eventually get back to the trip that I'm now apparently taking with some stranger named Nathan Jones. A trip I never in a bazillion years would have ever said yes to, and somehow ended up saying yes anyway. I'm in a constant state of nausea.

And Marie is totally on-board. She told the executive team about the trip and all the news coverage to give them a heads-up and make sure there were no reservations. I said many prayers there would be, but there weren't. Everyone was all for it. Of course they were—it's not their life being broadcast on the news or subjected to a trip in a different country with a complete stranger.

I had one last hope to get out of this whole mess, which was that the story would be rejected by the news station. Unlike what I told Marie, Quinn had never presented the idea to her producer, Jerry. So I figured if Jerry turned it down, I could tell Marie the station dropped the idea and then I could pretend to be sad about it, all the while feeling like I'd just won the lottery.

But I got a text from Quinn this morning with the words "IT'S A GO!!!!!!!!!!!!"

And now I'm walking to Hester's to meet up with my friends and I suddenly feel like I'm having one of those movie moments—I want to drop to my knees in the middle of this sidewalk and scream "WHY MEEEEEEEEE?" with a fist at the heavens.

"There she is," Alex says as I enter the restaurant. I'm sure they were just talking about me and this whole crazy trip and I don't even have it in me to care.

I glance over the table and realize I'm the one who's late today. Both Quinn and Thomas are even here. I don't think this has ever happened in all the history of me and my friends meeting up.

"Holly," Bree says. "You look terrible."

"Thanks," I say, slumping down in the seat next to Quinn.

"How you doing?" Alex asks, concern on his face. I had already been to his office earlier today to tell him Quinn's ridiculous idea was happening and how I got stuck doing it. I had to leave out the promotion part, since he can't know about that.

"Meh," I say, clumsily flopping my purse on the table. I look over at Quinn to see her eyes are red-rimmed.

"What's wrong?" I ask.

Quinn sniffs, her eyes filling with tears. "They want to give the feature to Moriarty," she says, her voice thick with emotion. A single tear slides down her cheek.

"The feature?"

"You—your feature," she says.

"What? Why?" I ask, temporarily forgetting I don't even want to do the feature.

Stacey Moriarty is Quinn's Tiffany—her arch nemesis at work. She likes to call Stacey by her last name because it makes Quinn feel like Sherlock Holmes (the Benedict Cumberbatch version). Plus, it's too fitting. Moriarty does the five o'clock news and is the station's darling. She's literally the face of the station. Practically every other billboard on I-4 is of her stupid, smug grill. She also hates Quinn and makes her life hell whenever she can.

"Yeah," she sniffs. "I'm sure it's because they think I'm too fat."

The table is suddenly filled with objections over this. Thomas's are laced with many colorful words, which Quinn doesn't even try to be mad about.

"Quinn, you are not too fat. You're not even fat," I say, putting an arm around her. "I'm sure they just think she's the veteran. Which is true. She was there before they invented television."

That doesn't even garner a laugh, and Quinn usually loves a good dig at Moriarty's expense.

"This was supposed to be how I made things right—how to get the station to see me for a real reporter and not someone who dropped an f-bomb that went viral."

Now I feel bad that I watched it today . . . twice. Okay, three times. But in my defense, I was feeling crappy and needed a pick-me-up, and what better way than from the person that owed me big time? I didn't know then the feature would go to Moriarty and now I feel crappy for a whole other reason.

I look around at the table, seeing a bunch of sheepish expressions from my other friends and feel pretty confident I wasn't the only one who watched it today. Really, we're the worst.

"You guys," Thomas says. "This is an easy fix. Holly," he gestures to me, "you just tell the station you won't do it unless Quinn has the story." He folds his arms, sitting back in his chair.

Quinn sits up taller at that. She sniffs, a bit of color returning to her cheeks. "You think that would work?"

"Of course it will," Thomas says, bobbing his head side to side. "You guys should know by now that I'm the smartest person here. I have all the good ideas."

We ignore him. "That could work. You would do that, right Hols?" Quinn turns to me, her red-splotched face looking so fragile. It's rare to see her like this.

"Of course," I tell her.

I will absolutely do this for Quinn. I wouldn't do it unless she's running the show anyway. That's definitely a deal breaker for me. Now if only I could hide this little blossom of hope that's begun blooming that maybe this could break the deal.

Quinn is suddenly feeling much better — I can tell this because she waves over the server and orders some chips and salsa — a big no-no for any diet she happens to be on.

"So, Holly, how are you feeling about this whole trip?" Bree asks now that Quinn seems to be feeling better. Bree's sitting back in her seat, her feet up on the chair, her knees pulled into her chest. She's got her martini glass in one hand, like every Monday night.

"I'm feeling a little better right now," I say and everyone smiles and nods thinking I'm referring to Quinn and the feature. I am — seeing the relief on Quinn's face and that I can help her does make me feel better. But also that little blossom — that morsel of hope that I might not have to do this — well, it's helping.

Maybe when I request that Quinn gets the feature, I'll request a bunch of other stuff to sweeten the deal. Like bumping the tickets up to first class and getting separate rooms in the hotel. Come to think of it, I'm not going if they don't do that, so I'm definitely requesting the separate hotel room thing. What else can I add? So many possibilities.

"You guys, can we turn the focus on me for a bit?" Thomas says, putting both hands on his chest. "Holly is stealing all the attention."

I scrunch up my nose at him. We've barely talked about

me. We were mostly talking about Quinn.

"Shut it, Thomas," Quinn says, adding an eye roll for emphasis.

"No, but seriously, I need to vent," he says.

"Fine," Quinn acquiesces, but not whole-heartedly.

He looks around the table, his eyes somber. "None of you," he points his index finger at each of us. "Not one of you got Mugshot Monday right."

"Oh, geez," Alex says.

"And you, Holly," he puts a hand on his chest, appearing as if he might be choking up with emotion. "You didn't even play," he says, his voice choppy like tears might start pouring at any second.

I shake my head at him. "I didn't feel like it."

He takes in a loud, horrified-sounding breath. "What kind of sister are you?"

I stare briefly at the ceiling, shaking my head. Thomas has taken the whole stepbrother/stepsister thing to new heights.

Alex snorts. "Poor Holly. You get to have Thomas as a brother."

"Hey," Thomas retorts. "She's lucky to have me. Even if she's terribly unsupportive."

I give him my best stink-eye. I may not have played Mugshot Mondays, but I did look. I always look, even if I don't submit answers. Just in case my mom's face shows up there. Thomas and Quinn have seen pictures of my mom and they know her name. Plus, you don't forget Melanie Murphy's face. She's a dead ringer for Susan Sarandon. Everyone was always saying that when I was younger. And that was the first thing out of Thomas's mouth when he saw her picture. So I know if he ever came across her mugshot he would recognize her.

Thomas's eyes go wide as if he's just remembered something. And then he slaps the table with his hand. "We haven't discussed the most important thing of all." He smiles with glee.

"What's that?" Quinn asks with no enthusiasm whatsoever.

"Holly's dad and my mom have picked a date for the wedding." He gives me a double eyebrow lift.

Oh, *S-word*.

"Holly," he crosses one leg over the other, placing his elbow on his knee. He leans in, his chin resting on his hand. He's *really* loving this. "Why don't you tell everyone?"

"When is it?" both Bree and Quinn ask at the same time.

"June eighth," I say, trying to keep my voice light.

The date doesn't register with either of them.

"Good for them," Alex pipes in obliviously.

"Tell them *where*, Hols," Thomas says, and I swear his eyes are sparkling. "Tell them."

I sigh. "The Luxemore."

"The *Luxemore*," Thomas echoes, his smile so wide his face looks as if it could split in two.

"Wait, that's your wedding venue," Bree says.

"Was," I pipe in. "*Was* my wedding venue."

"Right," she says.

"And wait, June eighth . . . the wedding was on the

ninth," Quinn says.

"Ding, ding, ding! We have a winner," Thomas says, slamming his hand on the table.

"Wait, Holly, your dad is getting married the day before your wedding was supposed to be . . . and at the same place?" Alex asks, confusion on his face.

I swallow. I had considered this would be weird, but then the practical side of me took over. There's a venue and a date—why not use it? Seeing my friends' response to it, though, I'm thinking I may have had a lapse in judgment. That seems to be my theme right now. I'm a super-judgment-lapser.

I decide I'm going to stand my ground, as ridiculous as it is. I sit a little taller in my seat. "They wouldn't give us the deposit back, and so my dad asked, and I thought it made sense."

"That's weird, Hols," Bree says and everyone nods. Well, everyone but Thomas, who's loving every minute of this. I give him my best side-eye glare. He's such an *A*-word. Obviously this would have come out eventually. But on my terms, not his.

"OMG," she says, her eyebrows lifted, her green eyes wide. "Did you send out Save the Dates? Because if you did, you should send out announcements that say 'we regret to inform you that Holly Murphy will not be marrying Nathan Jones, but we're pleased to tell you Holly's dad will be getting married instead.'"

Everyone starts laughing and Thomas yells out, "Epic!"

"Ha, ha, you're all hilarious," I say blandly. "It's not that big of a deal."

"Uh, it kinda is," Bree says.

"Whatever. Maybe I just want my dad to be happy. I mean, wouldn't you do this for your parents?" I use the old passive-aggressive tactic, playing on sympathies.

The table erupts with no's and deliberate head shakes. I forgot my friends are evil. Passive-aggressive doesn't work on them.

"Well, obviously, I'm a better person than the rest of you," I say, and then give them my best snooty duck lips.

"You really are," Quinn reaches up and pats my back twice.

"You should be sainted," Bree pipes in, and Alex concurs with a head bob.

"Besides," I say, feeling suddenly defensive, "no one but a handful of people will even know that was my wedding venue."

"Except the most important people," Thomas says.

"The most important people," Quinn repeats, with a head bob at the table, "won't tell anyone."

Bree and Alex both nod in agreement.

"Thomas?" Quinn says, giving him a very stern mom look with her head tilted to the side, her eyes glaring.

Thomas lets out a huge sigh. "Of course," he says, like he's resigned to it. He sits back in his chair, folding his arms. "Again with all the Holly talk." He throws his head back dramatically. "Can we talk about me now?"

CHAPTER 11

My plan didn't work.

I went to Jerry and demanded that Quinn have the story or I wouldn't do it. I also insisted they bump the flights to first class, get two rooms for the hotels in London and Paris, and I even required that they pay for all admissions to tourist attractions and throw in some spending money.

He agreed to it all. All of it. He didn't even flinch. I should have added something farcical—like requiring that I'm serenaded by Harry Styles every day.

Dang it. I should have thought of that.

It's all happening now. We taped the interview on Wednesday, it aired on Thursday, and now I'm here the day after the feature went live, dealing with the fallout.

Although, so far, there's been no actual fallout. In fact, I've been mostly praised, and oddly enough, mostly by my team. I honestly didn't think any of them would have seen it because they don't seem like a news-watching bunch.

"Are you gonna like, do a reality show?" asks Sarah-with-an-h. We're having our normal Friday morning meeting.

"No, I'm not," I say definitively.

"Oh my gosh, when I saw you on TV last night," says Sara, "I was like, that's my boss! Then I totally posted it on Insta." She shows me her phone where's she's taken a screen shot of me on TV — and of course in the shot she captured, I have one lazy eye and my chin is pulled in so tightly that I have triple chins going on. I look like an obese pirate. Couldn't she have tried for a better angle? "And it has, like, over three hundred likes," she says with a glint in her eye.

"Thanks," I say dryly.

"Is this going to affect your job here?" Avery asks.

This is a good question — a normal one. The answer though, is not normal. It actually could help me.

"I don't think so," I answer Avery.

"My favorite part," says Sarah, "is the part when you turned to the camera and said 'I'm looking for you, Nathan Jones.'" She tries to do an impression of my voice, all high and nasally. I'm pretty sure that's not how I sound.

That line was Jerry's idea and it took about ten takes because it was hard for me to muster up the energy he wanted behind it. It came out all stupid and forced. I cringe every time I see it, which is a lot — that's the line they are using as the teaser and keep replaying it during station advertisements.

"Anyway, that's not why I'm here," I say to my team. "I'm here to talk about the PFC report."

The Sarahs both whine, and Avery, Jim, and Brad all grunt.

Jim raises his hand as if we're in class. "Yes, Jim?" I ask, tentatively.

"Aren't you worried about going on a trip with some stranger?" he asks, peering at me through his black-rimmed glasses, his hair extra slicked back today, the ratty green polo looking extra worn out. "I mean, what if he ends up being a total psycho and he, like, ties you up and slowly mutilates you until you die, and then wraps you up in one of those huge carpet thingies."

"An area rug," pipes in Brad.

"Yeah, that. And then throws you in the Nile."

The room goes silent, everyone looking to me for an answer.

I swallow slowly. "Thank you . . . uh . . . Jim, for your concerns—as detailed as they are. But they'll be doing background checks on all the possible Nathans. Plus, we won't be anywhere near the Nile River."

"Aren't you going to London and France?" Jim asks, his brow furrowed.

"Yes," I say, drawing out the word. "In Europe."

"Right," he nods his head, still not understanding.

"The Nile is in Africa," I say, an unintentional what-the-hell tone to my voice. I couldn't even hold it back.

"Any more questions? Or can we get to the PFC report?"

Everybody's hands go up.

JUST A NAME

After filtering questions and bringing my team back around to the reason for our meeting, we finally got the changes to the PFC report squared away and I left the office feeling a little lighter than I usually do when I leave.

My team was actually interested in me. Granted, some of our discussion was a little ridiculous, but for the first time, I felt like we were bonding. I wish I could pick and choose when they do the supervisor assessments. I bet if they did it today I'd pass with flying colors.

"Yoo-hoo!" I hear Tiffany outside my office door as I sit down at my desk.

"Come in," I say, the good feelings growing large wings and flying away.

"Look at our little superstar," Tiffany says as she enters my office. She's wearing a slim-fitting, yellow sheath dress, perfectly tailored, of course. Her hair is pulled into a low-slung ponytail that hangs over one shoulder.

She shuts the door and takes a seat without my offering one.

"Can I help you?" I say, feeling disconcerted that she shut the door. She's never done that before.

"Look at you, with this whole crazy trip thing," she says, leaning forward in her chair, her eyes bright, her normal cheerful smile. Although it's tinged with something. Maybe psychosis. Yes, there's a hint of psychosis in that smile.

"Yeah," I say, unsettled. No, unsettled is too tame. I'm feeling a slight petrification in my bones right now.

"Are you doing this to get the attention of the executive team?" she blurts out. Her smile stays intact, though a little more nutter shines through. Also, a light red starts at the base of her throat and moves up her neck and to her cheeks.

"What?"

She takes a deep breath. "Holly, if you think this gimmick you're pulling is going to get you Mike's job, then . . . well . . . you must be kidding."

I chortle. "That's not the reason." Although it is. In a roundabout way.

"Then why all the hoopla? Why not go on a regular vacation like a normal person?"

Why, indeed.

I give her a thin smile. "I don't need to explain my reasoning to you, Tiff." I make sure I say her name with my best patronizing tone.

"Well, if you think it's going to get you the job, then you are very mistaken," she says, and I can't help but notice the slight shake in her voice. "I have it on good authority that the executive team is not happy about this."

Ah-ha! She's Lying McLiarson! I know for a fact Marie said they were fine with it. Even happy for the possibility of some free advertising for the bank. Not that they've mentioned the bank except for once in the initial interview.

I decide right now, with Tiffany, that I'm just going to be cool . . . like a cucumber. I can use this to my advantage.

I take a deep breath. "Well, I guess we'll have to see how this plays out, won't we," I say, now doing my very best impression of Tiffany's extra-fake smile.

Her red face darkens slightly and her eyes appear to be widening. "Yes, I guess we'll have to see," she says through gritted teeth.

"If we're finished here . . . do you mind?" I say with a head bob toward my door. Time for Tiffany to go.

She huffs and gets up to leave. She turns around before opening the door. "That job is mine." She yanks the door open and walks out of the room.

I hold off from yelling "in your freaking dreams, you crazy *B*-word!" as she leaves.

Huh. So far, this ridiculous trip has made my team more interested in me and has made Tiffany go a little psycho. Side benefits.

"Why are you doing this search thing?"

I just picked up my coffee at the Lava Java and was hopeful I'd avoid Logan this visit since he was busy on a phone call when I got here and didn't even notice me.

No such luck.

"I see we're avoiding pleasantries. Hi, Holly, how are you?" I say in a terrible impression of the male species. "Why, I'm fine, thank you for asking, Logan." I grab a packet of sugar and shake it in his face for no reason other than to emphasize my annoyance. I rip open the packet, imagining it has some kind of voodoo magic and would do something similar to the man glowering at me right now. There's actually a glower happening.

"Why are you doing it?"

I shrug. "For fun."

"For fun?" he echoes me, only his words are laced with irritation. "You said you weren't going to do the vacation."

"Welp, I'm a fun girl. And I changed my mind." I sound like I'm back in high school and realize I'm being sort of obnoxious right now. I don't know if it was the meeting with my team or the confrontation with Tiffany, but I'm feeling kinda punchy—in a good way.

He stares at me. "Is this about the spontaneous thing?"

"What?" My lip curls up at his question. "No, it has nothing to do with that."

He stares at me like he doesn't believe me, folding his arms as he eyes me.

I hadn't even considered Logan questioning my spontaneity. But here's another side effect—proof I can be spontaneous. These little side effects are adding up. If only I could reap all the side benefits without actually going on the trip.

"No, seriously. Quinn presented me with the option, and I figured, why not." I give him a little shrug for emphasis.

"There are a lot of reasons why not," he says, now squinting at me.

"Well, I think it'll be fun. Exciting even." I want to add *spontaneous,* but then he'd think I was doing it to prove him wrong. Which is ludicrous. I mean, honestly, he must think a lot of himself to think I'd do something this crazy because he said one thing.

"Couldn't you go with your friends?" he asks before I could point out how full of himself he is.

"None of them can go."

"Your dad?"

"He can't either." Because he's getting married in the place where I was supposed to be getting married. Wow. I really did not think that through.

He lets out a huff. "I'd . . . I . . ."

"What? You'd what?" I say watching him fumble with his words.

"I'd go with you."

"Huh?" I say, totally taken aback by that. What in the world?

"Let me go with you."

"You . . . I . . . you can't . . ." Now I'm fumbling my words.

"Just call the whole thing off, and I'll go."

I look at him, straight into his eyes to make sure he's not fooling with me. But Logan has never been one to say stuff he doesn't mean.

"You can't just offer to go," I say. "Not like that."

"Why not?"

I search my brain for the right words, letting out little huffs as I try to figure out what to say.

"Because, up until like three weeks ago, I was pretty sure you hated me." There. That's the truth.

"I—"

"I know," I cut him off, holding out a hand. "You like me just fine," I say, once again trying to imitate his voice and doing a crap job of it. "Excuse me for wanting to hang out with someone who likes me more than that."

"A complete stranger?"

"Well, at least there's the possibility. And he won't be a total stranger. We'll meet over the phone and Skype and stuff. And — you know what? I don't need to explain myself to you."

Why am I trying to explain myself to Logan? Am I so pathetic, a small part of me still wants him to like me? I never thought of myself as that kind of person, but maybe I am. Is that what's happening here?

"I think this whole thing is ridiculous, and . . . dangerous."

I lift a shoulder and let it drop. "I'm a big girl, Logan. I can take care of myself."

"I never said you couldn't."

We stare at each other for a beat.

"Just let me go with you," he says.

"No, thanks," I shake my head. "I'm good." I raise my coffee to him, my goodbye gesture, and I turn around and walk out.

CHAPTER 12

Not all the side effects of this trip are turning out so well.

I'm in my office a week later, checking out all the posts online about me. Yes, I Googled myself. Actually, I set up a Google Alerts to ping me every time my name shows up online. Which is both stupid and exciting. But mostly stupid.

It appears I'm trending. I've gone viral, and rather quickly too. The interview and follow-up news stories are getting tons of hits on the station's website. Jerry is giddy and Quinn's approval at the station is going up quickly.

I know the viral thing is part of it, I mean, we can't find any Nathan Joneses if word doesn't get out. And they've started showing up—five applicants already. There are five other Nathan Joneses out there in the U.S.A. who want to go on this trip with me. Perfect strangers who want to take off on a plane and go to Europe with someone they've never met. I find it all so strange.

Because there are about to be two Nathan Joneses in my life, we have been referring to the Nathan Jones we're doing the search for as Number Two so we don't confuse them in our conversations. Thomas has come up with many Number Two jokes and puns.

Even though I've gone viral, it hasn't been as big of a deal as it could be. At least not yet. It's only just begun. But I was hoping because this isn't the first time this was done that the bigger news outlets wouldn't care. Been there, done that, sort of thing. That seems to be the case so far. It's mostly been passed along by bloggers and social media. It's moved fast enough that way, anyway.

I've already been getting noticed around town, though. I've had quite a bit of experience watching Quinn get recognized when we go out, but it felt so foreign when someone noticed me over the weekend. Some lady practically pounced on me at the grocery store. It solidified what I already knew — fame is *so* not my thing. I've never wanted it. I've seen how it all can backfire like some of it has for Quinn, who always wanted it and pursued it.

I did get one call last night from a local production company asking if they could come with us on the trip and follow us around to film a reality show about it, one they could sell if Number Two and I were to fall in love. Because a love connection would mean big money, or so I was told. I told the guy *no way*, and he was flabbergasted that I would turn down this "once in a lifetime opportunity." A once in a lifetime opportunity to fake fall in love with some guy I don't even know on a trip I was supposed to be going on with my husband. Okay, sure. How about never in a freaking lifetime.

Speaking of my ex-fiancé, I got a call from Nathan early

last week claiming he was a little upset that I jilted him out of his plane ticket. I reminded him — nicely — that he was the one who gave the ticket to me. Like it was some consolation prize.

Then, after he got over that, which wasn't too long because Nathan's never been one to hold a grudge, he had the gall to ask me if I was doing this for him. To try to get him back. And I laughed. A bitter-evil-witch-sounding laugh. I said in no way, shape, or form was any of this for him. Because it's the truth. I don't want him back. He and that Christine chick can live happily ever after with their laid-back fairy-looking children, for all I care. The nerve of that guy.

Then he apologized — because that's Nathan, never one to want people to be mad at him — and then he told me he was proud of me. Like a father would say to his daughter. Which annoyed me even more. He doesn't get to be proud of me.

My phone beeps and vibrates, signaling I have a text. I'm now a little scared of my phone because of the Google Alerts. Maybe I should shut those down. So far nothing has been said, except the basic facts and a couple of people have called me a copycat. Initially I wanted to defend myself because I feel like it's different from how the lady in New York did it, and plus it wasn't my idea. Quinn is the real copycat. But then I realized it's not worth commenting on.

I pick up my phone to see I've gotten a text from Logan. I'm a bit confused by this because I'm pretty sure Logan has never texted me. Plus, I didn't think he had my number. I had his because Nathan put it in my phone once just in case I couldn't get ahold of him. But I never used it. In fact, I forgot it was there.

Logan: What about skydiving.

What the? What about skydiving?

Me: Skydiving?

My phone beeps again.

Logan: It's spontaneous. And not in a diff country with a stranger.

Oh my gosh. Why is he so against me doing this? Although, to be honest, *I'm* against me doing this.

Me: No, thanks.

I don't know why he'd even lead with skydiving. He knows I wouldn't do it with Nathan. Why would I start now?

Logan: Bungee jumping.

Me: No.

Logan: Swim with sharks.

Me: HELL NO.

Logan: Spelunking.

I had to Google that one. Exploring caves . . . small enclosed spaces.

Me: Pass.

Logan: I'll keep looking.

Me: I signed a contract.

Logan: So?

I want to tell him all of this is pointless. I didn't say yes to the trip because I was trying to be spontaneous. I signed up for it because I painted myself into a corner. And now, even if I wanted to get out of it, I couldn't. There's too much on the line. My job, Quinn's job . . . a contract. I won't deny I've thought about fleeing the state and starting my life over again. But that would be stupid. Mostly.

After about ten more texts from Logan, I leave my building and walk over to the Lava Java. Bypassing the coffee, I go straight to Logan's booth and have a seat. He doesn't notice me because he's got earphones on and he's peering down at his phone texting me. I know this because my phone beeps as I sit down.

I knock twice on the wood table that separates us to alert him to my presence. He looks up and pulls his earphones off, letting them hang around his neck like a DJ. Except that Logan would be the worst DJ ever. In all history. There would be no getting the party started with him.

"Stop bothering me," I say, holding up my phone as it beeps again with another incoming text. I'm assuming — with the utmost confidence — that it's from him.

The corner of his lip twitches upward. "I'm not giving up."

"Well, you need to," I say. "It's happening."

He huffs through his nose.

"Why do you care so much?" I ask, angling my head slightly to the side. I wanted to ask him this via text, but realized there's no way to text that and have it come out sounding inquisitively like I wanted it to. It sounds mean any way you type it. Also, I really am curious why he cares. How did we go from barely talking to this?

"I just do," he says.

131

"Well, I appreciate it. But really, I'm good," I say, and I feel a bit confident in this statement and wonder if maybe I'm starting to come to terms with the whole thing. Then a picture of me being rolled up in an area rug and thrown in the Thames appears in my head and my hands start getting sweaty. Dang that Jim. As if I can't scare myself enough on my own.

"I'd believe you if your face didn't say otherwise," he gives a little upward tilt of his head.

I purposefully relax my face and plaster on an extra-wide grin to show him I'm totally fine.

"Better," he says, overly sarcastic.

He reaches a hand up and pulls off his headphones and sets them on the table next to his laptop.

"So besides harassing me, what are you working on?" I nod over at the laptop sitting near him.

"A presentation."

"For?"

"AppLee."

"Right," I say. "When is it?"

"June fifteenth," he says, reaching up and swiping a hand down his face.

"June fifteenth," I echo. A month away. I'll be in London with someone I don't know. I hope I will have gotten to know him better at that point, and not been murdered. I need to stop going there.

"Hey, well good thing I didn't take you up on your offer to go with me—that's during my trip," I say, attempting to harness my thoughts.

He pulls in his brow. "I just found out this morning. I wouldn't have agreed to the date if I were going with you."

"But what if I asked you to go now?" I say, a teasing tone to my voice.

"Now?" Logan asks, his eyes moving down to the table between us. "Well, now they have executives flying in from California. So it might be harder to change."

"Right. Well, I'm stuck with this whole name search thing anyway. You're off the hook." I smile teasingly. "So how goes it?" I ask, with a nod at Logan's laptop.

"It's . . . a lot of work."

"And Nathan?"

"Not helping."

I give him an understanding smile. That's par for the course for them. Nathan doesn't prepare at all and then shows up and presents. Like me, Logan over prepares. Somehow it all works out. But I know it's always been a sore spot between them.

I chew on my lip for a second, not sure if I should ask him what I want to ask. I decide to just do it. "Do you think there will be a conflict of interest with Nathan dating someone from there?"

I've held off asking Logan about Nathan because I don't want it to seem like I'm fishing. I'm not. Okay, maybe a little. I don't even know why. I don't want Nathan. Even if he told me he'd made a mistake and wanted me back, I'd say no. We weren't right for each other. I see that now, I've seen it for a while. Maybe even before we broke up.

Logan looks to the side, frowning. Then his eyes move

back to me. "A little," he says. "I asked him to wait until after the presentation to ask her out, but . . ."

I can tell by the expression on his face that's all he's going to give me and I'm not going to push him on it. I never tried to ask Logan anything about Nathan when we were dating because, well, he barely talked to me. But I get the idea that if I had asked him about Nathan, he would've never said anything about it. I think he's loyal. The fierce kind.

Anyway, I can fill in the blanks there. Nathan can be laid back about so many things, so go-with-the-flow. It's one of the things that drew me to him in the first place. Perhaps the biggest thing. But he also didn't hold back when he went for something he was passionate about. Another thing that attracted me to him.

"Can I ask you something?"

"Shoot," Logan says, his eyes on mine.

"How come you hardly ever talked to me when I was with Nathan?" I've wanted to ask him this for a while.

He peers over at the service counter of the coffee shop, his face contemplative. He brings his face back toward me, but his eyes focus on the table.

"I guess I didn't know how to talk to you before—when you were with him."

"How's that? It's not rocket science. You just talk," I say, confused.

"I . . . what I mean is . . . I'm not good at knowing boundaries, so I tend to err on the side of caution."

"What boundaries?"

He stares over at the counter again. "Just . . . boundaries."

"Right," I say, now more confused. "Well, you aren't erring on the side of caution with my phone." I hold up my smart phone with the screen facing toward him and wiggle it around.

He looks at my phone, but both of his lips pull up into a smile. I kind of like it when I can get a smile out of Logan. It's so rare. It feels a bit like winning a medal.

It falls quickly, though, as a man approaches the booth.

"Hey, aren't you that girl from the news?" the man asks. Calling him a man is being a bit generous. He seems more like a college kid with his messy blond hair, basketball shorts and a T-shirt. And flip-flops, of course. It's the state shoe of Florida.

"I'm looking for you, Nathan Jones," he says, pointing a finger in my direction.

I close my eyes briefly, wishing I could disappear. I don't like this whole being recognized thing, and I definitely don't want to experience it with Logan here. It's more kindling for his fire. More evidence for his case.

"Yep," I say, resigned to the fact that this will be my life for a little while. I'm sure once the trip is over it will settle down. At least I hope. If not, there's always the runaway plan.

"Dude, you're a total hottie. I'd go with you," he says, putting a hand on my shoulder. I try to nudge it off, but he's not getting the message. He doesn't appear to be the smartest of humans.

I feel uncomfortable butterflies pooling in my stomach, and my instincts to go all ninja on him are coming out in full force. The only problem is I'm not a ninja, but I'm very skilled in the art of verbal butt-kicking.

"Dude, seriously. Can I go with you? I'll even change my name to Nathan Jones," he chuckles, and I hear his buddies laughing not far behind him.

I open my mouth to say something, getting ready to give this kid the most epic tongue-lashing if there ever was one, and then Logan says, "Take your hand off."

He says this quietly, but unmistakably. His voice has a gravelly undertone to it that reminds me of Batman. It's kind of awesome, if I'm being honest—masculine and brooding.

The kid immediately takes his hand off my shoulder and holds both hands up like Logan might arrest him.

"Yo, man, I didn't mean anything," he says.

"Then walk away," Logan says in his awesome Batman voice.

Without a word, the kid grabs his friends and hurries out of the coffee shop.

"Uh . . . thank you," I say after we sit in silence for a few seconds.

He replies with a nod.

I'm feeling . . . well . . . a little awestruck. I think that's the best word to describe it. I've never been one to like it when someone tries to rescue me—I'm pretty good at taking care of myself. I don't need anyone to stand up for me. But this time, I kind of liked it. I didn't feel challenged, or that my own strength was being stamped on. Rather, I felt a sense of support.

I never felt that way with Nathan—like he had my back. In fact, I can recall a couple of times that he got mad at me for sticking up for myself, and basically told me I should have just ignored the person who was pestering me. I never really needed his help, but it might have been nice for him to at least try sometimes.

"Thanks," I squeak out. I'm not sure why I say it again. I sort of feel like the thanking needs to be reiterated.

"That guy's an idiot."

"Yeah."

"This whole search thing—"

"Logan," I cut him off, a warning in my voice. I'm just getting all kinds of good feelings about him and his chivalrous gesture. I don't want him to ruin it.

"Fine," he says. I can tell it's a placating *fine*.

"I like your Batman voice," I say, changing directions.

"My what voice?"

"That low, gravelly thing you just did. You sounded like Batman."

The corner of his mouth tugs upward. "Batman," he echoes, bobbing his head as if he's considering the title.

And then the craziest thing happens. Both sides of Logan's mouth keep pulling up and then morph into a broad smile. An award-winning, teeth-showing smile.

Oh, *my*.

A tingle that starts in my head works its way down my arms, through my torso, cascades over my legs, and lands in my toes. I feel heat instantly rise to my face. His smile is doing weird things to me. Unexpected things.

"Your smile," I say, sounding slightly breathless—it feels like the air got a little thinner around me.

"Yeah?" his smile gets even wider at my reaction.

"You don't do that very often."

He pulls his lips in at my comment, and I immediately regret saying something. I didn't want him to stop.

"You should," I say.

"Should what?"

"Smile more."

He shrugs one shoulder. "Not that much to smile about, I guess."

"Except when comparing you to Batman."

His mouth pulls into a smile again. Not as grand as before, but still lovely. "Except for that," he says.

"Well, we'll have to remedy that."

Okay, whoa. I avert my eyes away from him because that came out all scratchy-voiced and flirty-sounding. What the *H*? That was not my intention. That smile of his must have messed with my brain.

My eyes move up from the table to meet his. There's no smile there, not even a hint of one. But there's a different look in his eyes, like something has ignited behind them. This does weird things to me as well. Similar to the smile.

Something has shifted here. The air between us cracks and pops. Unlike before, when the air between us was dull and stagnant.

There's only one explanation: there's some kind of

voodoo magic going on at the Lava Java.

"Well, I think I better get back to work," I say as I scoot out of the booth to make my escape.

"Unless you want to stay and see if I might smile more," he says.

My eyes widen. He's flirting. It's unmistakable.

"No . . . I have . . . uh . . . work ado. I mean, work I do, I mean . . ." Stupid flustered brain. I take in a deep breath. "Work. To. Do," I say, emphasizing each word.

"Okay," he says, his mouth settling into a smirk.

"Goodbye, Logan," I say, very formal sounding.

He doesn't say anything, so I walk toward the door. Before I leave, I peek over my shoulder and catch Logan looking like he's chuckling to himself as he puts his earphones back on.

I walk across the street to my office building feeling like I stepped out of a dream sequence. Logan and I flirted. I think. I'm pretty sure. I'm actually not sure of anything right now. That wasn't flirting; it couldn't be.

As I reach the tall glass doors to my office building, my phone beeps.

Logan: Zip-lining?

I don't even reply.

CHAPTER 13

"Is this about the wedding?" my dad asks as we sit across from each other at our regular meet-up—the Mexican restaurant off Orange Street. It's a busy night; every table around us is full, the clanking of utensils on plates heard all around. No mariachi band in sight this time, though.

"What? Why would this be about the wedding?" I ask him, pulling my brows in and squinting in his direction.

He's been grilling me for the past twenty minutes about this trip. I should have known when he called me earlier today to see if we could move our regular dinner up a week that this would be the reason.

He's known about the trip for a while, of course. He was the first person I called after I told Quinn I'd do it. I'm thinking he didn't understand exactly what was happening. Or perhaps I was so out of my mind with what I'd agreed to that I didn't explain it well enough. Probably the latter. Either way, it's all just hit him today: his baby girl is going to Europe with a stranger.

Fatherly pride is probably not one of the feelings he's

having right now.

"I don't know," he says, shaking his head and peering down at his hands, which are together on the table in front of him, his fingers intertwined. "I just thought maybe you were upset about it or doing some subconscious thing." His eyes move back up to me. "You know you'll always be my first girl."

"Dad, I know," I say. "And it's not about the wedding."

Why would it be about the wedding? Why does everyone think this trip I'm taking is about them? Logan and his spontaneity comment, Nathan thinking I'm doing it to get him back, Thomas wanting to be entertained. The only person who can lay any claim to it is Quinn, and I didn't even do it for her. It wasn't until Marie cornered me that it all happened.

My dad looks to the side, the corners of his lips pulled up ever-so-slightly, barely a whisper of a smile on his lips. I know this one well. He's worried. This smile was especially prevalent when I was younger, especially after my mom left. I'd often catch him looking at me with this expression. Even at that age, I got it. I was worried about us too. But we turned out okay, I think.

Obviously, his worry this time is warranted. I mean, I'm going to a different country with a complete stranger. I'd love to put his mind at ease, but I can't even mollify my own brain.

I reach across the table and place my hand on his. "This isn't about the wedding. I'm truly happy for you," I say. The truth is, I've been so caught up in all this vacation drama, I haven't had a moment to think about my dad's impending wedding. Maybe I can put that in the side benefits column.

"Now I'm wishing I'd have just moved things around so I could go with you," he says.

"Dad, it's all good," I tap the top of his hand with my fingers twice. "I'll be fine. I'm a big girl. I can take care of myself. Plus, you can't exactly change your wedding plans now."

I give him my most confident smile. It's a fake smile. In reality, his worry is making me worry, like maybe he has some sort of father's intuition and I'll be found tied up and left to die in the desert.

That was Jim's latest narrative. I told him I wouldn't be near the desert and he looked confused. Maybe for Christmas I'll buy Jim an atlas.

My dad's shoulders relax a bit, and the corners of his mouth turn up a little more. He chuckles once.

"What?" I ask, wondering how he could go from worried to chuckling.

"I was just thinking that this is something your mama would like."

My heart, which was already feeling weighed down from this conversation, plummets into my stomach like a lead balloon.

"Well, I hope she never hears about it, then," I say. I'm the opposite of most children. To rebel against my mother, I couldn't do anything crazy or foolhardy. No, I had to choose a life of structure and planning to be a disappointment. Not that she'd know.

"She's up for parole soon, you know," my dad says, his lips taking a downward turn. There's only a handful of topics that can take his smile away, and my mom is most definitely one of them.

He's kept track of her all this time, even helped her with money. He doesn't tell me any of this, of course. But I saw his bank statement once and saw a few transfers to a bank in Charlotte, and I just knew it was for her. But that's my dad for you. Giving even when he shouldn't be.

"Well, bully for her," I say, spiritless.

"She'll probably get it, this being her first offense and all," he says.

"Her first *legal* offense," I say. She has many other offenses—ones that don't count in the eyes of the law.

His lips pull downward, the ghost of a smile still there.

"She was bipolar, you know," he says, his voice lower and quieter.

I nod. "That was pretty obvious." I didn't recognize it until I was older, until I understood more. But the constant ups and downs—doing wild and spontaneous things for a while and then spending the next while never getting out of bed ... it wasn't hard to put two and two together.

"I worried about you . . . that you might—"

"Turn out like her?"

He doesn't answer; he just dips his chin once.

"Well, you had nothing to worry about," I say, confidence in my voice. I work very hard to make sure I'll never be like my mother. I may have gotten some of her facial

143

traits—high cheekbones and fuller bottom lip—but everything else is different.

"I sure didn't," he says, the corners of his mouth pulling up into his proud smile—the smile that I feel like he saves only for me.

I let out a deep breath. "Can we talk about something else?"

My dad's face immediately morphs. His lips pull up high enough that two small dimples form right above the corners and a warmth radiates from his eyes.

"Sure," he says. "So what's this trip all about, then?"

"Let's not talk about that, either," I say.

"Well, how about this," he says, leaning in toward me. "I'll stop grilling you if you promise to bring pepper spray."

"Already got it on my packing list," I say, giving him a wink.

He winks back. "That's my girl."

CHAPTER 14

It's been nearly three weeks of torture since I agreed to this crazy idea, but it now comes down to this: it's time to pick Number Two.

I should be feeling sick right now, maybe even verging on wanting to throw up. But I guess I'm resigned to it. Or apathetic. That might be the case—I'm now spiritless.

It does help that work seems to be going better. My team is still more interested in me as a person and even in our meetings as they seem to be actively participating in discussions. They've also been doing their jobs. For the most part. I mean, they aren't doing anything extra, and the Sarahs are still taking too many breaks. But generally, things are better.

Marie is over the moon regarding the trip. She wants updates all the time. I showed her the profile of all the applicants and she spent time weighing options and putting in her two cents.

Tiffany is . . . well, Tiffany. She's still putting in her digs whenever she can, of course. But she's laid off the notion that I'm using this trip to get the attention of the executive team. This should make me nervous, like she's heard something I don't know. But I have faith in Marie, so Tiffany can believe what she wants to believe. No one has more pull than Marie does. So if I have her on my side, I need not worry.

Now it's time to pick the stranger I'm going on this trip with. In all, sixteen Number Twos applied. If the tables were turned, I would never apply for something like this, so that means we already don't have *that* in common. Not a promising start.

Out of the sixteen, Jerry said only three met all the requirements and passed the background checks.

It's Friday night, and I've called my friends for an emergency meeting at Hester's. We've painstakingly narrowed it down to two. Painstakingly because Thomas is here and he makes everything painful.

So now there are two Number Twos. Tucson Nathan Jones, and Newport Beach Nathan Jones. I'll pick one tonight, Skype with him, and then if I get some creepy stalker vibe, I'll try the other one. I'll have a Nathan Jones, and a runner up Nathan Jones. If they both turn out to be creepy, I'll resort to plan C—which is my run away plan. I spend more time entertaining that plan than I probably should.

"I don't know, Hols," Thomas says as he sits across from me. "I mean, I think your best bet is the guy from Tucson."

"Why him?" Quinn asks.

"Yeah, why him?" Bree parrots.

"Because," Thomas says, picking up the picture of Tucson Nathan Jones's printed profile that is filled with information on him—where he works, single status, hobbies and the like, and also various pictures. "He just seems like a nice guy. I mean, look at him, he's got a picture with his grandma. How cute is that?"

"I don't know," Bree says. "My vote is for the Nathan from Newport Beach. Because abs." She holds up a picture of Newport Beach Nathan with his shirt off, and I do have to admit, I like what I see. He's ruggedly handsome, whereas Tucson Nathan is more boy-next-door cute.

"Holy *S*, that guy is hot," Quinn says, eyeing the picture of Newport Beach Nathan Bree's holding. "He's definitely the right choice."

"Just say the damn swear word," Thomas says, slapping his hand on the table. Quinn sticks her tongue out at him and he starts dropping all kinds of cuss words. In multiple languages, even. It's kind of impressive.

"You know you want to say it," he says, poking Quinn in the arm. "You know you do."

"Shut up, Thomas," she says, turning her body away from him and toward me.

"I like Tucson Nathan," Alex says, ignoring them.

"No, Newport Beach Nathan," Bree says.

"You guys," Thomas says, picking up Newport Beach Nathan's profile. "I think the only reason you're choosing him is because he's hot."

"That's not true," I protest. "He's also very successful. He owns a gym."

Thomas guffaws in a very condescending way. "A gym?

Please. I think Tucson Nathan is the safe bet. I mean, even I can recognize Nathan from Newport Beach is a good-looking guy." He puts down Newport Beach Nathan's profile and picks up the one from Tucson. "You need to pick the safe guy." He waves the profile around.

"The safe guy? None of this is safe. This whole thing is crazy," Alex says. "Holly, are you sure about this?"

"Yes, she's sure," Quinn interjects before I can say no. "Anyway, there's a contract now. Holly couldn't get out of it if she wanted to."

"I could get her out of it," Thomas quips, his lawyerly side coming out. I don't doubt it, even though I wouldn't want to deal with all of that. I'll just do what I signed up for. Or plan C. If I ran away, I could change my name to Megan. I've always liked that name.

"I think we have it narrowed down to Newport Beach Nathan and Tucson Nathan. Can we all agree on that?" Bree looks around the table and we all nod back. "Okay, let's take a vote. All in favor of Tucson Nathan, raise your hand."

Thomas and Alex both raise their hands.

"And those in favor of Newport Beach Nathan, raise your hand," Bree says then raises her hand, and Quinn does the same.

"Split down the middle, Hols," Quinn says. "You're the tie breaker."

"And as this affects my life the most, I'd say my vote is most important." Everyone grunts affirmations, including eye rolls from Thomas and Quinn. "I think I'm going with . . ." I cut off, biting my bottom lip. This is a big moment. I feel like I need a drum roll or something.

"You're killing me here, Hols," Thomas says.

Bree holds up the shirtless picture of Newport Beach Nathan, waving it around.

"I'm going with Newport Beach Nathan," I say, and Thomas and Alex both voice their disappointment while Bree and Quinn both cheer that they've won.

"Really?" Alex asks. "Are you sure?"

"Alex, all these guys have been vetted by the station. Background checks and everything. They've all come back clean. And Newport Nathan is just so . . . hot," Quinn says.

"Right? Maybe I should join you on this trip," Bree says, still eyeing Newport Nathan's picture. "Hey!" she protests as Alex snatches it out of her hands.

Quinn puts an arm around me and pulls me into her for a side hug. "I'm proud of you, Hols."

I smile back at her. I don't feel proud. I feel weird. Like, in-the-pit-of-my-stomach weird. Oddly enough, I don't feel all that nervous right now. But of course, I'm not on the trip. I'm safe in Orlando with my friends at our normal meet-up.

"Now on to more important things," Thomas rubs his hands together and everyone turns to him. "Not one of you got Mugshot Monday right," he says, appearing a little smug by that fact.

"What? I thought I nailed that one," Alex says. "What was 'Awful Alex's' offense? And why did you name him Alex?" His eyebrows pull together as he looks to Thomas for an answer.

"He resembles you, no?" Thomas looks around the table.

Alex's face falls and Bree laughs loudly.

"I'm missing something," I say. I only briefly glanced at it to make sure Mommy Dearest wasn't on there.

"That's because, once again, you didn't play along," Thomas says. Whipping out his phone, he pulls up a picture of 'Awful Alex.'

I start laughing when I see the picture. The only way this guy could look like our Alex is if he had kidnapped him and made a mask of his face.

"You're mean," I say to Thomas, who appears quite proud of himself. Bree is still giggling as Alex gives a half smile while shaking his head. Typical Thomas.

"Guess who got them all correct?" Thomas says.

"Who?" Quinn asks, though I doubt she really cares.

"Mr. Logan Palmer," he says, overly pronouncing his name.

"Logan? How did he win?" I ask, squinting at Thomas.

Thomas narrows his gaze at me, pushing out his lips — a glare he gives people when he finds them moronic — so, a look he gives often. "Because . . ." he drawls out slowly, "he got them all right."

"I mean, why is he even playing?"

"Because he gets the emails," he says slowly.

"Why?" I ask.

"He and Nathan asked to be on the list a while ago," Thomas says, still giving me his *you moron* look. "You know this."

I did know. I told them both about it over a year ago and they wanted in immediately. Which surprised me. Not

Nathan, but definitely Logan. It seemed very out of character. I don't know why I thought they wouldn't be on the e-mail list anymore since Nathan and I broke up. I just assumed, I suppose.

"Um, you should have taken them off the list when Nathan and Holly broke up," Quinn says the words I was not going to say out loud.

"Why would I do that?" Thomas seems appalled by the notion.

"Because, that's what friends do," she says.

"Maybe when you're a chick. Guys don't have time for that."

"Well, then you should be more of a chick," Bree pipes in.

"You guys," I say. "It's fine. They can stay on the list."

"Good, because I wasn't going to take them off," says Thomas.

"You're one of the good guys," Alex says, patting Thomas on the back.

"Right?" he says, ignoring the sarcasm from Alex completely.

Silence falls on the group until Bree says, "Can we get back to Nathan from Newport?" She once again holds up the shirtless picture of Newport Nathan Jones. I catch Alex's eye roll.

"Yes," Quinn nods. "Let's."

"Listen, Hols," Bree says, leaning slightly toward me, very serious-business-like. "If you don't make a love connection with this guy, do you think I could take a swing at him?"

"What?" I raise my eyebrows. "Love connection? No, not happening."

"Oh, yeah," Quinn says. "You're totally gonna make a love connection." She grabs the profile from Bree and peruses the picture of Newport Beach Nathan. I envision animated hearts jumping from her eyes as she ogles him. "I can just feel it," she says.

Well, that makes one of us. I don't feel like anything will come of it. My gut tells me that doing this—going out on a limb like this—will probably not end well, especially not romantically and hopefully not deadly. There are too many variables here—too many things out of my control. This is huge, and crazy, and let's face it—really dumb. But I'm in too deep now.

My phone beeps, signaling a text, and I pick it up off the table and click on the notification.

Logan: Wrestling gators.

I grin at the text. He's been sending me ideas since I saw him last week at the coffee shop. Which is the last time I saw him. Not for lack of me trying. I've gone twice with the purpose of drawing out that smile of his, but he wasn't there.

Me: Yeah . . . no.

Logan: Zip-lining over gators.

Me: What is your obsession with gators?

Logan: Cliff diving.

Me: Give it up, Logan.

Logan: Never.

I smile to myself. Luckily my friends are all still arguing

over the Nathans and don't notice me having this text conversation. They'd be even more shocked to know it was with Logan. So much has changed between him and me . . . but also it hasn't. We've never really had a meaningful conversation. Never discussed past mistakes or future goals like you do with friends. Yet I now consider him a friend.

My phone beeps again.

Logan: Stop twirling your hair.

I let out a gasp as I realize I am, in fact, twirling my hair. How does he know that? I mean, I do it all the time, especially when I'm contemplating something—but how does he know I'm doing it right now? Then from of my peripheral vision, I see movement outside one of the floor-to-ceiling windows at the front of the restaurant.

Logan. He holds up a hand, a quick wave at me, his mouth pulled into one of his classic barely-there smiles.

I look around to see my friends all engrossed in conversations with each other, so I make a quick excuse that I'm going to the ladies' room—which no one notices—and then make my way to the front of the restaurant and outside.

"What are you doing here?" I ask Logan as I walk outside.

"I was walking by and saw you in there."

This isn't too big of a stretch since Nathan and Logan's apartment isn't far from here. Still, I decide to goad him about it anyway.

"Are you stalking me again?"

"It's only stalking—"

"If you're ugly," I finish for him. "Why didn't you just

come in?"

He shrugs. "I didn't want to talk to everyone."

"We don't bite," I say.

"I don't know," he peers inside toward my friends, who are still deep in conversation with one another. "I think Thomas might."

I laugh. Louder than I probably should, but even the slightest joke from Logan is so funny to me. It's just so unexpected coming from him.

"You made a joke again," I say.

"I told you: I'm funny."

I shake my head back and forth, telling him without words that I'm not buying it. But I'm starting to wonder if he really is, or if it's so unexpected when he does joke that it makes it even funnier.

I then remember the conversation with my friends earlier. "Hey, you won Mugshot Mondays," I say, poking Logan in the arm with my finger. It's a friendly gesture I'd do with any of my other friends, yet with Logan it feels sort of intimate. He must feel the same because he reaches up and rubs the part of his arm where I touched him.

"Did I?"

"Yeah," I peek into Hester's to see that my friends still haven't noticed where I went. "I think Thomas owes you a drink or something. That's the payment for winning."

He shakes his head. "He never said anything. I only got a picture of a cat hanging from a tree that said 'you done good,' or something." He looks perplexed, like he doesn't understand.

I open my mouth to explain, then think better of it. Thomas obviously went back on the drink reward thing. I knew it wouldn't last long.

We stand again in silence, Logan staring at the ground, me looking out into the street. I feel his eyes move from the ground and up to my face, and I only have to turn my head slightly to meet his gaze. His eyes have that intensity in them again, and I find it doing the same thing to my insides as it did the other day. Very confusing.

"Did you have something else to say?" I ask, breaking the spell.

"Not really," he says, and I laugh. "Why are you laughing?" He eyes me dubiously, since no joke was intended.

I huff out a breath through my nose. "You're weird, Logan."

This gets me a smile. Not one of his bright, award-winning ones—but bigger than normal. I feel that tingling sensation move through my body.

I take in a deep breath to steady myself and decide my best course of action is to extricate myself from this situation. "Well, if that's all, I guess I'll head back inside," I say, reaching for the door.

He grabs my arm, pulling me back.

"Yes?" I say, looking down at his hand on my arm, an instant warmth radiating from his touch. My eyes move up to his, and I see an intensity there. But it's gone in a flash.

Logan lets out a breath, as if allowing some moment to pass, and then releases my arm. "It's just that . . ." He adjusts his stance as he tries to say whatever it is he wants to say. His hands are doing that nervous thing where he doesn't know exactly what to do with them.

"Yes?" I have no idea what he's thinking or what he wants to say, but it feels like it's important.

"It's . . . nothing," he finally says.

"Okay." I don't believe him, but I don't feel the need to pursue it either. "See you later," I say as I open the door and go back into Hester's.

He doesn't try to stop me this time.

CHAPTER 15

Saturday went by in a blur. I did all my normal things—at least on the outside, life for me seemed normal. But on the inside, my thoughts were moving all around at a rocket's pace.

Alex and Thomas were still trying to get me to change my mind as we were leaving Hester's last night. But I'm sticking with Newport Nathan. Well, for now, at least. I'm keeping Tucson Nathan as my runner-up.

Because we don't have a lot of time at our disposal, the station has already set up a Skype meeting for Newport Nathan and me today, Sunday. Right now, actually. Which would explain this pestering desire to vomit. I'm sitting at my dining room table drumming my fingers on the dark walnut wood, wondering if I'm going to be able to do it.

Nathan from Newport Beach doesn't know he's first in line to go on the trip with me; he only thinks we're chatting and that I've been chatting with other Nathan Joneses. Really, I'm just going to make sure there's no freaky vibes coming off him—not that I'm confident I'll be able to know via video conferencing, but here's hoping.

This should be fairly simple, but even so, I'm also on the verge of running away. My pits are sweaty, my breathing raspy, my heart palpitating. This can't be good for my body — or any body. Doing daring things is dumb.

I wish we didn't have to do this all so fast. I wish I could have had more time — more time to interview each person multiple times, to really get to know them. But there are only three weeks until the trip. Less than a month until Nathan — the first Nathan — and I would have been married. That all seems like another lifetime ago. Especially right now with this phone call I have to make.

I shouldn't do this alone. I should have Quinn with me. She wanted to be here, to document the whole thing — she wanted camera crews and an interview afterward, but I said no. That was just too much. I will, however, be doing a follow-up interview that will air soon. They have done little tidbits and teasers, keeping everyone up to date, and made a blog where Quinn's been keeping everyone abreast of the situation. *My* situation.

I keep thinking to myself that time goes by quickly, right? Soon it will be July and all of this will be a thing of the past. I will be moving onward and upward with my life . . . well, more like back to real life — back to my comfort zone. And hopefully with a new job. Not that this trip will get me the job, but it will show Marie I'm capable of taking time for myself and have the wherewithal to run a large department. The thought has been going through my mind that if I had listened to her in the first place — if I had agreed to the vacation when we first talked after the supervisor assessment, I wouldn't be doing something this crazy. But I can't dwell on that. It's too late.

I let out a deep breath and open the laptop as I sit at the dining table in my condo.

I've already put in Newport Nathan's information, and now all I have to do is click on his name. One little clickity-click of my mouse. A little tap of the pointer finger on my right hand. Just. One. Freaking. Click. And yet, I can't seem to make myself do it. I'm imagining him sitting in front of his computer awaiting my call, and it's making the panic in my stomach grow even more.

You can do this, Holly.

I blow out a large breath, big and slow, my cheeks puffing out as I do. I need to take a second to breathe. Yes, a few deep inhalations, the yoga kind. That's what I need. In through my nose, hold for a second, out through my mouth. I am one with the Universe or . . . something. I'm present and in this moment. They talked a lot about that in the yoga class I took with Bree. I found it all so confusing — I have no idea how to be present and in the moment. It's such a foreign concept. Especially with my future weighing so heavily.

I take one more breath and then I do it. I hit the button. It only rings for a second before I see that it's connecting. In a matter of seconds, I'll meet Nathan Jones from Newport Beach. Holy *every-freaking-word-in-the-book.*

"Hi," I hear a voice say, but no picture accompanies it. It only takes a second before the black screen disappears and he — Nathan Jones, aka Newport Nathan, aka Number

Two—comes into full view.

"Uh . . . hi," I say, when I see his face. I do an awkward waving thing, and then put my hands underneath my butt and sit on them in an attempt to control my arms. I need to control something here.

I'm sure I'm all kinds of red right now. I can feel the flush in my face.

"You must be Holly," he says, his mouth morphing into a smile. It's a nice smile—a *great* smile, actually. The pictures don't do it justice. The way it slowly pulls up, a dimple in his chin becoming more prominent as his mouth moves upward . . . I wonder, briefly, if seeing it in person will be even better.

"And you must be Nathan," I say, trying to return the smile. I have a nice smile, so I've been told. I'm unable to give him the full Holly grin right now, though. I'm still trying to not freak out. Because this is real. Nathan Jones—aka Number Two—the guy who is most likely going on this trip with me, barring creepy stalker vibes—is looking at me through the screen, and this is all happening.

"My friends call me Nate," he says, his grin still there.

I like that he wants to be called Nate. Many people tried to give Nathan the nickname and it was something that never stuck with him.

We both take each other in for a second, until Nathan—or *Nate*—lets out a nervous laugh. Okay, so he's nervous too. That's good; we can work with this.

"So, Nate," I say, and then I laugh nervously.

"This is weird, right?" Nate says before I can say anything.

"Totally weird," I agree, nodding my head. I must look like an idiot.

"Okay, so maybe we should start at the beginning," he says.

"The beginning?"

"Yeah. Like, tell me about yourself. If you choose me to go on this trip with you, we should get to know each other better, right?"

He's taking charge. I'd think I shouldn't like that—I usually like to hold the reins, but this time I don't mind so much. Especially with my muddled brain.

I let out a breath. "Yeah," I shake my head. "That sounds good."

"So," he smiles again, and I feel my stomach start to relax. "Tell me about yourself."

"Um, let's see, what don't you know?" I ask because he was given a profile of me, mostly the basics. I'm sure he's seen the interviews and the tidbits on the station's blog. Not that they tell much about me.

"Just start from the beginning," he says.

I peer up at the clock, it's 7:15 PM my time, which means it's 4:15 in California. "Oh, that's loaded. How much time ya got?"

He laughs lightly. "For you? I've got time," he says, adding a wink for good measure.

"Yeah, okay." That was a little cheesy, but I let it slide. I pull my hands out from under my legs and rub them on my knees. "How about the shortened version?"

"Sounds good," he says.

I tell him where I was born, briefly detailing my parents' divorce when I was in the sixth grade. I leave out pretty much all details about my mom. Not many people in my life know all that happened there, anyway. Even Nathan Jones—the first one—didn't know much. I never told him she's in jail. I only told him I didn't know where she was and haven't for a while.

Nate asks me how I ended up in Central Florida, so I tell him we moved here for my dad's job, which was mostly true. A fresh start for both of us was really the case.

"How did you get here?" he asks when I'm done.

"Where?"

"To this," he says pointing at the screen. "To this whole search thing."

There's something about Nate from Newport Beach that has me feeling oddly comfortable, and we've only been talking for all of fifteen minutes. But it really seems like he's genuinely interested in me. Like he actually wants to get to know me and not use me for a free plane ticket. I had expected him to jump right in and ask me about the trip.

So I give him a very brief version of how I got here. I tell him about breaking up with Nathan, and how my friend who works at a news station had this crazy idea. I leave out all the work drama he doesn't need to know. The only thing I tell him is that my boss wanted me to take a vacation.

"Well, sounds like a win-win," he says.

"Yeah, I guess," I say half-heartedly.

The jury is still out if it's a win for me. Telling Nate about myself makes me realize that despite what life has offered me, I've still managed to stay in my own little shell — my life has been full of calculated decisions with low risk. Until this trip, of course. I miss the old days. I like things low risk.

"What about you?" I ask, ready to move away from me. All this talk about myself is making me twitchy.

He leans back, rubbing his hands together, immediately reminding me of Nathan — the first Nathan. Maybe that's a Nathan Jones thing, to rub your hands together. Either way, it's slightly disconcerting. It doesn't matter though; I'm only going on this trip with him, not marrying him. Although I wouldn't have to change my Carrie Parker Planner . . . which is, of course, the *perfect* reason to marry someone.

"I'm a born and bred Californian," he says, taking me out of my reverie, a confident smile on his face.

He goes on to tell me that he's also from divorced parents. He tells me he stays close to his mom because he feels a need to watch out for her and protect her, and my heart melts a little. He likes spending time at the beach, working at his gym, and hanging with his friends.

He seems . . . normal. And nice. And not remotely complicated. He seems like he has things figured out for himself. And I find myself liking it — all of it. It seems like Nate might be someone I'd probably want to get to know if none of this had ever happened. I feel myself relaxing even more. Maybe this whole thing wasn't such a horrible idea. I mean, maybe it won't be the worst thing I've ever done.

"Okay, so tell me why you want to go on this trip?" I ask. It's kind of a "duh" question, but I feel like his answer will speak volumes.

He shrugs one shoulder. "Who wouldn't want to go on this trip? I've always wanted to travel, and I think I'd be pretty good company," he lets out a chuckle. "I'm just lucky I had the right name," he says.

I smile. That was kind of perfect. If he had said something like he wanted to go on this trip because he found me "smoking hot," or some other ridiculous line like that, I think . . . well, I don't know what I would do. No, what he said was quite perfect—honest and direct.

"Well then, I, uh, have some other candidates." I only have one—one other candidate. "I'll let you know when I decide." I say this knowing I've already decided. There were no creepy vibes. In fact, if anything, there were more vibes of me wanting to get to know this guy more. Beyond the fact that he's truly even better looking than in pictures, there seems to be more to him, and I wouldn't mind finding out what that is. Platonically, of course.

We hang up and I sit back in my chair, letting my arms fall to my side. Then I pick up my phone, which was sitting next to me, and pull up Quinn's name.

Me: We have a winner.

CHAPTER 16

Well, it's settled. I'm going on my honeymoon with Nate Jones. Or what was supposed to be my honeymoon. I need another word for it. My ex-honeymoon.

Or maybe something better than that.

On Monday, everything was put into place. Quinn informed the station, and then I told Nate I chose him. He was excited—really excited. Perhaps a little too excited. But then I thought to myself that in his shoes, most people would react the same. Not me. I'd never choose to wear those shoes.

On Tuesday, the station ran a quick story detailing that the Nathan Jones had been picked, and they posted a picture of Nate and then me, and seeing our pictures together on my TV screen made me a little sick to my stomach. This is real. My reality. I'm actually doing this.

Unless I run for the hills. Which, honestly, sounds super appealing. I need to stop entertaining that idea.

I can't ponder the news story for too long because I'm at work. Besides, I pondered enough last night. And the night before. And the night before that. There's been a lot of pondering happening.

I do feel like Nate is the right choice. At least he put my mind at ease when I talked to him. I'm actually scheduled to talk to him again tonight after work.

Today is Wednesday and right now I have to deal with the present. And presently, I'm meeting with my team and it's not going spectacularly. I had thought their genuine interest in this trip I'm going on had sort of brought us together—bonded us in a way. At least with a few of them. Avery couldn't care less, although she appears to not care about much. And Brad really couldn't be bothered. But today, even though the Sarahs briefly gawked over how hot Nate is, it's like we're all back at square one.

And I'm about to lose my *S*-word.

"Why did they change the script?" Brad asks, staring down at the piece of paper I've just given him. Since Brad can never seem to stay on the script anyway, this addition is not going well.

"They didn't change it," I say, for the umpteenth time. "They're just adding an extra promotion for next month and they need you to inform the customers who call in."

"So this isn't permanent?" Sara-without-an-h asks.

"Right," I say, trying not to do it through gritted teeth because this is also something I've said for the umpteenth time.

Avery hangs up her phone, finally done with a customer she claimed needed to be taken care of first thing this morning. I let her take the call and started the meeting without her. I walk over to her desk and hand her a copy of the additional script and give her a brief rundown. She's the brightest of the group so I don't think she'll need much explanation.

"So are we good here?" I ask, trying to get this show on the road. It's almost time for calls to start coming in.

"Yes," Jim says—the only thing he's said this entire meeting. I have half a mind not to believe him.

"No," says Sarah. She looks down at her paper, confusion on her face.

Dear Lord, grant me the serenity to accept the things I cannot change, courage to change the things I can, and the wisdom to not slap people.

"What seems to be the problem?" I ask after taking in a nice, calming breath. Which doesn't work at all.

"I just don't understand why they changed the script," she says.

Dear Lord, grant me the serenity . . .

I take another deep breath and will my eyes not roll to the ceiling as they are dying to do. It's like a magnetic force is drawing them there.

"As I've already explained," I say, controlled and artificially calm, "it's not a change, it's an addition. And it's only temporary."

"Right," she says. But what I hear is *I have no freaking idea what you're saying.*

"Are we good here?" I plaster on a huge smile that is so forced, my cheeks burn from the effort.

Jim raises his hand.

Dear Lord, grant me the serenity . . .

"Jim, if this is yet another deadly scenario you've come up with for my trip, then please put your hand down." Nearly every meeting we've had, Jim's got a new scenario for how I might die. Jim, I've found, is quite morbid.

His hand slowly drops back down.

"Great," I say. "Go and . . . uh . . . answer those calls." I try to add a bit of cheer into my tone, but fail miserably.

My phone beeps, signaling a text.

Logan: Kayaking with whales.

I smile to myself. I haven't heard from him since I saw him outside Hester's last Friday.

Me: Killer or Gray?

Logan: Which one seems more adventurous?

Why am I even asking? I'm not doing either. I text him this.

My phone beeps right away.

Logan: Volcano trekking?

Me: What is that? And also, no.

I stand up from my office chair and grab my wallet. Without thinking about it twice, I head over to the Lava Java. It's been a long morning and I'm in need of some distraction, which Logan is good for. Plus, maybe I can make him smile again.

My heart does a strange jumping thing when I picture his smile—his full smile—the one with all the perfect white teeth and the lone dimple on his left cheek.

I feel a thumping in my chest, which is a very weird re-action as I approach the door to the Lava Java, and I second-guess myself for coming here. Maybe I should just grab a coffee and go.

I open the door and feel the air-conditioning on my face and smell the scent of freshly brewed coffee and decide that this was a good decision. My eyes move over to Logan's normal spot and there he is, earphones on, working away on his computer. He doesn't notice me.

I order a coffee—still on Nathan's tab. I will definitely fix it next time. I wait for it, all the while peeking over my shoulder to see if Logan has seen me. Why do I even want him to see me? Not that long ago, if this scenario happened, I'd be thrilled at the chance to grab my coffee and go with-out him noticing. I've avoided this place merely for the fact that he might be here. What's so different now?

I guess I consider Logan a friend, that's what. I mean, I never thought he'd be my friend, and now I think he is. I'm pretty sure he is.

I actually have no idea.

So that's why when I grab my coffee, instead of leaving, I walk over to Logan's booth and take a seat.

He pulls off his headphones when he sees me and sets them on the table. His lip pulls up in the corner.

"Are we friends?" I ask, the words falling out of my mouth like I didn't plan it. Which I didn't.

"What?"

"Are you and I friends?"

"Yeah," he says, eyeing me with concern. "Why are you

asking?"

"Well, I was just thinking that not long ago we weren't . . . uh . . . friends. And now, I guess we are, and I wanted to make sure you agreed."

What am I even talking about? Why am I sitting here? What has happened to my world? If you would have told me last month that one day soon I'd be sitting down at Logan's booth talking to him like this, I would have laughed. Super hard. But also, if you told me I was going on a trip with a perfect stranger, I would have probably done a spit take.

But still, I want to hear what Logan has to say. Which is also not something I'd have said a month ago. Who am I?

He opens his mouth. "I—"

"If you say 'I like you just fine,' I'll reach across the table and slap you," I cut him off.

This gets me a closed-mouth smile.

"I wasn't going to say that."

"Oh. What were you going to say?"

"I was going to say that I've always thought we were friends."

"You lie," I say, exasperation in my voice.

"I never lie."

"Well, you just did. You didn't even like me until after I broke up with Nathan." I look down at my hands as I ponder what I just said. My eyes move back up to his. "Why was that?"

"I liked you just fine," he says.

I reach across the table to slap him on the arm, but he

170

stops me, grabbing my hand away. A tingle shoots up my arm at the contact. He lets go quickly, pulling his own hand away awkwardly. I feel my cheeks start to burn. Dang it.

"You—" I clear my throat and then swallow hard. "You did *not* like me. At all."

"I did."

"Then . . . why? Why were you so aloof? I didn't even think you could formulate a sentence until a month ago."

In all the time we spent together, I could count on one hand how many times we talked. Like really talked.

"Oh, wait," I say before he can say anything. "Boundaries."

He nods his head slowly.

"What does that even mean?"

"Just . . . boundaries."

"That's not an answer."

"I don't have an answer."

"I'm confused."

"You shouldn't be."

I stop talking, twisting my lips side to side as I think. I came here for a distraction, and I'm distracted all right. Befuddled. Perplexed. And I shouldn't like any of this, I should hate how I'm feeling right now. I don't feel fully in control of anything when I'm around Logan, yet . . . I don't know if I need to. I'm not compelled to try to control the situation—how I react, which way the conversation will go. I feel like I'm along for the ride. Like I want to see how this will unravel. This is a very foreign feeling.

"Base jumping," Logan says when I don't say anything.

"What?" I pull my brows down. Then, realizing what he means, I shake my head vigorously. "Hard pass."

"Do you even know what that is?"

"Um . . . jumping . . . off a base?"

This earns me half of a smile. There was actual sightage of teeth.

"I'm going to find something," he says.

"I don't think you can."

The smile grows wider. Not the full smile, but enough that the hairs on my arm stand up and goosebumps follow quickly after.

I should probably tell him his search is all for naught. I'm going on this trip. I'm in too deep now. And besides, this whole spontaneity thing wasn't even why I agreed to it. But I find I don't want him to stop. I like getting texts from Logan.

Which is a thought I'd never expected to think. Ever. Obviously, I have some sick, deep-seated problems with people not liking me. Or at least this person sitting across from me.

"You're smiling again," I say, which makes him stop. Dang it — I've got to stop mentioning it.

"My bad," he says.

We sit there in silence for a bit.

"Okay," I say, making my way out of the booth to stand. "I'll let you get back to work. I have work to do as well." I raise my paper coffee cup at him. "See ya," I say, and he nods his goodbye. A trace of a smile still on his lips.

CHAPTER 17

"What do you want to do when we're in London?"

It's Sunday evening, T minus two weeks until the big trip, and I'm on the phone with Nate. We've been talking on the phone or Skyping fairly often since the night I told him he was going.

I like Nate. He's easy to talk to and seems pretty normal. I'm, of course, still leery since I barely know him. But I find when I talk to him my mind is put at ease, I just forget that ease every time we hang up. Then my brain takes off at a wild gallop with deadly scenarios playing on repeat in my head.

Stupid Jim.

"Um, I'm not sure," I say reluctantly. Do I let the crazy out yet? Tell him I have an entire itinerary?

"Should we just see where the trip takes us?" he asks.

That sounds like a complete nightmare. "Well, maybe," I say, knowing there's no maybe about it.

This is the first trip to London for both of us, so it will literally be the blind leading the blind. Nathan had already been twice before to London and once to Paris. Even though I was glad he had been there before—because he could help navigate—I still planned the itinerary for our honeymoon. Down to the Tube stops.

Maybe I should have let him help plan. I see the error of my ways now. Sort of. I mean, I am who I am. And he knew that for the two years we were together. But it doesn't matter because it's in the past and everything happens for a reason and blah, blah, blah.

"You seem like the type of woman who has a plan," Nate says.

"What makes you say that?"

"I don't know. I just get that vibe from you," he says.

"Well, yeah . . . I mean, I like planning stuff." I shrug a shoulder even though he can't see me—like I'm a cool girl. A cool girl with a side of micromanaging, controlling, non-team-playing. Allegedly.

"I like that," he says.

I smile to myself. "You do?"

"Sure," he says. "When I'm training people at the gym, they have to have a plan if they want to stick with it."

"Right," I say. "When do you train people?"

"Oh, well, we all train at my gym," he says after a beat or two. "I'm a hands-on kind of boss."

"Gotcha," I say, picturing Nate walking around his gym—helping his staff, making conversation with the regulars. I wonder if he might have some tips for me regarding my team and my overly handsy approach with them. Well, overly handsy sounds bad. Too handsy? Nope. I'll think of a better phrase later.

"How is owning a gym?" I ask. Owning a business never seemed like an option for me. I always felt like I'd run whatever I did into the ground by over-thinking everything.

"Oh, you know — it has its ups and downs," he says. I get the feeling he doesn't want to talk all that much about work, which is fine by me. We'll have plenty of time to talk shop on the trip.

"So, what do *you* want to do in London?" I ask.

"Well, I guess see the sights, eat the food. Oh, and go to a pub. I've always wanted to go to a real British pub. You?"

"Same," I say. Although the pub idea never crossed my mind. When he says pub, I picture a grimy, moldy-wood smelling small space filled with burly men with missing teeth, spilling their beer and yelling "argh!" at each other. So, pirates.

I really do need to venture out more.

"Man, I'm just so pumped for this trip," he says.

"Me too," I say and feel grateful we aren't Skyping so he can't see my expression. It for sure doesn't match my words.

Later that evening I meet up with Quinn and Bree at Hester's for dinner. It's only the girls tonight, which I desperately need. Not that I don't love having Alex and Thomas around, but it's nice to talk about girl stuff without the peanut gallery (Thomas) piping in with a snide comment or feeling like we have to keep it tame because Alex will get all weird. He only has one brother, and therefore does not understand women. In fact, if he ever starts talking too much about sports, we just start talking about our periods and that usually shuts him up.

"So, how's it going with Nate?" Bree asks not long after we're seated and the server leaves with our drink orders. Bree gives me a double eyebrow raise and a sly smile, full of insinuation and innuendo.

"It's going fine," I say, giving her my best get-your-mind-out-of-the-gutter look.

"Give me the deets," she says. "How hot is he in person?"

"Well, since we haven't met in person, I wouldn't know."

She bats my words away with her hand. "You know what I mean. Skyping is practically in person."

"Not really," I say. "You can still hide a lot."

I've heard of relationships that have happened mostly via email and Skyping or calling, and I wonder how that would really work. I know it wouldn't work for me. I need to be face-to-face with someone. I need to see them in their environment and I need them to see me in mine.

Plus, everyone has skeletons in their closet. Even me. And some of them even my closest friends in the world don't know about. Like the fact that I didn't have my first kiss until I was seventeen. Or that my mom's currently chilling in a correctional facility.

"Has he taken his shirt off for you at least?" Bree asks,

her eyebrows now doing a silly wagging thing.

"What the *H*—he has!" Quinn says pointing to my face, which I'm confident has taken on a nice reddish hue.

I reach up and twirl some hair around my index finger and then quickly stop myself.

"Tell me everything," Bree says, leaning in toward me.

"You guys, he hasn't taken off his shirt while we were talking, but he has been shirtless when we've Skyped."

Bree picks up her menu and starts fanning herself.

I pull the menu out of her hands and set it down. She's creating a scene. "Stop it," I say. "Anyway, it's not like I've seen much. He's usually up close to the camera. I mostly see his face and his shoulders."

"How are his shoulders? I love a nice pair of shoulders," Quinn says, wistfully.

"He does have really great shoulders," I say, deciding to just give in to this conversation.

"Way better body than Nathan, though," Bree says and Quinn laughs.

"Yeah," I agree. Nathan didn't have a bad body, he was more lithe and lean. Whereas Nate is all toned and muscles.

The differences don't end there, though. Of course I'm going to pit Nate against Nathan, which isn't fair to either of them. I shouldn't compare, I know. But I can't help it. They are different in a lot of ways, yet sometimes Nate does remind me of Nathan. Not in obvious ways. Little quirks here and there.

"Tell me more," Bree says.

"Do you want me to give you his number after the trip?"

"No," she slaps my arm, lightly. "Well . . . maybe."

"Stop trying to take Holly's man, Bree," Quinn pipes in.

"He's not my man," I say. I'm pretty sure Quinn thinks this trip is going to turn out like some Hollywood movie where we ride away happily ever after. That's not going to happen.

"Well, he will be your man," Quinn says. "I have a feeling about you two."

Quinn has had a lot of "feelings" before and I've never put any stock into it, and rightfully so. I mean, after meeting Nathan for the first time, she was sure he was the one. We all saw how that turned out.

My phone beeps, signaling a text, and I reach in my purse and grab it to see who it's from.

Nate: Look what I got at the mall.

I smile when I see it's from Nate, which prompts Quinn and Bree to be completely obnoxious and try to get the phone out of my hand to see what he said.

I'm able to keep it away from them to see his next text. It's a picture of a red T-shirt that has a crown at the top and says, "Keep Calm and Go on a Fake Honeymoon."

I bust out laughing when I see it and Quinn rips the phone out of my hand so she can see it too.

"Oh, my gosh," Bree says when she gets the phone. "This guy is hot and funny? Holly, I'm not going to lie, I kind of hate you right now."

"You want to switch lives with me?" I ask, looking at the picture again.

"*H* yeah," she says, and Quinn gives her a motherly nod

of approval for not using the real word. I wonder how long we're going to have to keep this up.

"So you want to fall in love with a guy, have him ditch you three months before your wedding, and then go on your honeymoon with some random guy with the same name and have it all on the news for people to see?" I ask, the sarcasm oozing through my tone. The news, luckily, has died down. Not as many people are caring about it. Also, I turned off Google Alerts.

"Sure," she says. "Especially if he looks like Nate does."

"Keep your hands off," Quinn says to Bree.

"She can have him after the trip," I say. "I give you my blessing." Bree smiles brightly.

"Hols, you can't just give him away. He might be 'the one.'"

I roll my eyes and shake my head. "He's not 'the one,'" I say, imitating her voice, only making her sound like a man when I do.

"You never know, Hols," Quinn says, and my eyes dart to the ceiling and back down to her.

"Well, this might be the rudest thing you've ever done to me," a familiar voice says from behind me.

"What are you doing here, Thomas?" Quinn asks.

"I was getting take-out, but then I see you three sitting here all cozy-like." He stares at the table, his eyes wide with accusation. "How dare you."

"I told you we'd be here when we talked on the phone yesterday," Quinn says, shutting her menu and sliding it away from her across the table.

"You most certainly did not."

"I did, and I specifically said you weren't invited," she says, folding her arms.

"Of all the—"

"Just sit down, Thomas," Bree says, and Thomas pulls a chair out and takes a seat.

"What did I miss?" he asks, his head bobbing around the table, searching our faces.

Quinn takes a deep breath. "We were talking to Holly about her future with Nate Jones."

Thomas angles his body toward me. "How goes it with Number Two?"

"He likes to be called Nate," I say.

"Number Two is better," he says.

"Whatever." I sit back in my chair. "Things are fine."

"They're better than fine," Quinn says.

"Ah-ha, are we starting to like this Number Two?" Thomas asks.

"No," I say, emphatically. "I mean, he's not bad—"

"To look at," Bree pipes in.

"That's not what I was going to say."

"But it's true," she says.

I twist my mouth from side to side. "Okay, he's good looking."

"He's a total hottie," Quinn says.

I sigh. "He may be hot, but I'm still going to be happy when this is all over." In fact, three weeks from now, I'll be all done and maybe even meeting my friends here. I should make myself a countdown calendar. I'll title it "Countdown to the End of this Stupid Vacation." There will assuredly be no other countdown with that name.

"It might end up being the best thing you've ever done," Quinn says.

"Or the worst," Bree pipes in.

"Thanks, Bree." I give her my best sarcastic smile.

"I'm just kidding," she laughs. "It'll be great."

"As long as you don't muck it up with all your planning. Have you told Number Two about your trip itinerary?" Thomas asks, leaning his elbows on the table.

"What? How did ...? There's no itinerary," I say, appalled.

"Lies," Thomas says.

"Holly," Quinn and Bree both say at the same time, a chiding tone in both their voices.

"Fine, there's an itinerary," I say, slumping back in my seat.

"And did you tell him?" Thomas asks.

"No, not yet," I say. "I thought I'd ease him into it. Besides, he's already pegged me for the planning type. He said so today on the phone."

"Anyone would peg you for a planner," Thomas says, holding his hand out at me. I peer down at my outfit, which is a plain fitted white T-shirt and a cotton floral pencil skirt.

"How does this," I gesture to myself, "say I'm a planner? I'm not dressed like a stuffy librarian or something."

"Not that," he says. "You're too well put together. With the hair and the makeup. I mean, look at Quinn over here." He gestures at Quinn. "She's got 'I've given up on life' written all over her."

"Hey," Quinn says, slapping away his hand.

Quinn does look a little worse for the wear today. But even in her current state—navy T-shirt dress, messy bun, minimal makeup—she looks better than most.

"I've got a novel idea," Thomas says, putting an index finger to his chin. "How about, for this trip, you let your hair down, Hols."

"My hair *is* down," I say, reaching up and twirling some of my red locks with my finger.

He smacks his lips. "Not literally, I mean metaphorically. Gosh, you all are so thick-headed sometimes."

"I'm not thick-headed," Bree says.

"You," he points a finger at Bree, "are the most thick-headed of all."

She huffs at him, her mouth open, her eyebrows pulled in tight. Quinn and I don't try to defend her because Thomas is right on that one. Sometimes it's nice to have Thomas around to say the hard stuff.

"But we aren't talking about you, we're talking about dear Holly, here. And I think for this trip, sister of mine, you need to chill with this whole stick-up-your-butt vibe."

Nope. I take back that thought. It sucks to have Thomas around.

"Who invited you?" Quinn asks. "Oh, that's right. No one."

"Please, you all need me," Thomas says, leaning back in his chair, overly confident. "So, Holly, how about it?"

"How about what?"

"How about you go on this trip and vow not to do any of the crazy Holly things you do?" He holds his hand out moving it in a circular motion toward me. "No planning, no scheduling, no buying tickets in advance—none of it."

I nibble on my lip, feeling my heart pick up speed.

"I hate to side with Thomas the a-hole, but you're already doing something that's not like you, Hols," Bree says. "Why not go all in?"

I look up to see all three of them nodding at me.

I let out a big breath. I have a couple of options here. Tell them no. Or do what I normally do and tell them I'll think about it to appease them, and then do what I want.

"And none of this agreeing to it and then doing what you want anyway," Quinn says.

I hate that she knows me so well.

"Yeah, we need it in writing," Thomas says. "I'll law it up right now on this napkin. Give me a pen, Quinn." Quinn grabs her purse and gives him a pen.

He starts writing on the paper napkin, dictating as he writes. "I, Holly Anne Murphy, do hereby declare that I will not 'Holly up' this vacation to Europe. I won't make plans, nor will I plan to make plans, nor will I lie about making plans. I'll enjoy myself on this trip and let it happen."

He writes an x and a line after it and then hands me the pen. "Sign it," he demands.

"You guys, I'm not signing this," I say, trying to push the napkin away from me.

Quinn grabs it and brings it back to me, "Yes, you are. Come on, Hols, sign it."

I grab the pen and pull the napkin toward me. I could just sign it and be done. It's not like it's a legally binding document. Thomas can't sue me if I don't abide by it, although I wouldn't put it past him to try.

"Live a little," Thomas says, his voice carrying a rarely heard note of sincerity. "You can do this, Holly."

If I let go and fly by the seat of my pants on this trip, then what control do I have? I don't. This is not me. None of it. I don't want to live life by seeing where the wind will take me. That feels too much like my mom and her crazy hijinks. Those antics of hers always came with a heavy price. I've never aspired to be my mom, and I don't want to become her.

"What's holding you back, Hols?" Quinn asks, her motherly tone coming out.

I let out a breath. "I just feel twitchy."

"There's an ointment for that," Thomas says, and I peer at him through squinted eyes.

"You know," Thomas says, leaning his body toward me, "you can go back to all your stick-up-your-butt ways when you get back. It's not like you'll go crazy and forget who you are. You can't change all this," he gestures to me with his hand, "on one vacation."

"He's right, Hols. Just sign it," Bree says. "Try something different."

"This whole thing is different enough," I say.

"Well, then try something even more different. Something *differenter*," she says.

"That's not a word," says Thomas.

"It is now. I've just declared it," Bree responds, giving him her best snooty look.

I sigh. Would it kill me to give up even more? Probably not. According to Jim, there are so many ways for me to die on this trip, would an itinerary really change that? It's not like I could say, "Sorry, you can't kill me and dump my body in a river today; it's not on the itinerary."

"Fine," I say, reaching for the pen. "No itinerary it is."

CHAPTER 18

Agreeing to give up all my plans and expectations for my upcoming trip has been helpful. No, really. Since I'm no longer making plans—no longer rearranging or changing my itinerary, no longer researching or reading blogs, no longer considering what shoes to bring or clothes to pack—I have all this brain space back. Plus, I did so much research already, I'm armed with plenty of information. And Nate has pretty much taken over the job now, sending me links and pictures of places he wants to see. Now that I'm pushing any of my own trip planning thoughts to the side, I can put all that freed up mental space to use by working on my other plan—to get the promotion.

Marie is still starry-eyed about the trip, still wants to know all the details. On Monday, I told her about my new throw-caution-to-the-wind laissez-faire plans for this trip and she was giddy. There was actual clapping.

And, okay. I may have led Marie to believe this whole non-planning thing was my idea, and not something I was basically peer-pressured into doing (because that's exactly what it was). I believe I used words like "embracing new things" and "turning over a new leaf." Crap like that.

It was just what Marie wanted to hear. She told me that because of all these changes in me and how I'm handling my team — if I kept it up — she would be giving me her full endorsement when the CCM position — Mike's job — is publicized.

This bit of info carried me through the week like I was floating on a cloud. Every now and then, when I thought about the trip and the non-planning and scenarios in which I die, that cloud would dip a little, causing butterflies to dance in my stomach.

Now, on Friday, I'm finding my little cloud to have pretty much been absorbed back into the atmosphere.

"So I'm in charge?" Avery asks, her button nose scrunched up so that her glasses are askew on her face.

"Well, you're not in charge, per se," I say, trying not to let the frustration show in my voice. "I just want you to keep things going while I'm gone."

"Wouldn't that mean I'm in charge?" she asks.

"Why can't I be in charge?" Sarah-with-an-h asks.

"Do you want to be in charge?" I say.

She looks to the side, contemplating, her hair seems extra blond in the fluorescent lighting. "Yeah, probably not."

"How about this, you're all in charge of keeping things going. I'm only asking Avery, here, to make sure everything gets done and report back to me."

Avery is the only one I can trust. I don't want anyone running off to Marie or, heaven forbid, turning to someone like Tiffany if anything were to go wrong. So I've told her she should contact me if any problems arise. I've made a binder for her to follow and told her under no circumstances is she to tell Marie that I've told her she can call me during this trip. Marie would not like that. At all.

Sara-without-an-h looks up at me. "So if, like, I need to file a complaint, do I do it through Avery?"

"Why would you need to file a complaint?" I ask. She's never filed one since I've been her boss.

"I don't know. I mean, I might have something to complain about. Would I do that through Avery?"

"Um, no. How about you hold all your complaints until I get back."

"But what if it's, like, super important and can't wait."

"What would that be, exactly?"

She shrugs one shoulder. "I dunno. Like, what if Brad starts harassing me or something."

"Whoa," Brad says, holding up his hands, palms out. "I've never harassed you."

"But what if you started?" she says, turning toward him.

"Yeah, what if you started?" asks the other Sarah.

"I'm not going to start harassing you," Brad says.

"Well, you might. So what do we do if he does?" asks Sara.

I hold myself back from turning toward the wall behind me and banging my head repeatedly on it.

"Then you come to me and I'll tell someone," says Avery.

"Me," I say to Avery, louder than I mean to. "You tell

me."

"But you'll be on another continent," Avery says.

"You mean country," Jim pipes up.

"That too," she says, turning and giving him a side-eyed glare.

"Avery," I say, and she turns to me. "If anyone needs to report anything, you have my permission to contact me. Okay?" I'll have to pull her aside later and tell her to never let Marie know that or I will assuredly get in trouble.

"And when will you be back?" Brad asks.

"*If* she comes back," Jim says under his breath.

"I heard that," I say, my eyes on Jim. "I'll be gone for ten days, but I'm not even leaving for another week. So should you have any other questions or concerns, you can still talk to me."

Jim raises his hand. "Yes, Jim?" I question, tentatively. I never know what's going to come out of his mouth. He's at least chilled on all the ways I could die, thank goodness.

"If you, say, don't come back, would Avery be our boss then? I mean, shouldn't we have something in place, just in case?"

I stare at Jim, feeling heat travel up my face at a rapid pace. I can't be trusted to keep my cool right now, so without responding, I turn and walk out the door.

"Yoo-hoo!" Tiffany says brightly as she floats in my office later that day wearing a black pencil skirt and a light pink blouse without one wrinkle. Seriously, does she keep a steamer in her office? I need to know her secrets.

"Hello," I say, unable to hide the disdain in my voice. I'm finishing up making a PowerPoint presentation for my team with things they can and cannot do while I'm gone. I felt the need to make one after our earlier meeting.

"And how is Holly today?" she asks, taking a seat in one of the chairs that faces my desk.

"Just peachy," I say, plastering a super fake smile on my face, much like the one on hers.

"So," she places her hands palms down on my desk, her face very business-like. "Tell me all I need to know."

"All you need to know about what?" I ask, drawing my chin in, and wrinkling my nose.

"What I need to do for your team while you're gone," she says.

"For my . . . huh?" A feeling of unease creeps down my torso and spreads into my stomach.

"You know, your team. The complaints department. The one you manage." She says this like she's talking to a preschooler.

"What are you doing for my team while I'm gone?" I ask, the unease starting to shift into the beginnings of panic.

"Managing it."

"Why?"

"Because, silly," she smiles her very fake smile, "I was asked to. I'll be in charge of both teams while you're gone. Yours and mine."

Oh, hell no.

"Who told you that?" I ask, feeling my heart throbbing in my chest as it picks up speed.

"Marie, of course," she says. "Is that a problem?" She tilts her head to the side, her face full of fake concern.

I shake my head rapidly. This is not a problem. Not a problem at all. I tell myself this because I can't let my facial features show what I'm really feeling: this is the biggest problem in all history.

Tiffany can't take over my team while I'm gone. She will sabotage. She's a saboteur.

She pulls her head up straight. "You're not worried, are you? I mean, I can handle two teams. In fact," she leans her body toward me, "your team might even learn a few things."

"What's that supposed to mean?" I ask, my voice strained.

"Oh, now don't go getting your panties in a wad," she says. "All I'm saying is we manage differently and so maybe they might learn something from me. Just like if my team were managed by you, they might learn something." She lets out a little snort-laugh and peers down at her hands, her lips twisting like she's trying to hold back a smile.

She doesn't believe I could teach her team a thing or two. Well, I could. I could show them they're being managed by a two-faced B-word. I'm not exactly sure how I'd be able to pull that off. They're probably already brainwashed.

Oh, my gosh. She's going to brainwash *my* team. I can't allow this. My team is easily brainwashed. I mean, Jim isn't entirely sure where the Pacific Ocean is. And the Sarahs? No, no, no, I can't let this happen.

"Right," I say, willing my face to be calm. "Well, you don't need to worry about that," I say, feigning a calm disposition. I am one with the Universe. I sit up straight in my seat. "My team is a well-oiled machine that can fend for itself."

I force this out with as much confidence as I can muster, even though I'm lying through my teeth. My team of misfit toys is most likely to break while I'm gone, but that's why I've put things in place to make sure they don't. With Avery in charge, I'm mostly confident they will be okay. Mostly.

"Well, I'm sure they can," she says, her tone full of sarcasm. "But regardless, I've been asked to manage your team while you're gone, and that I will do." She slaps the table lightly with her hand.

"It's really not necessary. I'll have a chat with Marie," I say and then give her my best closed mouth condescending smile.

She mirrors the smile. "Regardless," she says, and then takes in a big breath, "it's what I was asked to do."

"Well, regardless," I say, imitating her use of the word, drawing it out as I do, "you won't need to after I talk to Marie."

She sits back slightly, tucking her bottom lip under her teeth as she stares at me.

"Why go to all the effort?" she asks after a few seconds of silence. "I mean, you don't need to. It's moot since I'll be running this department soon anyway."

"Well, that's pretty presumptuous of you," I say, feeling my blood start to boil. "How do you know *I* won't be running the department?"

She laughs, a wicked laugh. "Because I do," she says. "And this whole trip gimmick thing you're doing isn't working."

Her tone is so smug right now, I really want to reach across this desk and slap her face. My whole life I've never understood why women get into slapping and hair-pulling fights. But I see it now. I can actually envision myself jumping over this desk and pulling Tiffany's perfectly coiffed hair.

"It's not a gimmick," I say, internally trying to calm myself. "It has nothing to do with the job."

"Sure," she says, sarcasm oozing from her tone. "This whole plan was to get the executives to notice you. I'm not stupid."

Oh, but you are stupid, Tiffany. I know what she's doing here, and two can play this game.

"Well, that wasn't intentional, but it's definitely been a great side effect. They're loving all the free publicity for the bank," I say. This is a lie, of course. No one has mentioned it, except initially before anything even happened.

"No, they're not," she says.

"That's what I was told," I say.

"By who?"

"Oh, Tiffany," I angle my head to the side. "You know I can't tell you who I get my information from."

A tinge of red starts at the base of her neck and works its

way up her face. Her throat bobs as she tries to keep her best game face on.

She visibly swallows. "You should know I've also found out that when Mike retires, they're moving our teams under the CCM, which means if, and *when*, I get the job . . ." she trails off, her eyebrows pulled up toward the ceiling.

I don't respond, but I strain to keep my own game face on at this tidbit of information. I hear her loud and clear. If, by some evil mix-up from the Universe, Tiffany gets the CCM position, she'd be my boss. If ever there was a worst-case scenario for my career, this would be it.

I hadn't really given my brain a chance to run away with the idea that this job could end up going to Tiffany because of the way Marie has always spoken of me getting it. But what if it does? What if the Universe or karma or whatever is conspiring against me somehow gives Tiffany Mike's job? Then what would I do? Well, obviously, I'd make her life a living hell. And then plan a way to sabotage her and make it my life's mission to remove her from the position. She'd rue the day. There would be lots of ruing.

Or, I could just find another job.

But I don't want another job. I've been at CT Anderson Bank for five years. I've worked my way up to where I am, and I'm going to work my way up to the top. I want to sit on that executive team, dammit. That is, and always has been, my plan.

Tiffany stands up. "Don't you worry, dear Holly. I'll be the best boss ever. And if you don't want to work for me, I'll be sure to get you the best severance package. No skimping for you." She says the last part in a high-pitched fairy sounding voice.

And with that, she walks out the door.

CHAPTER 19

The following Monday I walk into the Lava Java feeling the air conditioning and the smell of coffee blast toward me as I open the door. The handle on the door is hot to the touch as it's sweltering this early June day.

I don't know why I'm here, really. I sort of robotically came down here after my meeting with Marie. Like my subconscious thought I might find some answers here at the Lava Java. With Logan. My subconscious must have lost its mind.

Regardless, I'm here now—although a glass of wine or something to numb my pain would be more welcome since my meeting with Marie went about as well as an all-vegan buffet at a Cattlemen's Association dinner.

I had made a PowerPoint—my last-ditch effort to get Marie to allow my team to manage themselves and pull Tiffany off the job. But the PowerPoint didn't do its magic. Marie refused to let my team manage themselves while I'm gone and is certain Tiffany will be fine running both teams. I tried to tell her Tiffany's evil (in so many words) and would try to sabotage everything, but she wasn't buying it. Marie's no fan of Tiffany, but even so, she felt confident Tiffany could handle both teams and that my team wouldn't be able to fend for themselves, even with all the time I'd spent making sure they could.

Marie then said, knowing me, I'd probably set my team up to call me while I was gone, and she was having none of that. I denied this profusely, of course, even though that's exactly what I was planning.

I finally had to acquiesce. Tiffany will be running my team while I'm gone. This is making a trip I don't want to go on that much worse. There are so many ways for Tiffany to ruin things. She could feed my team nasty lies about me, report fake stuff back to Marie, and tell everyone I've mismanaged my team. I don't put anything past her. I'm doomed.

I go to the counter and order a coffee, which once again I'm not charged for. I've put this off long enough and it's not fair to Nathan. In fact, I can't believe I let it go on as long as I have. I should probably pay him back. It's the right thing to do.

I force out a breath, my cheeks puffing up and my lips making a raspberry sound.

"So, I think you need to take me off Nathan's tab," I say.

"I'm sorry?" the barista — a woman named Denise says. She's been here for as long as I can remember.

"Yeah, I've been on Nathan's tab — Nathan Jones?" I say his full name when she still seems to not understand what I'm saying. "And you should probably take me off that."

I'll miss you, free coffee.

She's still giving me an odd look.

"We broke up, so I don't think it's fair to have him pay for my drinks," I say, not sure why I'm giving Denise all this information, but she's not making this easy.

"You're not on Nathan's tab," she says.

I scrunch my face. "Yes, I am. He put me on there a long time ago. Like two years ago." It was right after we started dating, not long before Nathan stopped coming to the Lava Java to work.

"Yeah, he closed that out not long after he opened it," Denise says. Then she points over to Logan's regular spot. "You're on Logan's tab."

"What?" I ask, her words not making any sense. "I'm on . . . Logan's tab?"

Denise smiles brightly. "You are."

"Does he know?" I ask, feeling suddenly horrified that Logan may have been paying for my coffee without even knowing.

She gives me an odd look. "Of course he knows," she says. "He asked to put you on there."

"He . . . he, what?"

"Here you go," she says, grinning at me while she hands me the coffee another barista made while we were talking.

My free coffee — that Logan's been paying for this whole time.

I grab it from her and stare at the cup like it's a foreign thing in my hand. I don't understand.

I walk over to the booth and slide into the seat across

from Logan.

"Hey," he says when he sees me, taking off his head-phones and setting them to the side of his computer. The corners of his mouth are pulled slightly downward. "I see you picked the guy to go on the trip with."

"Huh?" I say, still confused by the whole coffee thing.

"The guy for the trip? The . . . other Nathan Jones."

"Yeah, he's been picked," I say. I hold out an open palm to him. "Hey, why —"

"Have you met him?" he cuts me off.

"Met who?"

"The guy you're going on the trip with," he says, looking at me like I have two heads.

"Yes," I say. "We've met. Hey, Logan, have you been paying for my coffee?"

He glances over to the side and out the entrance of the coffee shop. "Yeah," he says quietly — almost inaudibly.

"Why?"

"Why not?"

"She said I've been on your tab for a while," I say, gesturing over to the counter where Denise is no longer standing. "That was back when . . ." My eyes lose focus as I stare at the table in front of me. That was back when Logan couldn't spare a word for me. Back when he could barely look at me.

I glance up to see Logan swiping a hand over his face, exhaling a long breath. "It's not a big deal," he says, his tone bordering on frustration.

"Yes, it is," I say, not sure what any of this means, but it's definitely a big deal.

"It's just coffee," he says.

"Two years' worth of coffee," I say. This whole time, I thought Nathan was footing the bill for my caffeine habit.

He shrugs.

"But . . . why?"

He sniffs while raising one shoulder briefly. "I probably shouldn't have. It wasn't really my place."

"What do you mean?"

"Boundaries," he says, the corner of his mouth pulling slightly up.

I scoff. "What are these stupid boundaries, Logan?" That freaking word is beginning to infuriate me.

"I'll tell you if you tell me why you're doing this trip," he says.

I stare up at the ceiling. This again. "You know why I'm going," I say.

"You never gave me a good answer."

I hold my hands out, palms facing upward. "My boss wanted me to take a vacation, and the vacation presented itself."

"There are a million other vacations you could be taking," he says, his face taking on a very condescending look I don't appreciate.

I stare at him for a second. "Yes, well, this is the vacation I'll be taking. I can't really go back now."

"Sure you can. No one's holding a gun to your head."

I feel heat begin to move up my face. His condescending glare is really starting to piss me off.

I grunt, the feeling rumbling through my chest. "I don't

get you, Logan. You don't even care."

"I care," he says.

"No, you don't," I say. "You never wanted anything to do with me when I was dating Nathan. You could barely be in the same room with us half the time. And now that we're not together, you're suddenly Mr. Chatty Pants?" *Dang it, I should have used a better word than chatty pants.* "And now I find out you've been paying for my coffee this entire time?"

He just sits there, staring at me.

"I don't understand, Logan. Help me understand."

His eyes move down at the table in front of us, not saying anything, his lips pulled into that same old flat line.

Actions are louder than words. But his actions and his words are like a big jumbled mess. My brain is spinning around, trying to put the pieces together, trying to understand.

"Let me ask you this," I say after the silence between us becomes deafening. "If you liked me 'fine' or whatever this entire time—if you liked me enough to put me on your tab—then why did you tell Nathan to break up with me?"

His eyebrows shoot up. "What?"

"The way he did it—the way he called everything off. It felt like he was repeating things you had said to him," I say.

Logan's looking at me like I've got more than one head again. "Are you crazy?" he asks.

"No," I say, even though I do feel a little messed up in the head right now.

"I didn't tell Nathan to break up with you," he says, his nostrils flaring.

"Then what *did* you say? What did you tell him when he told you he was breaking up with me?" Nathan never told me that he said anything to Logan. But of course he did. They're roommates, best friends, and business partners.

Logan sits there, staring at me. His lips turned downward, his nostrils still flaring, his stern posture telling me he isn't going to answer my question.

I purse my lips. Why had I even come here? "Never mind," I say as I edge my way out of the booth.

"Holly—"

"Take me off your tab," I say, cutting him off, not wanting to hear what he has to say. It's pointless anyway. I don't understand Logan and I don't think I ever will.

I walk out the door of the coffee shop and the hot, moist air instantly hits my face. I realize in my haste to leave, that I forgot my coffee. But I'm not going back for it. I may never go back there again.

My movements are swift as I go to cross the street so I can return to my office as quickly as possible. Just as I'm about to step onto the crosswalk on Church Street, a hand wraps around my arm and spins me the other way.

"I didn't tell Nathan to break up with you," Logan says, standing in front of me. His face now matches the tips of his ears—but more red than pink. His posture is rigid, except for the rapid lifting and lowering of his chest.

I wrench my arm out of his grasp. "It's fine, Logan," I say, briefly shutting my eyes. It was so dumb for me to come here, to bring up all the things I did.

Logan swallows. "I told him," he says, his eyes bearing

into mine, "that he was making the biggest mistake of his life."

"Huh?" I say, feeling my breath hitch. I was not expecting that. "You wh . . . what?" I stammer.

He takes a step closer to me, invading my space. So close that I have to look up at him. So close I can feel his breath on me.

"When he told me he was breaking up with you, I told him he was an idiot," he says in a lower voice, practically spitting out the words.

"But . . . why?" I ask, my voice timid. "You . . . you didn't like me and Nathan together."

He shakes his head slowly. "Still," he says, lowly, quietly. "It was his mistake."

My hands, which are hanging by my sides, are clenching into fists; I can feel my nails digging into my palms as I try to make sense of what he's saying.

"But you hated me."

"I didn't hate you."

"But you never acted like it."

He lets out a breath. "Boundaries."

"That word again," I fume.

I huff out a breath, readying myself to turn back to the crosswalk and get back to my office.

He grabs my arm again and turns me back. "You don't . . . I . . ."

"Don't what?"

He doesn't answer. Instead, he pulls me toward him until we're barely inches apart. He reaches a hand up to my face, cradling it, and when I don't pull away—for reasons I can't even understand myself—his other hand moves up to the other side of my face. All the while his eyes are intent on mine.

I'm—well, I'm frozen. I can't move. This is the most he's ever touched me. The most I've ever seen him touch anyone, actually.

"Lo—" I start to say, but before I can finish his name, his lips are on mine.

It's soft at first and slow, and I'm about ready to push him away from me, but then he moves a hand from my face to the back of my neck and pulls me in closer. His mouth is now moving over mine with intensity and drive and passion. So much passion that I can't control the reaction my body is having right now. My legs feel weak, my heart has gone off on a galloping pace. And to solidify that I'm no longer in control, my arms move up of their own accord and wrap around Logan's waist.

I can't think. It's almost as if I don't want to. I can't think of the past or the future, I can only focus on this moment—this moment right now. My mouth is moving against his, returning the intensity, and I can't stop. I don't want to. And I moan—I freaking moan—which only makes Logan's mouth move against mine with more intensity. His hand moves from the back of my neck to my back, and I can feel his fingers digging into my side as he pulls me close.

My brain, still not working properly, does conjure up one thought: I've never in my life been kissed like this. Not ever. I feel like I'm cherished, and desired . . . and wanted.

JUST A NAME

A car horn not far from us honks and someone yells something, and we pull away from each other. Our lips are swollen; our rapid breaths keep pace with one another. Logan takes a step back and I go to reach for him, but then drop my hand as my brain starts to take back over for my body and I'm able to focus on what transpired just now, and then all the things that transpired between Logan and me before this moment come rushing back.

I open my mouth to say something—anything. But before I can get a word out, Logan turns and walks away.

"Logan kissed me."

This is the first thing I say to my friends when I arrive at Hester's. I couldn't even bring myself to take a seat before I said anything. I'm standing in front of our regular table, my hair wet and matted to my face, my clothes—notably my shirt—plastered to my body, since the sky decided to downpour torrential rain just as I was getting to Hester's. There wasn't even time to pull out an umbrella, it happened so fast. I'm pretty sure I look like a madwoman. In fact, by the expressions everyone is giving me, I'm confident of it.

"'Bout time," Thomas is the first one to say something. "He's always wanted you."

Quinn, appearing quite concerned, motions for me to come sit by her.

"Wh-what are you talking about?" I ask Thomas as I take a seat. Quinn grabs a light cardigan from her bag and places it around my shoulders and I pull it around me, cocooning myself against the sudden cold I'm feeling with my wet clothes combined with the air conditioning in the restaurant.

"Uh, duh," Thomas says, wobbling his head, very teenager-like. "Logan? He totally wants a piece of that," he motions toward me. "Well, maybe not *that*," he says, scrunching up his face at my wet dog appearance.

"Logan likes Holly? No," Quinn says, shaking her head. But even as she says it, I can see her brain moving—like she's calculating things. Her head shaking turns into a slow head bob. Back and forth. Back and forth.

"Logan . . ." Bree says his name like she too is processing something.

"Oh yeah, definitely," Alex says, and Thomas nods his head at him, unspoken bro-words between them.

"He . . . he hates me," I say.

"Hate is kinda close to love, Hols," Thomas says like he's the foremost knowledgeable person on the subject. "There's like a fine line or something. Isn't there a quote? Alex, help me out here." Alex shrugs in response, nothing to offer.

"No, it's not. Hate is hate," I say. I feel my bottom lip wobble and I will myself not to cry. I don't like to cry. I don't want to do it in public, or even by myself. Basically, crying sucks.

"Tell us what happened," Quinn says.

And so I do. I tell them about the whole thing. The tab, the argument, the kissing.

"Whoa," Bree says when I've finished. "He just kissed

you—right there on Church Street?"

"Yes."

"And you let him?" Quinn says, her face screwed up with confusion.

"I . . . did." I'm still not even sure why I did. It was like the whole thing was out of my control, and I didn't care—I couldn't make myself care. I think I finally get how it feels to be in a moment. To be present. Although knowing that doesn't mean I can find it again. And certainly not now, when I can't keep my head from going back to that moment.

"So," Thomas says crossing one leg over the other, placing his elbow on his knee and his chin in his hand, a serious expression on his face. "Are you guys, like, a thing now?"

"What?" I sputter. "No. There's no thing. It was . . . I don't . . . I . . ." I have no words.

After Logan walked away—after he kissed me—I robotically went back to work, not speaking to anyone. Not that I needed to; it was basically the end of the day anyway. I wrapped up everything for the day on autopilot and then walked here. *Logan kissed me* were the first words out of my mouth since leaving the scene on Church Street.

"You okay?" Quinn asks, rubbing large circles on my back.

"Yeah," I shake my head. "I'm . . . it was . . ." I sigh.

"Wine?" she asks, half a smile on her lips.

"Please."

CHAPTER 20

"Holly, what are you doing here?"

Crap. Busted.

I give Marie a sheepish grin. "I had a few things to finish up." Also, I don't want to leave my team with Tiffany or go on this trip. *Please don't make me do this. Pleeeeeease.*

"I told you we've got it," Marie says, standing at the front of my desk, her hand on her hip, her lips forming a straight line. She must have gotten wind that I was here because she rarely comes down here. Freaking Tiffany. I know it was her.

I lick my lips. "I know you do. It's just that—"

"Don't you have to pack? You have a trip to get ready for. And a wedding tonight?"

Oh, yes. A wedding. Tonight my dad will marry Miranda at what was to be my wedding venue, and they're also using my photographer. They picked a different color scheme and flowers, and I'm pretty sure the music will be a lot different since getting the party started isn't really my dad and Miranda's jam. There will be lots of jazz and I'm sure some 70s and 80s hits. And Thomas will officially be my stepbrother.

As for the packing—that's been done for a while. Now I just keep remembering things and unpacking and repacking so everything will fit. I'm usually pretty good at packing, but this time, I seem to be forgetting even the essentials. Like underwear. Thank goodness I remembered last night.

Is it any wonder I'm here? Who wants to think about all that? I wasn't planning on coming in, but I just felt itchy, like something was unfinished. My team knows Tiffany will be babysitting them. Well, that's what Avery called it. She was pretty ticked that I had to renege on having her be in charge. I may have told her she was still in charge and to report to me if Tiffany pulled anything.

"Right," I say to Marie. "I need to finish one little thing, and then I'll be on my way."

"Wrong," Marie says.

"Wrong?"

"There's nothing left for you to do; it's time for you to go. To get away from this place. To show me," she points at me, "you can get away from this place."

"I can totally get away from this place," I say, sounding defensive. "I leave here every night."

She tilts her head to the side, eyeing me disapprovingly. "You know what I mean," she says in low tones.

"Right." Placing my hands on my thighs, I look around my desk, wondering if I could do a quick re-organize before I leave, but a glance up at Marie tells me I better just grab my purse and go.

She wraps an arm around my shoulder as we walk out of my office — after she had to pry my hand off the handle of my door — and gives me a little squeeze.

"Promise me you'll have fun," she says.

I swallow. "Well, there are no guarantees of that," I say. It's not like I can control the fun, especially since I promised not to plan anything.

"Holly," she squeezes a little tighter. "Having fun is a choice."

"Right," I say, disbelieving. I'll add that to my list of things I need to figure out, right under learning to live in the moment.

After saying goodbye to Marie, I take the elevator down to the first floor and make my way to the exit, the clicking of my nude-colored high-heels echoing through the grand marble entrance as I go. I stop in the middle of the vast lobby, looking around. In the five years I've worked here, I haven't taken much time to really see this building. I've been so focused on getting to my office. I've always thought it was pretty, but taking it all in now — the building is actually quite stunning. With tall ceilings, white marble floors, neutral colored furniture, and gold accents . . . it's lovely.

I take a deep breath and walk out the grand door and look across the street at the Lava Java. I haven't been back since Logan kissed me on Monday — only four days ago. Without realizing it, my hand moves to my mouth and my fingers lightly touch my lips as I remember what happened on the sidewalk across from me not that long ago.

I had half expected to get a text from Logan, but I didn't

get anything. No grand adventurous ideas, no "Hey, sorry I kissed you on the corner of Church Street—that was weird. *Amiright*?" Nothing.

That kiss had been weird. It was out of the blue, totally unexpected and thoroughly . . . thoroughly . . . strange. It was also spine-tingling, mind-numbing, and knee-weakening. I try not to think about it too much because my mind seems to run off when I do.

My brain runs off in a lot of directions when I think of Logan. Like, what *was* that kiss all about? It felt like it had been a long time coming for him. First kisses can sometimes be awkward and fumbling, like my first with Nathan was—there was way too much tongue on Nathan's part. But that kiss with Logan seemed planned. Or at least like it had been thought about.

And what did it mean? Has he always had a thing for me like Thomas said? Then why was he so standoffish? Why did he always seem so annoyed when Nathan and I were together? Even as I think this, though, I can hear Logan's voice in my head saying "boundaries." Is that what that was?

Deciding I don't want to go home right now, to ponder over my already packed suitcase—there's been too much pondering on that as it is—I take a deep breath, and looking both ways for traffic, I cross the street.

Before I can let myself think too much about it, I open the door to the coffee shop and walk in. The coffee aroma does weird things to my stomach. Butterflies spin around—and it's a combination of the good and bad kind of butterflies,

211

mixed in with some nausea. I have no idea what I'm going to say to Logan, but I feel like I should say something.

But the butterflies were for naught, because Logan's not here. At least he's not at his normal table. I walk over to it to verify. I'm not sure why—it's not like he'd be under the table or something. Then I turn and go around the corner to the tables in the back to see if he's there, but there's no sign of him. No laptop sitting on the table, no messenger bag on the seat.

Why is there a sinking sensation in my stomach over him not being here? Did I really want to see him? The answer is . . . kind of. I kind of want to see Logan. I'd like to ask him what that kiss was all about. What he was thinking.

"Looking for Logan?" someone asks from behind me. I turn around to see Denise the barista standing there with a rag in her hand.

"Um, no," I say shaking my head vigorously. "I was just—"

"Not here," she says, obviously not believing me. "He hasn't been in since Monday, actually."

"Oh," I say with a nod. "Well, I wasn't looking for him anyway, so I'm glad he's not here."

I really hope I'm never required to lie for a life-saving reason. I'd surely die.

"Sure," says Denise, not even trying to keep the sarcasm out of her tone.

"Okay. Well, thanks," I say and then, pulling my shoulders back in a pseudo-confident manner, I turn and walk toward the exit.

Once outside, I grab my phone and think maybe I'll send him a text. Just a "how are you?" or "what are you up to?" But none of that feels right.

As I consider my options for what I could say to him, my phone beeps and my heart starts pumping, wondering if it's Logan. But my stomach does a little sinking thing again when I see it's Nate.

Nate: Two days!

He's added some dancing lady emojis for emphasis. Nate is big with the emojis. Every text he sends is full of them. And lots of exclamations points. He's an energetic guy—at least from what I gathered when we Skype. He's fidgety, but not in an annoying way, more of an endearing way. Like his energy could be contagious. I'm not lazy, but I've never been one to be called over-energetic. I'm not really an emoji kind of girl either. I gave them up a while ago when I accidentally sent a laughing emoji to a friend who'd texted me to tell me she'd broken up with her boyfriend. It was Bree, and it could have been Freudian. She really does make the worst choices with men.

Despite that, I text back a smiling face because I have no words to say. Two days seems like too soon *and* too long. I'm torn between wanting to get this done and wanting it to take as long as possible for it to happen.

"As your new brother, my first task is to tell you your hair color is dull," Thomas says with a quick chin dip toward my head.

We're sitting at a round table at what was supposed to be my wedding venue, watching my father and Miranda — his new wife — walk around talking to people. There are a lot fewer people in attendance than Nathan and I had planned to invite. They ended up using the smaller upstairs ballroom, rather than the larger, grander one on the main floor. So at least the whole time I haven't been comparing or wondering where I would have stood or been, since it's different.

My friends are all here, everyone came to be here for my dad's and Thomas's mom's wedding, but also to support me through my "darkest moment," as Thomas keeps calling it.

It hasn't been a dark moment, though. It's been . . . well, good. My dad is beaming and Miranda seems so smitten, she actually looks like she's glowing. I suppose I have found myself comparing — not for what might have been, but rather for what wasn't meant to be. My relationship with Nathan was never like theirs. I was never smitten with him the way Miranda appears to be with my dad.

"Hello? Holly? Is this thing on?" Thomas pretends to tap an imaginary microphone in his hand.

I take a deep breath. "You told me my hair color was dull the other day." I reach up and grab a tendril of it, wrapping it around my finger.

"Yes, but that was when we were just friends. Now we're related, so I have to say it more. It's the sibling code," he says.

"You're my stepbrother. And how would you know what the sibling code is? You've never had a sibling."

He tilts his head to the side. "Help me out here, Quinn. Isn't being straightforward the sibling way?"

"Sometimes," Quinn says, her eyes briefly glazing over as she probably thinks of her sister Tessa, who most definitely tells it like it is. "But you've always been that way."

"Yes, but that's because I think of you all as family," he bobs his head around the table. "Except for you," he says to Bree. "You're like the relative I can't get rid of."

"Wow," says Bree. "Thanks, Thomas." She raises her champagne glass in his direction. "I'd say the feeling is mutual."

"And how's my favorite table?" my dad asks as he and Miranda approach.

Responses from "good" and "great" to "awesome" (Alex), and "I've been better" (Thomas), erupt from the table.

Miranda walks up behind Thomas and puts her arms around his shoulders, laying her cheek against the side of his head. She closes her eyes as she gives him a squeeze and Thomas reaches up and wraps his arms around hers. It's the perfect picture moment. Thomas is a mama's boy, through and through. Even though he's also close to his dad — who happens to be sitting at a table across the room from us with his wife. Yes, Thomas's dad is here to see his ex-wife marry another man, and everyone is all smiles and happy about it. What a world we live in.

I doubt my mom would have wanted to be here. At least,

not how she was when I was younger. Well, she might have come to sabotage in some way, but I don't know the person who's sitting in the jail cell any more than I do a stranger on the street.

My dad walks around the table to me and I stand up and go to hug him. We've hugged dozens of times already today, but I find my eyes getting a little misty with this one. I'm not sure if it's all suddenly hit me now that I've watched my dad happily walk around the room with Miranda on his arm, or the burst of love I felt for him when he approached the table. When I pull my head back, I see his eyes are also a little damp.

I lean in to whisper in his ear. "I'm so happy for you, Dad."

"Thanks, darlin'," he says, giving me another tight squeeze. He pulls back and looks me in the eyes. "You ready for your big trip?"

"Sure," I say, but I can tell instantly by the expression on my dad's face that he thinks I'm lying. He's got his I-don't-believe-you smile on his face.

"Got that pepper spray?" he asks with a wink.

"Packed and ready to go."

He pulls me in for another hug. "I want you to be happy," he says in my ear. "I want all of this for you." I know what he means by all of it — love, happiness, marriage to the right person. Even though I had my reservations about him getting married and all of it happening so fast, Miranda really does seem to be the right person for him. But I will punch her if she hurts him. This is probably something I should have told her before they got married, and it's certainly not appropriate right now. I'll just have to hope. By the love in her face as she looks at my dad, I don't think I have to worry.

"I *am* happy, Dad," I say, pulling back so he can see my face—see the sincerity in my eyes. Because I am happy for him—happy he's getting all he deserves. He's a good man, my dad. A great one.

"Darlin', I'm sorry I won't be here to send you off Sunday," my dad says, his smile taking on a regretful tone.

"Dad, I'm pretty sure I can make it to the airport," I say and give him a wink. "Besides, I'm not asking you to hold off your honeymoon so you can send me off on what was supposed to be mine."

He chuckles, his head moving slowly back and forth— giving me that what-am-I-going-to-do-with-you smile. It's not one he's given me often since I've rarely been one to deserve such a look. "I sure love you, kid," he says.

"Love you too," I say, and then give him another hug for good measure.

CHAPTER 21

"Are you gonna throw up?" Quinn asks, a real expression of concern on her face.

It's two in the afternoon on Sunday and we're in a bathroom at the airport waiting for Nate's flight from L.A. to get here.

The station was unable to connect his flights, so Jerry had to get him a flight on another airline. It's also possible Jerry said that because it saved the station money. That's what Quinn thinks, at least. Jerry is definitely the type to cut corners. I made sure to double check that we had first class seats when he told me we did—I wouldn't put it past him to try to pull one over on me. But he came through. He also got us separate rooms at the hotel, and when we got to the airport, Quinn handed me an envelope of cash to use for the trip.

Now we wait for Nate. The other Nathan Jones that's going with me on what was to be my honeymoon. Number Two. I've been so nervous I haven't even had time to think about the wedding that wasn't. I figured on the actual day I would have had thoughts like, "Right now I'd be walking down the aisle," or "Right now we'd be dancing our first dance." But I didn't think much about it. Plus, Quinn kept me busy most of the day yesterday. I think she had it planned all along, but it wasn't necessary since I haven't been thinking about the first Nathan much at all.

My mind is not on my canceled wedding as we wait for Nate's plane to get here. It's not even on work, crazily enough. Nate's set to arrive in fifteen minutes, and then we have to grab his bag and go check in for our flight. Then we have to do a quick interview with Quinn—after Joe, the cameraman who's with us, gets footage of us meeting for the first time. All in the name of entertainment.

So, yeah. I might throw up. I also might run screaming out the building, take the next flight to India, and live out my days there. I could probably find a job fairly easily; they have lots of call centers, and Indian food is my favorite. I've also heard the shopping is excellent. I'd miss my dad, of course, but never being found again seems like a good option right now.

Or I could suck it up and just do this trip.

I sigh as I stare at myself in the mirror of the airport bathroom, with its cream-colored tiled walls and warm overhead lighting. My hands are grasping tightly onto the edge of the beige laminate counter.

Quinn reaches up and rubs slow circles on my back. "You'll be fine, Hols. Everything'll be great." She's wearing a charcoal gray pantsuit, and her hair and makeup are all done up. She's camera ready. I, on the other hand . . . my hair would not cooperate, and my eyes look glossed over like I didn't get any sleep. Which I didn't.

"I might not be fine. I might end up floating down the Nile wrapped in a rug," I say, feeling my stomach do a little flipping thing. I let go of the counter and stand up and face her.

Quinn regards me as if I've lost my mind, and I realize I never told her about Jim and his crazy stories. "You won't even be near the Nile."

I bat a hand at her. "It's still possible."

She puts a hand on my shoulder. "You're going to be fine," she says, her voice taking on a very mom quality. "And if I know you, you've got a can of pepper spray packed."

"Well, of course." I also considered bringing a Taser, since I read online you can pack that as well. But I don't own a Taser, and by the time I thought of it, Amazon Prime couldn't deliver it fast enough. The pepper spray will have to do.

Quinn chuckles. "See there? You're covered."

"Yeah, but I can't bring it on the plane. I had to pack it," I say, sounding whiny, even to myself. "What if he tries something on the plane?" My eyes go wide at the possibilities. Before I can even stop myself, in a split second my brain has taken off on a scenario where I end up being pushed out the emergency exit, falling to my death. These little anxiety-ridden brain tangents seem to be happening more and more lately. I blame Jim.

"Maybe he *will* try something on the plane," Quinn says

giving me an insinuating double eyebrow lift. "Ever heard of the mile-high club?"

"What? No," I say, scrunching my face. "Have you ever been in those tiny bathrooms? How is that even possible?"

"Oh, it's possible," Quinn says.

"Did I hear mile-high club?" I hear a familiar voice behind me and see Quinn's face morph from surprised to a bright smile.

"You found us," Quinn says loudly, and I turn around to see Bree standing there.

"Well, you texted where you were," she says, holding up her phone as proof.

I look to Quinn, who shrugs, and then back at Bree. "You came to see me off?" I say, feeling a sudden overwhelming love for Bree.

"Wouldn't miss it," she says. "Thomas and Alex are here too."

I'm having all the warm fuzzies right now as I wrap my arms around Bree. We aren't huggers, my friends and me, but my nerves have made me all kinds of sappy, so a hug is in order. I feel Quinn's arms wrap around me from the back and now we're in some kind of hug sandwich.

After a few seconds of the sandwich hug, we let go of each other. Bree starts messing with my hair, tucking it behind my ear. "You ready to meet hottie Nate?"

"No," I say emphatically.

"Oh, come on," she says. "You're going to have so much fun." She gives me the same insinuating eyebrow lift that Quinn was giving me only a minute ago.

"You guys," I roll my eyes. "Do you know me at all? I'm not really the 'having fun' type," I say.

"Hols, you're lots of fun," says Quinn.

"Name the last time I was a lot of fun," I say, glancing from Bree to Quinn, taking a challenging stance with my hands on my hips.

They both appear to be contemplating this, as Quinn puts an index finger to her chin. "Well, I always have fun with you," Quinn says and Bree nods her head in agreement.

"You're both biased."

Quinn pulls her phone out of her purse and looks at the time. "Okay, you ready?"

"No," I say, now honestly contemplating moving to India.

The main door to the bathroom inches open. "I didn't come all the way here so you could hang out in a bathroom," Thomas yells through the crack.

"Shut up, Thomas," Bree yells.

"Come on," Quinn says, wrapping a hand around my upper arm and tugging gently.

Bree grabs my bags and we exit the bathroom to find Alex and Thomas there. Joe, the cameraman, is off to the side leaning against a wall, fidgeting with his camera equipment.

"You ready for this?" Alex asks when he sees me. He puts an arm around me and gives me a side hug. The question is rhetorical. He knows I'm not.

"What are you wearing?" Thomas asks, an expression of

disgust on his face as his eyes travel from my barely made-up face down to my black flip-flops.

"What?" I look down at the black T-shirt and olive green jersey knit pencil skirt. "What's wrong with my outfit?"

"You could have at least tried," he says, his face changing from disgust to disappointment.

"I did try," I say, feeling defensive. "And I'm flying overnight to Europe. I was going for comfort."

"Maybe a little too comfortable," he says, his nose scrunching up like he's smelled something stinky.

"You look great, Hols," says Bree as she gives a side-glare to Thomas. Alex and Quinn chime in with words of affirmation.

Thomas sighs. "Fine. Whatever. Can we get this dowdy princess off? I was promised lunch."

Bree hands bag duty over to Thomas who surprisingly makes no argument as he takes them from her. Quinn and Joe start walking ahead of us, their heads close as they discuss where we're going. The rest of us follow along after them.

"You can still back out, you know," Alex says as he sidles up next to me.

"No, she can't," says Bree, who's on my other side.

"She's right," I say. I briefly imagine going back to work tomorrow and seeing the look on Marie's face. No, if I ditched out on this vacation, I'd have to go into hiding for a week, and then spend that week making up stories about the trip. And since lying is not a talent of mine that would never work. There's also the tiny fact that parts of my trip will be detailed on the news as I'm supposed to send pictures to Quinn. I'm sure Marie will be watching since she's been so thrilled about this entire thing.

"Well, if anything goes wrong, you call me. I'll be on the first plane out," Alex says.

"Wow, aren't you chivalrous." Bree says this like it's a bad thing.

"Thanks, Alex," I say after giving Bree a questioning glance.

We arrive at the waiting area for arriving flights. It's a large atrium space with huge vaulted ceilings and windows all around. A large cardboard cutout of Mickey is front and center holding a sign that says, "Welcome to Orlando."

There's already quite a bustle of people coming and going since this is also the departures area, and there's a large line queuing up to go through TSA. I've never understood why Orlando is such a tourist trap in the summer. The weather is terrible this time of year—with the heat index twenty degrees higher because of the smothering humidity, and the daily thunderstorms that, rather than cooling down the temperature, only add more moisture to the thick air.

But people come here. By the boatloads. We locals avoid any of the tourist traps during this time because of it. You'll find us getting our fill of Mickey and the gang during the winter months when the weather is perfect—low humidity and bright blue skies. Although you will rarely find me in a tourist space any time of year. I haven't set foot in any of the amusement parks in a long time.

I watch as Quinn and Joe find a place to the side where

people are arriving from all over the world, Alex and Thomas are standing near them. Bree and I wander over to the large screen that shows arrivals and departures and we look up Nate's flight, which is flashing "landed" next to it, and my stomach does a couple of flips.

"He's almost here," Bree says, putting her hands together like she's in some yoga prayer stance.

This reminds me to breathe, so I take a big, deep, yoga breath and wonder if I should try meditation right here in the middle of the airport. It's never worked for me in the past, but maybe this time.

"Come on," she grabs me by the hand before I could sink into a meditation position and leads me over to where everyone else is waiting.

Thomas, who still has my luggage is talking quietly to Alex, and Quinn and Joe are discussing the lighting and where she should stand when she does the interview. We get a few looks from people as they pass by, wondering why there's a news camera at the airport. I doubt if anyone knows, but maybe some of the people who work here might recognize why we're here and the thought gives me nervous butterflies. I'd hate to draw a crowd, although when the cameras start to roll, I wonder if that's what will happen anyway.

"I think I see him," Bree says, and we all turn to the crowd of people coming down the hallway. I stand on my toes and extend my neck to have a look.

And I see him. My stomach does a sinking, flipping thing that makes me feel all kinds of strange. Nate smiles big and waves at me, and then tries to get around the crowd of people exiting, but then realizing he can't, just keeps walking with them.

"Oh, my gosh," I hear Bree from close behind me. Her voice is low and she's obviously talking through her teeth. "He's even hotter in person."

She's not just saying that. Nate approaches with his big, bright-white smile, that dimple in his chin even more pronounced, a sprinkling of shadow on his jaw, his dark blond hair tousled just right, and a perfect surfer tan. He's . . . well, he's definitely not ugly. He's got on basketball shorts and a fairly fitted navy blue T-shirt. I thank the heavens he didn't wear his "Keep Calm and Go on a Fake Honeymoon" shirt.

"Holly?" he asks as he finally reaches us, the crowd of people walking around us as they head toward the baggage claim area.

"Yeah, um . . . yes, I'm Holly," I say, all flustered and ridiculous sounding. I have to look up at him as he probably has about six inches on me. "You must be Nate."

Nate drops his bags next to him, takes a large step toward me, and before I can reach out a hand to shake his, he's wrapped his arms around me and spins me in the middle of the airport. I let out a sound that's like a half growl, half scream from the surprise of the gesture.

"Perfect," Quinn says, and I turn my head to find that Joe has been taping the entire introduction. "I couldn't have planned that better myself." She looks quite proud, as if she *had* planned it.

Nate puts me back down and then with reddened cheeks

and flustered breath, I introduce him to everyone. He shakes everyone's hand as he meets them, and I have to tell Bree to let go when she shakes Nate's hand for much longer than necessary.

First impressions are usually pretty telling about someone—barring Logan, who I'm trying not to think about—and my first impression of Nate, at least the real, in-person Nate, is I like him. I can't say I have a feeling of comfort or that his presence helps my unease, but I'm not sure the Dalai Lama would make me feel any better about my current predicament. Nate is full of energy, and that smile of his . . . I mean, it's a *great* smile. It's definitely even better in person.

"Okay," Quinn says, her work persona now on. She gets very serious when she's working. I find I like this rare version of Quinn. She's confident and commanding. "I just need to ask you a few questions and then we'll get you checked in and on your way."

Thomas, Alex, and Bree have moved over to the side behind the camera, and by the obvious glances in our direction, I know what they're talking about. At one point Bree makes eye contact with me and her eyes go wide like she can't believe my luck. My eyes go wide back, trying to get her to stop. I quickly glance over at Nate, whose attention was thankfully on something else and didn't see the exchange.

Alex is standing rigidly, his legs shoulder-width apart and his hands down at his sides, one of his hands repeatedly opening and closing into a fist. Thomas says something to him and he nods, both of them looking not too thrilled. I wonder if they're still thinking I should have gone with Tucson Nathan Jones. For a minute, I picture him standing here, at least what I can remember of him. I know his hair and eyes were dark brown, but I can't remember the details of his face. It feels all wrong, though. I think I made the right choice. My mind is made up, even though my stomach is still in knots over the whole thing.

As if he could hear the thoughts going through my head, Nate reaches over and grabs my hand. He doesn't weave his fingers through mine; it's a simple hold. Even so, the gesture feels quite intimate for two people who have just met in person. My initial instinct is to shake his hand off, but I also don't want to be rude.

"Nervous?" he asks. I'm sure my sweaty and clammy hand already answers his question.

"Yeah," I say, taking the opportunity to take my hand out of his grasp and wiping it on my skirt.

He leaves his hand down as if he wants me to take it again, but I can't. It feels wrong to be holding his hand at this point, or any point. I don't want to give him any ideas, and I need to set boundaries now.

Boundaries make me think of Logan. I know what I mean by boundaries right now — establishing them with Nate — but I still don't understand what Logan meant when he said it. I suppose he must have meant that he didn't want to cross any — at least not ones that might affect his friendship with Nathan. And somehow a boundary between him and me was necessary. Although I still don't really get it. I mean, it didn't seem hard for Logan to be a complete arse when he was around me. Was it all just a front? A cover for how he really felt?

And where were those boundaries when he grabbed me and kissed me like he did? And why hasn't he tried to contact me since?

Nope. I have too much going on right now. I'm not going to think about Logan.

Quinn has Nate and me move over to a wall where the backdrop is a mural of modern art. It's not far enough away from the hustle of people, and I wonder how we will be heard over the noise and if anyone will stop and watch.

Sure enough, once the camera is rolling we get some head turns and some people stop and stand behind the camera to watch. We have to redo one question because a couple of teenagers decided standing right behind Nate and me and jumping up and down would be cool. One glare from Quinn and they both ran.

Quinn asks us if we're looking forward to the trip and Nate answers with a resounding "Yes!" My yes is a little more reserved. I'm mostly looking forward to it being over. I'm not planning to live in the moment this entire trip. Each day will be one day closer to me being home and this nightmare being over. I know I'm supposed to be going on this trip with no preconceived notions, no planning or whatever. But I can't help myself.

As I look at Nate though, with his chiseled jaw, his attractive smile, and his contagious demeanor—the guy has a ton of energy after a long flight—I can't help but hope it won't be such a nightmare. Maybe . . . just maybe, I might actually have some fun. Can you have fun but still want it to be over?

"One last question," Quinn asks, angling her body toward Nate.

"Now that you've met in person, what do you think of each other?"

She puts the microphone toward Nate first, and I'm grateful because it gives me a moment to formulate my answer.

Nate puts an arm around my waist and pulls me toward him. I let out an uncomfortable laugh—a combination of a gasp and a chuckle. "I thought Holly was great over the phone and Skyping. But seeing her in person, well, I think I like her even more." He leans his head in, resting it on mine. The audience—yes, there's now an audience—says "aw" practically in unison. You can see the giddiness in Quinn's eyes even though her smile doesn't let on. She's got her I'm-a-TV-personality smile on, which is nothing like her normal smile. I'm sure she's thinking this is ratings gold and she's loving every second of it.

She turns the mic to me. "And you, Holly?"

I pause, thinking of what to say. How do I feel? Well, I'm a mixture of things, really. I want this trip to be over, but Nate's quite attractive and full of energy and although I feel nervous I also feel okay—like I'm not going to die on this trip (stupid Jim). I'm supposed to be letting go, aren't I?

"I feel . . . the same," I say tentatively, and then without really thinking about it, I lean into Nate, his arm around me tightening as I do. I reach my arm around him, lightly settling it on his waist, which feels taut and sinewy even under his shirt.

What was I just saying about boundaries? Right, must establish boundaries. A side hug is a friendly gesture, isn't it?

As we stand together, arm in arm, a camera in front of us, an audience behind it, I suddenly feel a little as though I'm having an out-of-body experience. That my life is really not my own. Is this what letting go feels like? If so, I'm not sure I like it.

I turn my head up to see him — and instead of Nate's face with his rugged good looks, for the briefest of seconds I imagine Logan standing there. His lips pulled into a half-frown, his gaze casting judgmental glances at everyone around us. An odd sense of comfort washes over me and I find myself suddenly wishing it were Logan standing here instead of Nate, which ranks up there with one of the most ridiculous thoughts I've had. Ever.

CHAPTER 22

I survived the flight.

Actually, I survived the flight, finding our hotel (which is a lovely little boutique hotel near Hyde Park), a half day of seeing a few things that weren't high priority—places that didn't require too much brain power since the jet lag was something fierce—going to bed early in a foreign place (literally), and another full day of tourist attractions.

I'm still alive. Not that I thought I'd die the first day. I never had any notions of dying at all until Jim started up with his stupid stories.

Also—and this is officially day one since the first day was more just trying to acclimate to the time change, so I can't make a fully educated decision—but I think I might be enjoying it so far. Today has been fun. Like, actual, real fun that I haven't experienced in a long time. And if I'm being honest, even in my over-caffeinated yet tired state, yesterday was fairly entertaining as well.

Even the flight was good. I'm afraid now that flying first class has ruined me and I'll never be able to fly any other way again. But even with all the comfort first class provides, Nate and I didn't get as much sleep as we should have because there was so much to talk about. Nate, it turns out, is a really great listener, and a great conversationalist.

It also turns out that Nate is more of a planner than I thought he would be. He seemed so fly-by-the-seat-of-his-pants when we chatted before the trip, so it surprised me when, not long after we took off on the plane, he pulled out of his travel bag an entire list of things to do and see, and each grouped by location and travel time so we could get in as many sights as possible while we were here. He even made one for Paris.

I mean, sure, it was written sloppily on a piece of paper that was haphazardly ripped out of a spiral notebook. Not on index cards or in the notes section of a phone like I would have done. And honestly, it looked like chicken-scratch—I wasn't sure what most of it said—but the point is, he made a list. Nate is a list-maker.

He scored us the London Pass, which is a prepaid card that gets you into all the major attractions and bypasses lines, saving us time and money, and he also got us the Oyster Card for transportation. Nate, I've found, is quite resourceful.

I had obviously found out about all this in my research, back when the original Nathan Jones and I were supposed to be going on this trip. But I hadn't expected Nate to find it as well. Or to even bother. Had I known, I could have sent him all my info and saved him the time. But since I was trying to throw caution to the wind—or rather, was bullied into it by my friends — I didn't think of it. I didn't even bring my Carrie Parker planner, and I'm only a little twitchy about that.

First on Nate's list for today was St. Paul's Cathedral, which was gorgeous itself, but the views from the top of the dome were incredible. Nate was quite impressed that I made it up the stairs without needing a break. I probably did need a bit of a break, but since he was traipsing up them like it was no big deal, I made sure to keep pace with him. I faked I was overwhelmed by the beauty of it all while I caught my breath once we got to the top.

Then we saw the Millennium Bridge, Tate Modern, and now I'm sitting at a bench near the Borough Market where Nate is off getting us drinks.

Nate is . . . well, he's great, actually. He's witty, and talkative, and so freaking energetic. It's contagious, that energy. I've found myself talking more animatedly than I normally do and using lots of hand gestures as I mirror him. Nate is big on hand gestures. Even when he was explaining what he thought the symbolism meant on a piece in Tate Modern that was basically a bunch of orange squiggly lines on a white background. It wasn't until after we left that he admitted he was making it up and that he doesn't really get modern art. Another thing we have in common. I mean, I can appreciate it, but I can't see the meaning behind it.

I know I compared him and Nathan in the beginning, but there really is no comparison. I mean, of course there've been a few times that I've thought about how different it would be to be here with Nathan. Nathan, who's so go-with-the-flow and would have never made a list of things to do or see—he would have figured I'd do it (which I would, and did), and he would have been along for the ride. That's how it always felt with Nathan. Until our wedding plans were too much of a ride for him and he abandoned ship.

My phone beeps in my purse and I jump at the noise. I wasn't sure if my phone was going to work over here even though I put everything into place to make sure it would. I wasn't about to be stuffed into a rug and sent down the Thames without some way to contact the police, after all.

When we first got here, I got a little nervous because the connection seemed shoddy when a text to my dad wouldn't go through and I had a momentary freak-out that my team wouldn't be able to get a hold of me, but it appears to be working now as I pull it out and see a text from Quinn.

Quinn: Have you made out with him yet?

Typical Quinn. Actually, that feels more like a Bree thing to ask. I would have expected Quinn to ask me if I got here safely, how I was feeling, etc. But apparently, she's more interested in whether I got some action rather than all that other nonsense.

I text back a simple "none of your business," to let her stew over that for a bit.

Quinn: OMG!!! You totally did!

I roll my eyes and put my phone back in my purse. I'm not even going to answer. She has to know her best friend of fourteen years would not make out with someone she barely knows. I told her I'd let go, but I'm not going to let *that* much go.

If I'm being honest, I'm finding it's not all that hard to let go around Nate. I was nervous initially, but now I find I'm relaxing a lot around him. Which goes against his demeanor since, like I said, he's a ball of enthusiasm. It has an opposite effect on me, though. I find his energy endearing, even if the guy can't sit still for a minute.

But no, there's been no kissing. Not even a moment for something to happen. Even as we stood close together looking over the Millennium Bridge at the spectacular views of the city, Nate's arm up against mine, our faces only inches away from each other. There was no inkling, no worry on my part that he would cross any lines. He's been a perfect gentleman so far.

I'll admit I do find Nate attractive. Who wouldn't? The guy is hot. As in H-O-T. I can't deny that as the day has gone on, I've felt tinges of . . . something. Maybe it's the jet lag. Or gas. I did eat what may have been a dodgy gyro from a food truck earlier.

Dodgy. Look at me speaking like the locals.

"Here you go," Nate says as he approaches. His skin looks sun-kissed and he's wearing a pair of tan chino shorts and a black tee that hugs all the right parts of his muscular upper body. He has a pair of aviators on and the scruff around his jaw only adds to the appeal.

He hands me a bottle of water. The coldness of the bottle feels good in my warm hands and I quickly unscrew the top and take a few big gulps, keeping my eyes on the market rather than the man standing in front of me.

Nate sits down next to me, our bodies close together on

the small bench. We both stare out toward the market; the green, red, and yellow awnings that cover some of the booths make the place seem bright and cheery. People move in and out through the stands, perusing and stopping to make purchases or try samples.

Nate opens his water and gulps it down quickly. There's only a quarter of the bottle left when he comes up for air. Then he pours what's left over his head and rubs it into his hair, the water trickling down his face. It's a hot day in London and I feel slightly envious I can't do the same. My hair would frizz up like I stuck my finger in an electrical socket if I tried.

"Feel better?" I ask as I watch him tousle his now fairly wet hair around.

"Yeah," he says, his mouth pulling up into a grin, that dimple on his chin quite prominent.

He fusses with his hair for a minute, only making it worse as he does.

"Do you want some help?" I ask finally after watching him move his hair one way and then back the other way, trying to get it into place.

"Yes, please," he says.

He leans his head down, and I reach up and comb through his damp hair with my fingers, trying to style it the way he had it when we left the hotel this morning.

He sighs as I run my fingers through his dark blond locks. "That feels nice," he says on a long exhale.

"Look up," I say so I can have access to the front part. My fingers go to work, as I push the hair back from his face. His hair feels lush and soft and I find I don't mind doing this. Not at all.

When I'm basically finished, and now just fixing some pieces, trying to get them to stay in place, I look at Nate's face and see he's watching me with those pale blue eyes of his.

The intense stare he's giving me isn't something I've seen a lot from this happy and energetic guy I'm on this journey with. A tinge of something pulses through me once again and I instantly pull my hand away, afraid it might grow a mind of its own and caress that stubbled square jaw of his.

"There you go," I say, looking away from him and back out at the Borough Market. Warning bells have started going off in my head. I liked that way too much.

Boundaries. Must keep boundaries.

"Thank you," Nate says.

I take a quick breath, my shoulders raising as I do. "You ready to go?"

"Let's go," he says, rubbing his hands together.

"You know," Nate says after taking a big gulp of his beer, "I'm having a great time."

We're at a café in Piccadilly Circus eating pizza after a long day of walking and sight-seeing.

"Are you?" I ask.

"Yeah," he says, reaching over and brushing a couple of his fingers up my arm. Nate's found ways to touch me throughout the day — nothing that would cause any warning bells on my part. Just small gestures here and there. A hand on my back as he guides me through a door. A quick tap on the arm to show me something. He even grabbed my hand once as we were leaving Tate Modern, and I wasn't put out at all.

"I'm having a great time too," I say.

"You say that like you're surprised," he says, giving me a teasing smirk.

"Yeah," I say, reaching up and twisting some hair around my finger. "I wasn't sure how this all would go."

"Right," he says, putting his hands in his lap. "I wasn't sure either. I mean, I hoped, but it's definitely weird going on a trip with a stranger."

I smile because once again, Nate has made me feel like I wasn't alone in my feelings. Although I doubt he was as crazy as I was.

I clear my throat. "So, tell me about your work," I say. This is a topic Nate seems to always shut down. He can go on and on about his mom, which I find quite endearing.

He can also go on and on about his friends — he has a tight-knit group of friends like me, but no women in his group. Just a group of guys who hang out regularly, go out on the weekends, play basketball during the week, and work out together at the gym Nate owns. But when it comes to work, it's like he doesn't want to talk about it.

"There's not much to say," he says.

"What's it like owning a gym?" I prod.

"It's," he looks off to the side, down at the unfinished pizza on his plate. "It's kind of boring, to be honest. Lots of paperwork and dealing with complaints."

I nod my head. Not that I fully understand, but I can sort of relate. There are parts of my job I don't find boring, but rather more annoying. Like my team. And Tiffany. Which is the bulk of my job and makes me wonder what I actually do like about my job. I like the reporting part. I hope there'll be more reporting in the CCM position.

"What are you thinking about?" Nate asks, pulling me out of my thoughts.

"I was thinking of the parts of my job that I don't really like."

"What're they?"

I twist my mouth from side to side before responding. "I guess I don't like managing my team so much."

"Really?"

"They're . . . hard to manage," I say. This is the understatement of the year.

He cocks his head to the side, squinting. "What do you do again?" he asks.

This is a conversation I know we've had a few times, and I feel a sliver of annoyance creep down my back. Nathan—the original Nathan Jones—rarely listened to anything having to do with my work either. It was like his mind couldn't retain anything work-related that I shared with him. I get it, my job isn't that interesting. Working at a call center isn't glamorous. But it's a big part of my life, so of course I'm going to talk about it.

I could deal with it when it came to Nathan, because on paper he was everything I was looking for: stable, successful, raised by both parents (I already had enough baggage there), relaxed — he could be the yin to my yang of need for structure. He had all those things and more. He was also supportive, but not in all the ways I needed him. At least where work was concerned.

Looking back, I realize now that even if things seem good on paper, even if someone matches my mental list of what I think I want, it doesn't mean it's the right fit.

This is all moot now, since Nathan and I are over, and I'm sitting with Nate, who has had so much information about me thrown at him in a short amount of time. Of course he's going to forget some things. At the end of the day, what I do for work carries no weight here, since what Nate and I have is temporary.

Nate nudges me with his elbow. "You okay?"

I give him a closed-mouth smile. "Yeah, I'm good. I—"

"You ready to get out of here?" Nate asks, interrupting me.

I hmph and then chew on my bottom lip. Didn't he just ask me about work? I guess my work is a topic all Nathan Joneses find boring.

"What?" Nate asks, his brow pulling down.

"Nothing," I say and then give him a confirming smile. "Yes. I'm ready to go."

CHAPTER 23

I haven't thought about work in two days. Well, okay, I've thought about it, but not half as much as I figured I would. Sure, thoughts of Tiffany brainwashing my team and taking my job and the promotion in one fell swoop have filtered through. But Nate and I have been so busy that I haven't even had the time to really entertain them. Marie will be so proud.

Like right now, for instance. I had a temporary moment where I felt like I should send a note to Avery to make sure they were all surviving (aka, making sure I still have a job) as we exited the elevator on the 68th floor of the Shard. It might have been because, unlike the other tourist attractions we've been to, the Shard has more of a corporate feeling to it, like you're in an office building rather than the tallest building in London. Maybe it was the reddish hue of the hardwood floors and dim lighting in the stairway as we made our way to the sixty-ninth floor to see the first viewing gallery.

But then we got to the top of the stairs and walked into a

three-story-high atrium with a 360-degree view of the city, and I couldn't remember why I wanted to contact Avery. Well, I remembered, but it was like it didn't matter anymore.

"Holy crap," Nate says as we stand near a window looking out toward St. Paul's Cathedral where we were only two days ago. I thought the views were fantastic there, but from here, it seems like a little miniature toy I could squish between my fingers.

We spend some time pointing out places we've been over the past couple of days. Big Ben, Westminster Abbey, the Tower. Nate claims he can see our hotel, but I think he's full of it.

"Isn't it crazy that we're up here and there's a whole world going on down there?" Nate asks rhetorically. He's having one of his "deep" moments. Which, to be honest, are not that deep. Like when we were at the Tower of London and he asked me, in all seriousness, if I thought it might be haunted by Anne Boleyn's ghost. I laughed, but then seeing his face, I realized he had actually been considering it. At least he has his history right. Jim would have probably asked me if the Tower is where they found Tutankhamun.

Nate is pretty smart, I've found. Not that Jim isn't smart, he just doesn't know anything about geography . . . or history . . . or how to talk like a normal person on the phone and not sound like a robot. I forgot where I was going with this . . . Oh yes, Nate. Nate has surprised me with his knowledge of history and especially with the places we've visited. Like when we were at Big Ben, he whipped out a ton of facts

I didn't know, not that I knew much to begin with. I mean, it's a clock. But as he rattled off points—like the fact that Big Ben is actually the name of the largest of the five bells, and not the tower or the clock—it became more than just a clock to me. Plus, we sort of had a moment there.

We were standing outside and studying the structure since you can't go inside unless you're a UK resident, and it suddenly started pouring down. I had seen the ominous clouds and wondered if we would get some rain—we'd been lucky thus far and had only beautiful blue skies. The sky didn't give us a warning, no drop or two, just instant rain in mass amounts.

Nate, in a flash, pulled an umbrella out from his backpack and had it over us, but not before we were both soaking wet. He guided us over to a large tree for more shelter. At this point I was shivering and my white T-shirt was pretty much transparent. He wrapped an arm around me, his other hand still holding the umbrella over us, and pulled me into him when he saw my chattering teeth.

At first I was rigid, like this was definitely crossing boundaries. But the warmth of his body—even though his shirt was as wet as mine—radiated through me. I found myself relaxing and sort of snuggling into him, and we stood like this for what seemed like a long time, under the tree, an umbrella over us.

I'd love to say I just enjoyed the moment, but of course I couldn't. I kept arguing with myself—telling myself I should pull away, create some distance. But my body would not move. He was too warm and strong . . . and listen, if you were all plastered up against that body with all the muscles and the tightness, well, you'd be hard-pressed to step away too.

I was present enough to know I liked what I felt. Nate, his tight-muscled-hotness aside, made me feel something I hadn't felt in a while: he made me feel taken care of. That's something I've always counted on myself to provide. I plan, prepare, keep things in order because it provides the safety net I desire—I don't need other people to provide that for me. But, for a moment, it felt nice to be taken care of by someone other than me.

It didn't end there. After the rain was over, Nate reached into his backpack and pulled out a long-sleeve shirt and put it on me. He actually put the shirt on me, rolling up the sleeves so my dwarf arms—that's what they felt like in his massive shirt, at least—could fit through.

I could have kissed him then, after he helped me with the shirt and then started rubbing my arms to warm me. His face was so close to mine, and I think he wanted to. There was a moment when we looked at each other, and it would have been a small upward turn of my head, just a little bit of a nudge, and I think he would have taken advantage of the moment. But I didn't. The word *boundaries* crept into my mind, and instead I forced myself to step away, giving him the subtle—or perhaps, not-so-subtle—signal that it wasn't going to happen.

Now as I stand near him at the Shard, looking out over the city moving and pulsing below us, I kind of wish I would have just gone for it. I mean, this trip was all about me throwing caution to the wind. Why not with Nate?

Because he's a person with thoughts and feelings, and although flings sound fun in books and movies, I know in reality they only complicate things—I've seen what they do to Bree. That's why. And I don't need this trip to get complicated.

"Where's your brain off to?" Nate asks, briefly rubbing my upper arm with the back of his hand.

"What?" I say, realizing I've been staring off at the view before us, daydreaming, for who knows how long. I feel heat start to move up my face.

"You seemed lost in thought," he says.

"Oh . . . well . . . I was—I was just thinking about what you said."

"Huh?" Nate pulls his eyebrows downward.

"You know, how we're up here and everyone else is down there." I point out the window at the view.

"Right," he nods, his lips pulling into a closed-mouth smile.

"You ready to see more?" I ask quickly, trying to stave off Nate from coming up with another deep thought. I know I said they were endearing, but only at a minimum.

"Sure," he says, his grin slowly morphing into a grand one. He's got a great smile. Not exactly the spine-tingling, award-winning smile Logan has. But then again, Logan's smiles are hard earned. Nate's very free and giving with his grins. And who cares about Logan? I've done a fairly decent job of not thinking about him, and I plan to keep that going.

That's not so hard to do when Nate reaches over and

takes my hand, weaving his fingers through mine. It's a gesture he's done before—holding my hand—but the finger weaving is a new thing. I find I don't mind. Not at all.

"I could live here," Nate declares as we eat fish and chips at a pub with outdoor seating overlooking the Thames. It's nearing dusk and purples, oranges, and blues from the sky reflect off the water. We're alone out here, the only other table that was occupied having left a few minutes ago.

Nate's chosen to sit next to me rather than across from me this time, and I was taken aback by that at first, but then I relaxed and just enjoyed the companionship. We're sitting at an old-fashioned wooden picnic table, his leg pressed up against mine, a lit candle in front of us dancing around in the soft breeze.

"Really?" I ask, wondering how he could think about living here after only being here for three days, and one of those days was mostly walking around in a jet-lagged stupor.

"Yeah," he nods his head. "I mean, I love the city, and the people, and the history."

I look out at the river, watching the water move in slow, lazy patterns. "I think I like where I'm at," I say.

I see in my peripheral vision that Nate has turned his head toward me. "You don't like change, do you?" he asks.

I turn my head to him and grin. "Who me? What made you think that?"

He laughs at my sarcastic tone. "I mean, it's not anything you've done, it's the vibe I get from you."

"Yeah, I've been trying to be less rigid on this trip. I'm trying something new, doing something I wouldn't normally do."

"What would you have done differently?"

"For starters?" I say, angling my body more toward him. "I wouldn't have even gone on this trip."

Nate puts a hand over his heart, an over-dramatic expression of hurt on his face. "What? You don't want to be here?"

"No," I say, putting my hand over his and pulling it away from his heart and down into his lap. I go to remove my hand, but in a swift move, he turns his over and grabs a hold of mine. "I'm glad I'm here. I . . . I just . . . well, this wasn't my idea. None of this is like me."

"Explain," he demands, angling his body more toward me, his hand still holding mine.

"This whole trip? This was Quinn's idea, and I did it to help save her job," I say. I don't feel like mentioning that, in a way, it's also been to save my own job. That's a much longer explanation I don't feel like giving.

"Quinn's career?"

"Yeah," I say, looking down at the candle as the flame moves and shakes around. "She had this video go viral where she cussed on air."

Nate's eyes focus out on the river, a look of concentration on his face. Then his eyes go super wide. "Oh, my gosh," he exclaims, slapping his hand on the wood table in front of us, which causes our empty plates and glasses to shake and rattle and the candle to nearly extinguish. "I totally saw that!"

"You have?" I ask, scrunching my brow. It now has over thirteen million views, but that's a drop in the bucket compared to the billions of people on this planet.

"Yeah," he says, still chuckling. "My boss showed it to us. The woman got all mad at that other reporter and then she totally dropped an f-bomb." He hits the table again, this time with less force.

"Your boss?" I ask, confused.

His eyebrows fly up. "No, not my boss. I'm the boss." He looks away from me and down at the table in front of us. "I mean, sometimes my partner acts like my boss," he says, giving me a sheepish grin and adding in what sounds like an uncomfortable laugh. He shakes his head. "It's been . . . um . . . an issue."

Okay, so I sort of get that. I mean, Tiffany acts like she runs the call center. She's pretty bossy. But regardless, that feeling creeps in again, the one where I think Nate is holding back. Something kind of feels . . . off. And I don't like it.

Nate shakes his head as if to pull himself out of a thought. "How does doing this trip help Quinn's career?" he asks, just as I was going to ask him more about the gym.

I take a breath as a feeling of unease wraps its tiny tendrils around me. I'm torn between wondering if this is my womanly intuition and I should actually be worried, or if I'm just projecting my anxieties about this whole trip onto Nate. The projecting makes the most sense. Especially since my intuition lately has been hit-or-miss.

"Holly?" Nate asks, confusion in his voice at my lack of response.

"Sorry," I say and then clear my throat. "I got lost in thought there." I let out a graceless chuckle that may have included a snort. Go, me. "Yes, Quinn. She needed something to get her boss off her back. A feature she could do that would get everyone to forget about the whole video thing."

"Right," Nate says, nodding his head as he understands. "So she gets this story idea to get her boss off her back and makes you do it."

"Well, she didn't make me," I say. "I mean, I had a choice." Sort of. I sort of had a choice.

"And? Did it work? Did it help her?"

"I think so," I say. "I mean, I guess we won't know until after the trip's over." Every night I've been sending her pictures that we've been taking as we tour around the city for her to use. She hasn't sent a response yet, so I hope she's getting them.

"Well, then this horrible vacation wasn't totally in vain then," he winks at me, the side of his mouth pulling up into a half smile.

I punch him lightly on the arm. "Oh, yeah," I dead-pan. "I hope my suffering has been worth it."

"So, none of this trip was your idea?" he asks.

"No," I say emphatically. "This whole thing is *so* not me."

His lips curve downward as he appears to be mulling this over in his head. "I wouldn't have thought that about you."

I cock my head to the side. "Really? You don't see that? I'm not really the spontaneous type. I'm more the planning type."

He chuckles. "Well . . . maybe I can see that. I mean, you haven't let me pick any of the restaurants."

This is true. I've stayed true to my word and let Nate be my tour guide. But I had to stop it at where we eat. No one chooses my food.

"Well, you wanted to eat at that sketchy seafood place."

"Hey, that place looked all right," he says, a fake defensive tone to his voice.

I scrunch my nose, "It looked not clean."

He laughs. "Okay, you've picked the food, but you've gone along with all the other plans I made."

"Yes," I say taking my hand out of his and rubbing my palms on my cotton skirt. "That's because my friends made me."

"Your friends made you?" He squints. "Are we still in middle school?"

I laugh. "Yeah, you don't know my friends."

"Well, I got a bit of it back at the airport."

"They're protective," I say.

"I gathered that. Well, all except for your one friend — Bree, I think it was? She seemed like she wanted to come with us."

I laugh, louder this time. Nate is quite perceptive. Bree wanted to do a lot more than just join us on this trip.

As we talk, I notice the unease has gone and is taken over

by a feeling of comfort. Or maybe it's camaraderie. Nate is a good guy. At least, he's never shown me any reason to think otherwise so far. Whatever he has going on at work — if that was even anything — is none of my business. I'm just projecting. Actually, right now I'm kind of feeling silly for having any of those unwarranted feelings.

"Has it been horrible for you? Being here in London with me?" Nate asks, this time the hurt on his face doesn't seem so fake.

"No," I say, putting my hand on his arm. "I'm having a really good time," I say and I mean it.

"Good," he says, reaching over and taking the hand that's not on his arm. "Because I like being here with you."

"Good," I say, looking at Nate and giving him a reassuring smile.

"Good," he says quietly, his pale blue eyes on me, his smile echoing mine.

Our eyes lock, and something snaps between us. There's a definite shift. Nate's smile slowly fades and is replaced by a more intense look — a more serious expression. He leans in toward me and my breath hitches at the proximity.

"Good," I say, trying to un-snap what's been snapped, but it doesn't seem to work. It's like Nate's in a trance, and whatever I say won't pull him out of it. Or maybe it's because I also feel under a spell of sorts.

"Yes, good," he says. His voice is low and breathy and does all kinds of things to my insides. He reaches up and tucks some hair behind my ear, his eyes searching my face.

I should pull away. I should remember that word . . .

what was it again? It started with a B. B . . . something. Whatever it is, I should remember it and pull away.

But I don't. Not even an inch. When he angles his head slightly to the side and moves in even closer, I still don't move. When his lips brush mine slowly and softly, I find I couldn't move even if I wanted to.

My thoughts are all over the place, all at once. One voice is saying "Woo-hoo, let's do this!" and the other is saying "B word! Remember the B word!" Which I still can't recall.

I decide to ignore the side of my brain that can't come up with the right word; it obviously has no idea what it's talking about anyway, and I go with the voice who approves this whole thing.

I lean into Nate, parting my lips and giving him permission to deepen the kiss. A low groan from him tells me that this was a good choice on my part. Especially when I feel his tongue move along the edge of my bottom lip. This does more things to my insides. Wonderful, magical, things.

We're still holding hands as Nate's lips move over mine, the pacing getting more frenetic. I place my other hand on his chest and I can feel his heart thudding through his shirt.

The voices in my head are still arguing and for a second, I wonder if I should maybe push him away. I know one tiny nudge from me and he'd get the message. But instead, I move my hand up his massive, sinewy shoulder, then to his strong neck, and I bury my fingers in that soft, thick hair of his—sending an entirely different message.

The message is this: I like it. I like it a lot.

But even though I know I like this, I still can't calm those other voices in my head. The ones that don't approve of what's happening between Nate and me right now. I want them to shut up. I want them to shut up so badly, but I can't keep them from swirling around, and it's ruining this perfectly amazing moment.

I tell myself to ignore them — these annoying voices in my mind — but then one word pops out that's so unexpected, it makes me pull away from Nate so suddenly I don't even have time to realize what I've just done.

Logan. That's the word. Freaking Logan. And it wasn't only his name, but also his stupid face. Why, oh, why would Logan pop into my head right now?

"Are you okay?" Nate looks at me, his eyes searching my face. "Was that too much? I . . . I didn't mean — "

"No!" I say, shaking my head. "I mean, that wasn't too much . . . that was . . . it was . . ." I trail off as Nate reaches his hand up and places it on the back of my neck, gently tugging me toward him. Instead of going for another kiss, he leans his forehead against mine.

I just ruined this amazing moment. Actually, it wasn't me, it was Logan. Why would I even think of him?

Wanting to make up for my abrupt end of the kissing, I pull my forehead away slightly and then lean in and press my lips against Nate's. It's a soft kiss, the spell that had been cast before now gone because of stupid Logan. No — nope. I'm not going to think about him. No Logan. I'm here with Nate, and right now I'm thinking about him and how I'm going to kiss him and let him know everything is okay. Which is what I do. Nate's response is to put his arms around me and pull me into him.

We do this for a bit more, kissing here and there, never getting back to the frantic, crazy pace before he-that-shall-not-be-named entered my brain. Then Nate pulls away.

"I've wanted to do that for a while," he says.

Despite myself, I let out a laugh. "A while? We only met three days ago."

"Actually," he says, "we met weeks ago."

"True," I say, dipping my chin once. "But you know what I mean."

"Is it cheesy to say that it feels like I've known you longer than that?"

I twist my mouth from side to side. "Kind of," I say after a beat. Then I smile to let him know I'm teasing him.

I *am* teasing him. Sort of.

CHAPTER 24

Boundaries. The word is boundaries. I finally remembered after Nate walked me back to my room, giving me a kiss by my door and then a little eyebrow lift — the universal facial expression for "can I come in?" That's when the word slammed back into my brain so fast, I almost yelled it out loud: *BOUNDARIES!*

Luckily, I didn't. Instead, I placed a soft kiss on his cheek and told him I'd see him in the morning. If he was disappointed, he didn't let on.

My mind whirls about from the events of the evening, and I find sleep not coming easily. I briefly wonder if I should check my work email, just in case. But that's probably not the best idea since I did try to check it the first day we got here and there were three messages from Marie.

From Mariepeters@CTAbank.com: YOU BETTER NOT BE SEEING THIS

From Mariepeters@CTAbank.com: IF YOU ARE, GET OFF NOW

JUST A NAME

From Mariepeters@CTAbank.com: I WILL FIRE YOU
IF I FIND OUT YOU CHECKED YO . . .

The last subject title was truncated, but I got the point. I
logged off and haven't looked since.

I pick up my phone and stare at it. It's been strangely
silent, the only text I've gotten was from Quinn asking if I'd
kissed Nate. I smile to myself thinking about the fact that I
did kiss him. I probably shouldn't tell her because she will
for sure blow up my phone with a bunch of texts and probably phone calls wanting all the details, but I can't help myself.

I pull her up in my messages and write a quick text and
send it before I lose my nerve. It's two words: Good kisser.
She's going to freak out.

It's dinnertime in Orlando, so I wait a bit for her to respond. But after twenty minutes of nothing, I decide I probably should try to sleep and I silence my phone knowing
that once she does see the text, my phone will start buzzing
and ringing and will undoubtedly wake me up. I'll just let
her stew over it a bit before I give her details. *If* I give her
details.

After a fairly decent night's sleep, I wake up early and
decide to go for a walk around Hyde Park before I'm to
meet up with Nate in front of our hotel to do more tourist
stuff. We only have two more days here before we leave for
Paris.

There are only a handful of other people out this early in
the morning, and I almost feel like I have the place to my-

self. My mind feels clear and I think about all the things that transpired to get me here, walking around Hyde Park. For a minute, I entertain thoughts of Nathan back in Orlando, maybe wondering how I'm doing and perhaps even wishing he were here. Actually, he's probably off with Christine and hasn't thought twice about me.

Because I was thinking about Nathan, of course my brain would move to Logan. I don't want to think about Logan right now as I approach the Serpentine, the breeze rippling through the water, a bevy of swans swimming across the picturesque scene. I want to think about anything else.

But Logan is where my brain wants to stay, and apparently my brain wants to replay the kiss we shared on Church Street so long ago. Well, it was ten days ago, but it feels like it was a long time ago. I feel like I've lived a lifetime since then.

Of course, my brain is now spinning around comparisons of the kiss I had with Logan and the kissing with Nate last night. Whoever said fresh air clears your brain is a liar. Or maybe my brain is broken.

There's no comparison, though. I mean, they were both good in their own way. But Logan . . . that kiss was, well, it was incomparable. Which I find irritating. I don't want to have been incomparably kissed by Logan. Couldn't that have happened with a more emotionally available guy? Someone who didn't get under my skin so . . . so . . .

Nope. I'm not going there. This is the last time I'm going to think about Logan and that kiss. In fact, I'm going to start pretending like it never happened.

JUST A NAME

All my thoughts of . . . that other person . . . seem silly now. Now that I'm sitting with Nate, eating lunch on a bench in St. Dunstan-in-the-East, surrounded by the ruins of a church that has now become a city park. To say it's picturesque would be an understatement; it's enchanting with the ornate arched windows, and the vines weaving up and around the broken stone walls. Nate and I have been snapping a ton of pictures, but I don't think any of them will do it justice. There's a feeling here, one you can't capture in a picture. It's tranquil and calm.

I pull my phone out of my bag and look at it. No text from Quinn yet, which surprises me. I was sure I would wake up to a gazillion texts from her wanting me to kiss-and-tell. But there's been nothing. She has yet to even comment on the pictures I've been forwarding her of the trip so far.

"What are you thinking about?" Nate asks.

"Huh?" I say, realizing I'm just staring at my phone.

"Hello?" Nate says, nudging me with his elbow.

"Sorry," I say, slipping the phone back into my bag. "I was just thinking about how beautiful it is here." This is sort of true. That's what I was thinking about before I started wondering why Quinn hasn't texted me back yet. I would have expected at least something by now.

I see Nate nodding his head in my peripheral vision. "I

don't know," he says, his voice low and deep, "I think my view is better."

I peer up to see his eyes are on me and I laugh uncomfortably. He's been doing this all day — little comments here and there that are meant to be romantic, but out of his mouth sound kind of . . . well, cheesy. I've never been one for cheese. I mean, I like a good compliment like every other woman — or person, for that matter. But from Nate, sometimes they sound a little like . . . well, like this isn't his first rodeo. He's done this whole seduction with his words thing before. I'm not the type of woman who can be seduced by words. I'm more of an actions gal.

Plus, I don't know how to react to them, to be honest. I mean, what do you say? I can only say "thank you" so much.

Here I am, reaching again. Who gets annoyed by compliments? Even if they do feel like they were said before. Something keeps nibbling at the back of my mind, though. Like it's all too good to be true. Sitting here with Nate — a guy I picked randomly to go on this trip with me. Well, it was sort of random. It almost feels like it's too easy. Like it was handed to me on a platter. A very muscly, blue-eyed, chiseled-jaw, platter.

I'm definitely reaching.

"Never have I ever gotten a tattoo," I say, and then Nate laughs and takes a drink of his beer. "What?" I search him, surprised I would have missed that detail. "Where is it?"

"Maybe I'll show you later," Nate says, a wink of his eye insinuating it's somewhere that would be inappropriate to show here.

We're sitting up at the bar at a pub that's next door to our hotel, getting drinks and eating authentic pub food. My Toad-in-the-Hole—sausages baked in batter—is yummy, and Nate is eating Cockles, which are some sort of clam. His meal doesn't look yummy at all.

I scrunch my face. "Oh no, where is it? I have to know," I say and then, thinking twice about what he could garner from that line, I add, "Please tell me it's not a lower back tat."

Nate laughs heartily. "Nah, it's on the back of my shoulder." He pulls the sleeve of his gray V-neck T-shirt up and moves it over. It's a Chinese symbol that looks sort of like the letter H, about two inches in diameter.

"What does it mean?"

"Strength," he says, pulling his shirt back down into place.

I squint at him. "Are you sure? What if they told you that but it really means 'nerd' or something?"

He shrugs a shoulder. "I'd be okay with that."

I smile because I believe him. "You don't let things get under your skin, do you?" I ask.

He tilts his head back, looking as if he's contemplating. "Not really," he says. "I mean, sometimes if it's something really irritating. But most of the time it's not worth it."

"Like with work?" I ask, not being able to help myself

since this seemed like a good enough segue. I still want to know more about what he does.

His eyes move down to his nearly empty plate and then back to me. "Yeah, that can be annoying."

I give him an expression that hopefully conveys that I want him to elaborate, but he looks away.

"Okay, my turn," he says. "Never have I ever made out in a pub."

I eye him dubiously. "I don't believe you."

"What?" he says, feigning innocence.

"You've totally made out in a pub."

"No, I haven't."

"Ah," I say, realization dawning on me. "You've never made out with someone in a pub in London. But I'm sure you've made out with someone in a bar."

"Ding, ding, ding," Nate says, tapping his nose.

I roll my eyes and then I look at my drink, which is mostly full since never have I ever done much of anything. I probably should find that sad, but I don't. My life is how I want it. It's how I set out for it to be. Barring the last few months, of course. But I'm finding that to be okay too. At least this part—being here with Nate and experiencing all this with him. I'm not just okay; I'm really enjoying myself.

I turn my face toward Nate and find him staring at me.

"Neither of us have made out in a pub in London," he says, his eyes earnestly on mine.

"That's true," I say, feeling suddenly a little breathless.

"We should fix that."

He leans in and kisses me gently on my lips and then

pulls back and searches my face. Probably to gauge my reaction. He hasn't tried to kiss me all day, and I'm glad he hasn't. There was touching and hand-holding and I was okay with all that. It felt like too much to be prancing around London like a couple of twitterpated teenagers making out at every stop. Not that I'd do that with anyone anyway. Plus, I've only known the guy for four days. Well, in person.

My reaction to his kiss is a smile because I like Nate's lips on mine. They're soft, and warm, and tender. I want him to kiss me again right here in this pub. So I lean in toward him and he meets me halfway, and when our lips meet, I melt into him.

It all happened so fast, I'm not even sure how we got here. All I know is we were kissing at the pub and then the bartender made a comment about how we should get a room or something, and then he threatened to spray us with the hose, so we paid our bill, made our way to our hotel, making out in the elevator up to our floor, and when we got to Nate's room, he invited me in to see his view and then he started tickling me and we ended up on his bed . . . kissing.

So, I guess I do know how we got here.

But man, this is fun. I haven't had this much fun making out in a long time. We're on the bed, Nate half on top of me, my fingers tangled in his hair as his mouth traces kisses down to my neck and collarbone.

His mouth works its way back up to mine and we kiss for what seems like a long while, the intensity picking up as we go. Hands feel like they're everywhere, like Nate suddenly has more than two. They're in my hair, on my face, stroking my arm.

Then Nate slides a hand down my side, over the light pink cotton T-shirt I'm wearing, and finding the bottom, he tugs my shirt up slightly and places his hand on the bare skin at my waist, his thumb making circle motions on my stomach.

This does not have the effect I think he was going for, because all it does is send off warning bells in my head.

Boundaries, boundaries, boundaries.

This is going too fast. Way faster than I'm comfortable with. I allowed the imaginary no-kissing line I made in my mind to be crossed. While that's been fun, I'm not going any further than that. That's not my kind of thing. I fear this whole in-his-hotel-room-kissing-on-the-bed is leading Nate to believe we might go further than that, when that was never my intention.

"Nate," I say as he nibbles on my ear. "Nate," I say again, this time a note of impatience in my voice.

"Yeah," he says, pulling his lips away from me, he lifts his head up so I can see his face.

"I think . . ." I stop, trying to catch my breath. "I think maybe we should call it a night."

"What?" His eyes narrow.

"Yeah," I say, moving my hands to his chest. I push lightly to move him over, which he does, and then I pull myself to sitting. I reach up and grab a tendril of my hair, wrapping it around my finger.

"Okay," he says, dragging out the word.

"I'm . . . I just . . . this is great and all, but I'm, well, I'm not . . ." I trail off. The understanding dawning on his face lets me know I don't need to finish that sentence.

He reaches up and rubs the back of his neck. "Right. Got it."

I lick my lips. "I'm sorry if I led you to think that. Honestly, I didn't even expect us to kiss on this trip," I say.

"Oh," Nate says, his eyes on mine. "And now you regret it?"

"No," I say, shaking my head. "I like it. A lot." I give him a reassuring smile. "It's just that . . . well, it can't go any further than . . . that." I start nibbling on the side of my bottom lip.

"Right," he says, running a hand through his hair. He appears a little lost in thought.

"Okay?" I ask, a feeling of regret settling on me. This trip had been going well without the kissing. I thought it was going well with the kissing, but now I wonder if that crossed a line.

"Yeah. I mean," he huffs out a frustrated laugh. "I guess I was thinking we might have something here," he says, his eyes focusing on something on the bed.

"We do," I say, and he looks up at me. "I think we're becoming friends."

"Friends?" he says, the hint of irritation in his voice duly noted.

"Well, yeah. Friends. I mean, where did you see this going?"

This was not the right thing to say, or at least not what he wanted to hear, because Nate now looks mad. Or at least I think he looks mad since I've never seen him this way. This tidbit of info reminds me of how little we really know each other and although I was already firm in my decision, this solidifies it.

"I don't know, but I was willing to find out," he says. "But you . . . I guess you've already made up your mind about it."

"Well, I mean, I'm only being logical. You live in California. I live in Orlando. I just figured—"

"We'd go on this trip and that would be it."

"Well . . . yeah," I say.

He lets out a breath. "Okay, whatever you want."

"What's that supposed to mean?" I ask, feeling anger rush through me.

He huffs out a breath. "No, you're right," he says, his voice full of irritation. "Best that we just leave it like it is."

I want to say it wasn't going any further than this anyway, but it feels moot at this point.

"I'm sorry, Nate," I say. "I didn't mean to—"

"Whatever," he says, throwing a hand back as if to dismiss it all.

Feeling like I should probably leave, I stand up and grab my purse. "I'll see you tomorrow?" I ask since the expression on Nate's face and the tension in the room makes me wonder if I will.

"Yeah, sure," he says flatly, lying back on his bed, a bulging, muscly arm going underneath his head.

"Okay," I say, looking at him hoping his eyes will meet mine one more time, but he stays put, staring at the ceiling. I quietly let myself out.

CHAPTER 25

I wake up early with unease in my stomach over last night. I feel bad about how things went down with Nate. I could have said things better, I realize. I could have sugar-coated a little. Of course, had I been totally upfront with him regarding what I would and wouldn't be doing on this trip, none of that would have ever happened. None of the kissing or the hand holding.

This is why I have boundaries in place. Because when I allow myself to go outside of them, everything gets compli-cated. Well, I can't say I know that — because I rarely go out-side of them. But I assumed, and I was right, and now things are all kinds of complicated.

How will the rest of the trip go? Tomorrow is Paris, and we still have five more days together. I don't want this awk-wardness between us. I want things to go back to where they were before. Before we kissed — back to the casualness of it all.

I get out of bed with purpose. I'm going to make this right. Nate and I will have a talk, we will iron out any feelings of awkwardness, and maybe we can start over. I'll run and grab breakfast first, though, as a peace offering.

During my shower, I second-guess myself about this whole thing and I realize the one person who could help me with this is Quinn. Bree wouldn't be helpful; she'd tell me I should have gone for it. Quinn, even though she's been pro Holly-gets-some-loving on this trip, knows me. That's why it's still so weird I haven't heard from her since I sent the text about Nate and me kissing the other night. I double checked last night, and I'm pretty sure my text went through.

I find my phone in my bag and stare at it. Nothing. No texts, or any notifications, for that matter. It seems so out of character for Quinn. The fact that I haven't gotten a text from any of my friends in the past couple of days seems curious.

I wonder briefly if my phone is broken, or maybe the connection isn't working out here even though I paid a lot of money to ensure it would. I don't know much about how phones work, so I do what anybody in my position would do: I reboot.

It takes a couple of minutes for my phone to boot back up and I get dressed while I'm waiting, putting on a black cotton weekend skirt and a mossy green fitted V-neck tee.

A picture of my dad and me—the one I use as my wallpaper—shows up and I put in my password. Sounds and vibrations erupt from my phone, the dinging and pinging coming in so fast I almost drop it from the noise.

That was the problem then. Stupid technology. My texting app says I have fifty-two new messages. So my friends really do care about me.

I open the app and see a list of unopened texts. I see Quinn's name first—I'm willing to bet at least forty of the messages are from her. There are also messages from Alex, my dad, the group text I have with my friends . . . and Logan.

I decide to start from the top, so I open Quinn's texts first. I press on her name and see that, indeed, most of the texts are from her. I scan through them, most of them not making a lot of sense since she was having a one-sided conversation.

> **Quinn:** Call me.

> **Quinn:** Holly, we're all worried, can you please just call?

> **Quinn:** None of my calls are going through. Your voice mail isn't working.

> **Quinn:** Your stupid hotel won't answer.

They keep going like this. The last one, time stamped from Thursday morning is the most confusing.

> **Quinn:** Don't be mad at Thomas, okay? He didn't think. I don't know what compelled him to put that on MM. Are you freaking out? I'm so sorry. I had no idea. Don't freak out, Hols. It's not as bad as it seems. Too much to text. Call me when you get this.

Not as bad as it seems? What's she talking about?

I go back to the message list and click on our group text—the one I have with Quinn, Bree, Alex, and Thomas, and see the time stamp is for yesterday.

I open it up and the top message of our group text is from Quinn and all it says is "OMG."

I scan down to the bottom of the texts where the conversation started, my eyes quickly scanning the OMGs from both Bree and Quinn, and a "what the hell" from Alex.

The original message is from Thomas.

Thomas: Early rendition of Mugshot Monday, out today since I'm gone on Monday. Hols, you might want to pay particular attention to number three.

Why would I need to pay attention to anyone on Mugshot Mondays? What's he even talking about?

And then my stomach sinks as I realize what it has to be. It's finally happened.

Thomas has found my mother's mugshot.

I feel suddenly sick, sinking down on the edge of my bed. I swallow hard, and with shaky hands I pull up my email app and wait for the emails to load. I stare at it, willing it to load with my brain, but it just says "checking for mail" at the bottom and nothing is pulling up.

I shouldn't jump to conclusions, but what else could it be? How am I going to explain this to my friends? The shame of it all has kept me from saying anything to anyone. I don't want their looks of pity, which they will inevitably give me now that they know: mommy's in jail.

I'm going to murder Thomas. Couldn't he have sent it to me personally instead of putting it on Mugshot Monday for everyone to see? Nathan's on that list . . . as well as Logan. Oh gosh, I might be sick.

I cover my mouth as if to keep myself from throwing up,

and blink back the tears that are prickling behind my eyes. Maybe it's not that bad. Maybe Thomas didn't even mention that it was my mom. He did say for me to pay particular attention to it. But then why did my friends all have that reaction?

My phone dings a bunch of times, jarring me out of my thoughts and causing me to almost let out a scream from the sound. I look at my inbox, scanning down through all the new messages until I see it.

From Thomasmoore@JJandS.com: *Mugshot Monday, early rendition!*

My finger hovers over the email, not sure I want to open it. I swallow hard and press on the message.

The text pulls up, but the pictures are taking their own sweet time to load. I can't bring myself to scroll down to the third mugshot, not wanting to see her face load on my phone. I've seen the mugshot before, having looked it up myself. But to see it on here will be so much harder. I just know it.

The pictures start to load, the first mugshot pulling up. My hands still shaking, I use my index finger to scroll down the email until it gets to the third one. The last mugshot.

As the picture finally starts to load, I prepare myself for it — for her.

As the face comes into full view, I take in a sharp breath, my stomach taking on a whole new level of sickness. The mugshot is not of my mom.

It's Nate.

CHAPTER 26

I drop my phone as if it's just burned me.

And then I pick it back up and read what Thomas wrote.

> *A familiar face on Mugshot Monday. Recognize this guy? Our friend Holly will. We'll call him Nate Number Two . . . or Number Two for short. Looks like Number Two got himself into some trouble.*
>
> *Was his crime:*
> *A) Theft*
> *B) Possession*
> *C) Disorderly Conduct*

I'm so confused right now as I stare at Nate's mugshot, his hair disheveled, his lips turned downward. It almost doesn't look like him—the lively, energetic man I've been spending the past five days with. The one I was rolling around on a bed with last night. But it's definitely him. I'd know that chin dimple anywhere.

What the *H*-word. Actually, Quinn is not around and this deserves the full word. It deserves all the words. *Hell.*

Hell, hell, hell.

Without thinking about it, I grab the key card to my room, and walk—or rather, stomp—down the hall to Nate's. I want answers and I want them now. I pound on the door. When I hear nothing from the other side of the door, I pound even harder.

"Hang on," I finally hear him say, his voice muffled through the door.

I'm breathing so heavily, I feel like I might hyperventilate. At least I think that's what this feels like. I've never experienced this before.

"Holly?" he asks when he cracks open the door. His hair is a mess, and his eyes struggle to fully open. I've woken him up.

Not caring, I hold up my phone. "Do you want to tell me what this is?"

"Huh?" he asks, his eyes focusing on my phone. "There's nothing on it."

"What?" I ask, turning the screen toward me, I see my phone has timed out and gone into sleep mode. Not exactly the confrontation I was going for. Stupid phone. I click on the home button and put in my passcode.

"Can we talk about whatever this is later?" Nate asks, rubbing his eyes as we wait for my phone to open back up. "It's, like, six in the morning."

"No, we can't," I say as I pull his picture up—his mugshot—full frame and shove it in his face. "Can you explain this?"

He looks at the phone and then lets out a long sigh. He

curses under his breath and swipes a hand over his face.

"What the hell is this, Nate?"

He opens the door wider so I can come in, but I stand in the hall, my feet set in place. I'm not going in there with him. No way am I falling for that trap. I will not be wrapped in a carpet and dumped in a river because of my own stupid choices.

"Holly, it's not that big of a deal," he says. "Just come in and I'll explain." He motions with his hand for me to come in.

"No thanks, I'm good right here," I say, still holding the phone toward him.

He breathes out again loudly. "I got caught with some of my buddy's stuff," he says, motioning toward the phone with an outstretched hand.

"Stuff?" I ask, but I think I know what *stuff* is and I feel my stomach turn.

"My buddy's medication," he says.

"Drugs?" I echo, my stomach not only turning, but doing a bunch of somersaults.

"Yeah, his prescription. I was holding them for him," he says. "I got pulled over for speeding and the cop found them and took me in. He was a real jerk. He wouldn't even listen to me."

"You were . . . holding them," I repeat.

My mind instantly replays a voice in my head . . . my mom's voice. Back when I was only ten, before she left and after I'd found not just one, but three bottles of pills in her purse. *"They're not mine, baby. I'm holding them for a friend."*

"W-when?" I ask, hoping this was something in his past—something from a while ago, but this picture on my phone would say otherwise.

"A few months ago," he says.

"A few months ago?" I swallow. How is that possible? It would have been on his record a few months ago. They would have seen it in his background check.

"Yeah," he nods his head. "Look, I should have told you, but I didn't think—"

"But there was a background check," I say, cutting him off. "That would have shown up."

"A background check?" Nate asks, his eyes scrunching up. "I don't remember hearing anything about that."

"Yes. That was part of the deal—a background check on whoever came on this trip with me."

He shakes his head. "I was never told about a background check."

I run a hand through my hair, my fingers getting caught in the damp locks since I never got a chance to blow dry it. I don't even have shoes on; I didn't think to put them on.

What does he mean, he was never told about a background check? Don't you have to disclose that? And drugs? Of all things . . .

I close my eyes slowly as I realize what happened. Jerry. Freaking corner-cutting Jerry. Of course. He never did the background check. That has to be it. I will seriously punch him in the face when I see him. What was he thinking? I could have been out here with a serial killer! Although that probably wouldn't show up on a background check because serial killers aren't usually free to roam the planet. But still.

"There was a form," I say through gritted teeth.

"Yeah?" Nate's eyebrows pull up.

"You were asked on the form if there was anything you needed to disclose and it specifically said felonies and misdemeanors." I know this because I read every one of the applications and paid close attention to that particular part. Especially after dimwitted Jim got into my head.

"I didn't think to put it on there," Nate says. "It's not even resolved yet. I still have to go to court for it."

"You didn't *think* to put it on there?" I ask, my eyes going wide.

He huffs out his nose. "Well, I did think to . . . but then I thought it might ruin my chances."

"Oh, my gosh," I say holding my phone to my stomach. "You lied."

"Come on, Holly," he says, sounding exasperated. "It's really not that big of a deal."

The thing with me is I can tolerate a lot. Well, I can't tolerate all that much—but one thing I definitely cannot handle is lying.

To think I was going to come up here and make amends and ask him if we could start over. I mean, if he can hold this bit of info back, what else is he not telling me?

"What else?" I demand.

"What else?" he parrots, leaning against the door, folding his big, muscly arms. Arms that could wrap around my neck and . . . Holy crap, I can't believe I ever thought his too big arms were attractive. Now they look all wrong and gross and maybe a little sinister.

"Yes, what else did you not say on your application?"

He reaches up and rubs his chin with his index finger and thumb as if trying to recall what he wrote on the application.

I think about it too. What else could he have lied about? Then my eyes go wide as I remember how evasive he's been about work. "Do you own a gym?"

This time he has the decency to seem nervous, if only slightly.

"I work at a gym," he says, like this answer will suffice.

"But do you own it?"

His eyes peer down at the floor. "I don't," he says.

"Oh, my gosh, I knew something was going on there. I knew it," I say, my voice suddenly shaky.

He shrugs briefly, like he doesn't care all that much.

"But why? Why would you lie about that?"

He looks up, but not at me; his eyes are focused on something down the hall.

"I just embellished."

"That's lying," I say through my teeth.

He relaxes his arms, standing straight, his form taking up most of the doorway. "Maybe, but everyone does it."

"Lies on applications?"

"Sure. I wanted to go on this trip, so making myself sound a little more appealing so I might have a chance seemed like a no-brainer. It's a sales tactic," he says, one of his big hands gesturing outward, palm up as he states his case.

"A *sales* tactic? Seriously?" I ask, nausea rolling through me. "Is your name even Nathan Jones?"

He looks at me, his head cocked to the side. "Holly, it's on my passport."

I huff out my nose. I don't know what to believe anymore.

"You lied," I say since this seems to be my strongest defense.

"Tell me this, would you have picked me if I had said on my application that I'm part-time trainer, part-time guy who passes out towels?" He stares into my eyes, his face so serious I hardly recognize it. Five days was not long enough for me to see this side of Nate. Which is more fodder for why I should have never done this in the first place.

"Yes, I would have," I say with full confidence. "What would have probably pulled you out of the running is the felony."

"I'm not a felon," he says, his voice louder.

"Misdemeanor, whatever," I say. "The fact is you lied."

"Well, then it's a good thing I left that off," he says.

This is the wrong thing to say and I wonder if Nate's brain decided to leave the building.

"Are you serious right now?" I know my face is probably as red as a tomato, but I don't care.

"I'm not sure what else to say," he says.

"Well gee, Nate, you could start with something like 'sorry I lied'?" I say, wondering who I'm even talking to. It's like everything I knew about Nate went out the window.

"Sorry," he says, but he doesn't sound all that confident.

I shake my head slowly, steadily. "I don't think we can continue this," I say.

"Continue what?"

"The trip . . . this whole thing," I say.

His eyes widen. "Holly, you can't be serious."

"I'm totally serious. You lied . . . and I can't . . . I don't do this," I say as tears fill my eyes.

I turn and run back to my room, Nate calling my name as I fumble to open the door.

Once I finally get inside, I slide down the door and, covering my face with my hands, I cry.

I don't know how long I sit here crying. Maybe an hour. Maybe more. I just let the tears fall. I let them fall for so many things. Being on this trip, not knowing what's going on back home with my job and all the drama there, being lied to by Nate. I cry about Jerry—freaking corner-cutting Jerry. Can I sue him for this? I should on principle.

Once I'm down that rabbit hole I cry about other things. Like the fact that my team probably still hates me and I don't know how to fix it. And my dad is now married, even though I'm honestly happy for him. I cry about Nathan moving on already, despite not wanting him back. I also cry about my mom, which makes me angry because she doesn't deserve tears from me.

I have released the floodgates.

JUST A NAME

My mind keeps going back to my current predicament and the tears start to come even faster when I go there. What do I do now? I knew this wasn't for me—this whole trip—and yet instead of putting my foot down with Quinn, with Marie, I still ended up here, and look where it got me.

Nate and drugs . . . of all things. What were the other options on Mugshot Mondays? I believe it was theft and disorderly conduct. I could have dealt with that, I think. But the drugs hit too close to home. Maybe he was telling the truth—maybe it was just a friend's, but I don't know if I can believe him now. Especially since he lied on the application. I can't handle liars. I have such a limited amount of trust as it is—once someone loses what's there, it's nearly impossible to get it back. That's why I surround myself with people who tell me the truth—some of them don't know how to sugarcoat it. Like Thomas.

Thomas . . . I can't believe him. How could he send that picture out like that? How could he do that to me? But even as I think about it, I know. He didn't think he was causing any harm. That's Thomas. He thought he was being clever and funny—going for the drama of it all. Thomas knew Nate's crime, unlike everyone else who saw the email. He probably didn't think it was that big of a deal, and he couldn't know it would affect me like it did.

I haven't read the rests of the texts. I'm sure they all say the same thing. I did send a note to the group that I was fine and not to worry. Quinn's called me probably ten times since I've been sitting here. I don't want to hear what she has to say. Not yet. She's got to be feeling guilty about all of this. Because unlike Thomas, she does know me. She knows how I'd be reacting right now. It's her fault I'm here. Well, it's a lot her fault.

A knock on my door jolts me back into reality. I know it's Nate. He's been knocking every now and then, trying to get me to talk. I get up off the floor, not to answer it, but because I need tissues to blow my nose. I go into the bathroom and grab the entire box of tissues and bring it out to the bed where I sit down and cross my legs and proceed to blow so hard into the tissue my head feels wobbly.

The knocking keeps going.

"Go away, Nate," I yell at the door.

The knocking doesn't stop and he doesn't say anything. I guess this is his new tactic. Just keep knocking until I'm forced to open the door.

The tactic works, because after a minute of this, I get up and crack open the door.

"I don't want to talk," I say.

But the eyes that meet mine are not Nate's pale blue ones. They're an unmistakable sea-blue.

"Logan?"

"Holly?" he says, his voice full of concern.

"Wha-what are you doing here?" I say, still leaving the door cracked. Logan Palmer is standing at my hotel door. He's wearing his classic outfit of jeans, a plain colored T-shirt, and flip-flops. He's got a backpack on one shoulder and a computer bag on the other.

With my snot-filled head, I almost wonder if I'm somehow home and this whole trip has been a nightmare I'm just waking up from.

No such luck. I'm pretty sure I'm still in London. The question is, how is Logan here?

"Can I come in?" he asks.

I open the door and let him in, my mind still unable to reconcile that he's here.

"What are you doing here?" I ask again. My tone is not demanding, it's more awestruck. It also has a very frog-like quality since I've been crying for who knows how long. I briefly wonder how I must be looking right now. Big splotchy red patches on my face and puffy eyes, I'm sure.

"I flew here," he says as he enters my room and shuts the door behind him.

"I know that," I say. "But . . . why?"

He puts his bags down on the floor and then grabs me by the shoulders, his eyes looking me over, searching my face—as if he's wanting to make sure I'm really here.

"Are you okay? Did he hurt you?" he asks.

"No," I say, shaking my head. "He didn't hurt me. I'm fine."

He drops his hands from my shoulders and then starts pacing the floor back and forth. "Why didn't you answer your phone? Everyone's been worried," he says, his tone full of tension. He looks as if he hasn't gotten any sleep.

I've never seen Logan like this—so frazzled as different expressions cross his face. Expressions I don't recognize since Logan doesn't display many of his feelings.

But this Logan pacing the floor in front of me seems to be having all kinds of feelings right now.

"It's not working," I say, pointing to the bed where my phone is. "I haven't been getting any texts or calls. Not until this morning."

Logan stops pacing and releases a breath like he's been holding it in for a long time. He runs a hand over his face and then looks at me, his hands dropping to his sides. He closes his eyes for a moment and then opens them.

"You're okay," he says as if he's not sure he believes it.

"Yes," I say, trying to convey through my tone that I'm fine. I'm sure my puffy eyes are making it hard for him to believe me. "You came all the way out here," I still don't fully understand how or why.

"I got the email," he says.

"The . . . email?"

"Mugshot Monday."

"Right," I say.

"I saw his face on there and the only answer Thomas had was that it was possession, but he didn't have any other details."

"Prescription drugs," I say.

He exhales out again, his shoulders sagging slightly. "I didn't know what to do."

"So you . . . you flew out here?"

"Well, someone needed to," he says, exasperated.

"How did you find me—how did you find where I'm staying?" I ask.

"Quinn," he says.

I stare down at the ground in front of me, contemplating that. Quinn told him where I was? Why didn't she tell me he was coming? Maybe she was trying to, all those times she called me. But not even a text? A little heads-up?

"Logan, I . . . I can't believe you're here." My eyes find his. I feel tears start to fill the base of my lids and I blink them away. "Thank you."

That doesn't feel like enough, just saying thank you.

Logan's lips form that straight line he always makes. He takes a step toward me and, putting a hand on my shoulder, he pulls me into him and wraps his arms around me, holding me tightly.

I bury my head into his chest and I take a deep breath. He smells of airplane and dingy taxis. But I don't care. He's here. As I let him hold me, the weight I've been feeling since seeing that picture of Nate lifts off me and I feel a thousand times lighter.

CHAPTER 27

The feeling doesn't last long.

I didn't see Nate the rest of the day yesterday. I didn't try to find him, and he never knocked on my door again. At least, not after Logan showed up.

Logan spent the night in my room—on the floor, of course. He offered to get himself a room at the hotel, but by the time we had dinner and came back to the room, the jet lag had hit him hard. I told him he could have the bed, but he wasn't having it.

So Logan Palmer slept in my room. I wish I could go back to Holly from two years ago and tell her this—back to the beginning when I was first dating Nathan and Logan was his cold, aloof self. Younger Holly would never believe it. Oh, sweet two-years-ago Holly. How naive you were.

Honestyl, the current me is still having a hard time accepting it. I almost thought I had dreamed he was here until I woke up this morning and saw him on the floor only a few feet from the end of my bed, his chest rising and falling as he slept.

Last night during dinner, Logan wanted to know every-thing that happened, so I told him. I left out the kissing bits because I doubt Logan would want to know. Plus, I'm hav-ing a hard time believing I did it, now that I've taken a step back from it all and seeing the whole thing through differ-ent eyes.

Even more odd, the kissing felt—in a way—like a be-trayal to this man who traveled all this way to, well, rescue me. That's what he did, didn't he? I mean, I'm no damsel in distress; I could have handled it on my own. But having Lo-gan here and not having to do this by myself has me feeling relieved, in a way. It doesn't make any sense that I've be-trayed him by kissing another man—yet that's where my mind keeps going.

Logan was mostly interested in what happened after I confronted Nate, after I saw his picture on the Mugshot Monday email. I appreciated that he didn't scoff or make me feel dumb for reacting like I did. I didn't tell him exactly why—just that drugs, in any form, don't sit well with me. Or lying. That was two strikes for Nate. Two big ones.

If anything, Logan agreed and would have acted the same in my shoes. That's the thing about Logan I realized last night over pizza that tasted a bit like cardboard—he gets me on some level. Maybe on more levels than I've given him credit for.

There was no "you should have listened to me" or "I told you so," nothing of the sort even implied in his tone or his facial expressions. In fact, the only time he seemed to even be upset was when I told him about corner-cutting Jerry and the supposed background checks. That seemed to get his blood boiling. Mine too, actually. Jerry and I will be having words when I get back. Lots of words.

So I went to bed last night feeling so much lighter than I have in a while. But then I woke up this morning and felt the weight of it all again. It was much more stifling this time.

My brain had a hard time turning off once I awoke. I went through many emotions—frustrated, sad, overwhelmed, and an odd sense of failure. That emotion hurt the worst. I've failed this vacation. I can't go back to Orlando feeling refreshed because this trip hasn't been refreshing. It was at first, I suppose, but now it's been tainted. Marie won't like this, and she won't understand. She might even demand I take another vacation . . . or wonder if I'm so tightly wound that I can't ever relax no matter what. That wouldn't bode well for the manager position.

Because I couldn't get my brain to stop bothering me after I woke up, I did what I do best. I take action.

"What are you doing?" Logan asks through puffy and sleep-filled eyes. He's propped himself up on his elbow and is watching me as I frantically pack.

"I'm packing," I say.

"Yes," he says, acknowledging with a head bob at the suitcase I have on the bed and the fact that I'm folding my clothes.

"I'm supposed to be going to Paris today for the second half of this trip." I want to add this *ridiculous, stupid* trip and throw in a few cuss words for good measure, but I don't.

"Okay," Logan says. "What about that . . . Uh, Nate." He says his name like it's hard for him to get out.

"I don't know," I say. "I guess I should talk to him."

"Is he going with you?" he asks, his voice sounding tentative with a hint of irritation.

"No," I say. "Because I'm not going."

"You're not?"

"No." I start picking up clothes and haphazardly folding them and putting them in the suitcase. "I think I just need to go home. This trip has been . . . well, it was a mistake. I think I should call it good and go home."

Logan sits up. The blanket that was around him falls down so his shirtless self is in full view. It's a good view — a great view, actually. I purposefully avert my eyes and focus on my packing since I don't need to be looking at Logan's naked chest and my mind doesn't need to be wandering off like it is. Like, wondering how it would feel to touch him, his toned and muscled torso under my fingertips. Or maybe, you know . . . lay my head on him.

Get a grip, Holly.

I've gone mad. That's what's happening here. I've finally flipped a switch and have lost my mind. I was kissing another man not even days ago, and now I'm in my room with a different man — one who flew across an ocean to make sure I was okay — and my mind is now conjuring up the craziest of things. I should get therapy when I get home.

"What if," Logan says, pulling his knees up to his chest and wrapping his arms around them. *Yes, that's good, cover that thing up.* "What if I come to Paris with you?"

I drop the shirt I was attempting to fold and it lands on the floor, missing my suitcase completely.

"What?" I ask, thinking I heard him correctly, but not entirely sure.

"Why don't you still go to Paris," he says, his voice low and quiet, "with me?"

I stare at him for a moment. He stares back.

"You want to go to Paris . . . with me?" I ask.

I know Logan kissed me and I remember what my friends said after he did. Specifically, Thomas's words are running through my mind right now. But for two full years, I was under the impression — a very strong one — that Logan Palmer hated me. No, that he couldn't even stand to be in the same room as me. Whether that was out of "boundaries" or whatever he keeps calling it, or if it was because of some unrequited feelings like Thomas said, it's kind of hard to reconcile that he's sitting on the floor of my hotel room, half naked, telling me he wants to go to Paris with me.

"I don't think so, Logan," I say.

"Why?"

"Why? Because . . . because this trip has turned out to be a disaster. And I think I just want to go home." I pick up the shirt I dropped and put it in my suitcase.

He gets up from the floor and walks over toward me, his torso now in complete view, his pajama bottoms hanging nicely on his hips. I swallow hard as he approaches and find myself wishing he would put a shirt on.

He stands near me, resting his hands on his hips, his eyes on mine.

"What can you do at home? Go back to work?" he asks.

"Well, yeah," I say, taking my eyes off his body since I just realized I've been staring, and resume my packing.

"But aren't you supposed to be on vacation?" he asks.

"Sure, but—"

"Wasn't it your boss who wanted you to take this trip?"

"Yes, but—"

"So," he puts a hand on my arm and I look up at him once again. "Finish the trip . . . with me."

"Why?"

"Why?" he echoes.

"Yes. Why do you want to go?"

He gives me a half-shrug. "I've never been. And I'm here."

I let out a breath and then, pushing my suitcase over to give me some space, I sink down on the edge of the bed. We've both never been, and he *is* here. I have a train ticket and two hotel rooms booked in my name.

"I don't know, Logan," I say, still conjuring up reasons why it's better if we just go home. "I mean, don't you have work to get back to?"

"I have some time," he says.

He sits down next to me, pushing the mattress down with his weight, the force of it making us lean into each other. I don't think he meant to sit so close, but he doesn't try to move even with his leg and arm pressed up against mine.

"If you want, I can provide a background check," he says after a few beats of silence, only the hum of the air conditioning bouncing around the room. The corner of his mouth pulls up. He's teasing me.

I laugh, louder than I mean to, and it feels good. "Too soon, Palmer," I say and punch him lightly on the arm.

"I have good references," he says, and then he does the oddest thing I've ever seen him do — he winks. Logan winks at me. It does things to my stomach. Twisty, strange things.

"So, what do you say?" he asks, his voice low and soft.

I let out a breath. I envision myself home and sleeping in my bed — my very own bed. It sounds so amazing right now. Even the thought of getting off the plane, the muggy summer Orlando air surrounding me, sounds welcoming. Then I picture myself in Paris with Logan. Winking-naked-torso Logan. Seeing the sights, eating pastries. And although it doesn't sound as great as being home — it does sound . . . interesting.

"Let's go," Logan says. "And if after a day or two you still want to, we can go home."

We . . . home. Why do I like the way he says that? Why does putting those two words near each other make the hairs on my arms stand up? Therapy. Must get therapy.

I cover my face with my hands. There are a gazillion reasons to go home, and very few to stay here.

Logan nudges me with his elbow and I release my hands.

"Okay," I say.

"Okay?" he repeats, sounding as if he didn't expect me to say yes.

"Yes," I say a note of resignation in my voice. "I'll go to

Paris. But—" I say, holding out a finger. "I get to plan every-thing. Where we go, what we do, where we eat—every-thing."

"I wouldn't want it any other way," he says, his lips pulling up into a smile. Not the grand one—but one that still does funny things to my insides.

"Okay, then," I finally say after I shake myself out of the trance that is Logan's smile. "I just have one thing I need to do."

"Are you serious?" I ask, gaping at Nate, baffled by what he's just asked me—by the entire conversation, actually. He's got some nerve, that one. I suppose I'd be impressed if I didn't want to poke him in the eye.

We're in the small entrance of the hotel, where I told him to meet me. Logan is standing off to the side, watching. He wanted to be here with me—standing next to me like some sort of bodyguard, but I told him I'd be fine and to give me a minute to figure things out with Nate. I'm not scared of Nate, but I don't mind having Logan here for the support.

"I just figured since I'm on this trip too, that the money the station gave you for food and stuff for the both of us—half should be mine," he says.

I gawk at him. I have no words, really. I don't want to argue, and I suppose he has a point. I grab my purse, quickly counting what's left of the cash, and give him half.

"Well," he holds out a hand after pocketing the money.

"I guess this is goodbye," he says.

"I guess so," I say, taking his hand and shaking it.

We've mutually decided to part ways. I found this initially annoying because I wanted to be the one to tell him that the rest of the trip was not happening — at least not together — but apparently Nate had come to that same conclusion as well.

As it turns out, he's going to stay in London for the rest of the trip. Or maybe longer, so he said. Apparently when I wouldn't talk to him yesterday, he went out and did some exploring around the city on his own and he "met someone." And they "totally clicked," according to him. So I guess he's going to stay here and explore . . . all that.

I did not see that coming. There have been a lot of things in my life recently I did not see coming.

To think I kissed this man — made out with him, even. I'm not proud of myself. Lesson learned, though — always go with your gut. Don't talk yourself down even if you think you're reaching. I'm going to listen to the voice from now on, even if it tells me to jump off a bridge. It clearly knows better than me.

CHAPTER 28

Quinn: Heads up, Logan is on his way there.

I got this text the morning of our second day in Paris, I'm guessing a couple of days after she sent it. Stupid phone.

It was too little, too late. And I'm actually okay with it. Paris is . . . well, I don't regret coming here. Not so far, at least.

It was love at first sight. Well, technically it was after we'd taken the train from London, then a taxi ride to a quaint café that came highly recommended online where I had the best chocolate croissant I've ever had. *Then* I realized I was in love. So maybe it was love at first pastry.

I wonder if I had gotten the text before Logan showed up how different this would have been. Would Logan have been able to talk me into this if I'd known he was coming? If I'd had time to consider everything? I'm not sure what I would have done, honestly.

Regardless, so far I'm glad Logan talked me into coming here, to finishing the trip. I'm even glad to be here with him.

He fits in well with the French. They don't smile all that much either.

That's generalizing, I realize—but I mean it in a good way. In my not-so-educated opinion—which only consists of a day and a half or so of research—the French aren't rude so much as they're straightforward. They know what they want, and they don't give their smiles away freely. You have to earn them. I bet if we looked it up, Logan's ancestry would be mostly French.

For Logan's part, he's been very patient with me, letting me plan it all and then drag him around. After we arrived from London and I fell head-over-heels for that croissant, we went to Sacré-Coeur and saw amazing views of the city, Eglise Saint Pierre—one of the oldest surviving churches in Paris, and some of the covered passages where we browsed through shops that can only be found here. Logan was a champ about the whole thing. He even held my purse while I tried on this gorgeous dress I saw in one of the boutiques we passed.

This morning we got up and headed to Versailles, where we toured the palace and the amazing gardens. I wish we had at least another half day to see more. It was amazing.

After Versailles, we headed back to the Latin Quarter where our hotel was and grabbed some dinner, and then walked along the Seine.

Logan's been a pretty great traveling partner. Maybe vacation Logan is more talky, because it's never felt like there's been a lack of conversation with him. We've talked about families, a little bit about work, and we've even dabbled in politics and religion. We have a lot more in common than I thought we would. Which makes me feel like we wasted a lot of time when Nathan and I were dating. We could have had real conversations if he would have just tried. We could have been friends. Logan and his stupid boundaries.

I find that I keep stealing glances at him—still wondering how this all happened, how we ended up together in Paris. Even on day two, I still haven't wrapped my brain around it. I mean, I know how it happened. But how did *this* happen?

Normally I would have called Quinn to talk about it, but she's off the grid at fat camp. She warned me before I left that they weren't allowed to have cell phones with them.

Truthfully, I don't need my friends knowing I'm here with Logan. Not right now, anyway. They'll find out soon enough. For all they know, I sent Logan home and went to Paris with Nate the felon. I know he's not really a felon, but it feels more dramatic to call him that.

"Is this boring for you?" I ask Logan as we walk along *Rive Gauche*—the left bank of the Seine.

It's dusk and the cobblestone pathway is not quite so crowded. Mostly people are sitting in groups near the banks or off to the side on some of the grassy areas. Some are on blankets having picnics, and some seem to be there for the view, relaxing as they watch the colors of the sky change from oranges and pinks into the dark blues of twilight.

"I'm not bored," Logan says, walking next to me, our

pace now relaxed after I made him rush around Versailles today.

"But wouldn't you rather be cliff diving or jumping out of a plane or something?"

Nathan and Logan were always off doing random adventurous things. Deep sea diving, diving with sharks, night diving in Devil's Den . . . there was a lot of diving. It's Florida, after all. Not a ton of high mountain adventures there, unless you consider riding Everest at Disney World a high mountain adventure, which you shouldn't.

It bothered Nathan that I didn't want to do any of the daredevil things he and Logan did, but it never appealed to me.

I see Logan lift his shoulders briefly. "I like doing those things, but I also like doing this."

"Nathan didn't like that I'm not very adventurous, did he?" I say. I know the answer to this already, but part of me wants to know if he ever said anything to Logan. I don't know why I ask; it's not as if I'm fishing for information to win Nathan back. I don't want to be with Nathan. Not anymore.

"He never really said," Logan says.

"Liar," I say, and that earns me a half Logan smile.

"He may have mentioned it a time or two."

"And what did you say to that?"

"I told him he was being an idiot," he says, his eyes focused on the pathway in front of us.

We walk in silence for a bit after that because I don't know how to respond. I want to ask Logan so many things, but I also don't. Like, if he was creating "boundaries" or whatever, then why did he have to be so standoffish, so rude? You can create boundaries and still be a nice person.

"Why don't you like it?" he asks.

"The daredevil stuff?"

"Yeah."

I lift my shoulders briefly, blowing air out of my nose. "I like having my feet on the ground."

"Did you try something and get hurt?"

"No," I say.

"Then you've formulated your opinion on what?"

I peer down at my feet, one foot moving in front of the other as we walk. "My mom was into all that."

"So?"

I look over at him, furrowing my brow. How does he not understand that? But then I remember Logan probably doesn't know all that much about my mom. Not many people do.

"My mom isn't someone I aspire to be like."

"Right," he says, understanding dawning on his face. "And you think if you do something adventurous—something like she did—that she might approve of it?"

I think about this for a beat. "I guess. I mean, it's not like she would know since I haven't seen or talked to her in over a decade."

"Then why?"

I feel the churning of my stomach—the feeling I usually get when my mother is the topic of conversation. "I just don't want to be like her," I say.

"I get that. My dad chose a hard life."

I'm quiet, wondering—or maybe hoping—he'll say more. I feel like getting Logan to open up is like peeling a mango with your fingernails, it's hard to do.

When he doesn't say anything, I say, "How's that?"

"He was always working different jobs; we never knew if food would be on the table."

"Oh," I respond. When I was dating Nathan, I had thought maybe the fact that Logan and I were both raised without moms would be some common ground between us—something that would help us become friends or at least be friendly. But from what I gathered from Nathan, and from what Logan's saying now, it seems we had very different upbringings.

"That's why you're so driven, then," I say after a few seconds.

"I work hard because I don't ever want to live like that again," he says.

"And I like structure and keeping my feet on the ground because I don't want to be like my mom."

There. I guess we do have common ground.

"How old were you when she left?"

"Nearly twelve."

"And you haven't seen her since then?"

"Nope," I say. "We talked a couple of times on the phone when I was a teenager, but that's it."

"Do you know where she is now?"

"Only because my dad keeps tabs on her."

"Where is she?"

I sigh. Do I tell him? I could give him the answer I give everyone else, which is *last I heard she was in North Carolina*. I've never said the truth out loud to someone other than my dad. Part of me wonders if it would be freeing to just say it. Logan is the perfect person — being the man of few words that he is. I know he will keep my secrets.

I let out a long exhale as I ramp up the courage. "She's . . . in jail, actually."

I don't know what I expect Logan to do. If it were Quinn, she would have screamed "WHAT?" so loudly it would have echoed down the Seine, disrupting the family of ducks currently swimming near us.

Logan keeps walking, nothing but stoicism on that handsome face of his.

"What for?" he asks.

"Um, she stole from a pharmacy," I say. It feels weird to say out loud, but it also doesn't punch me in the gut like I thought it would. "More than once, apparently. I guess she was self-medicating or something."

"Oh," he says, dipping his chin just once.

He doesn't seem taken aback by this info at all, and I wonder what would surprise Logan. If I told him the sky were falling would he give me a one shoulder lift and that would be that?

"Nathan —"

"I never told him," I cut in, knowing what he was about to say since this might have been something Nathan would have told him. Nathan wasn't the best secret keeper.

"Were you afraid to tell him?"

"No," I say. "More like embarrassed."

He glances up at the sky, tilting his chin upward. "So that's why with that Nate guy . . ."

"Yep," I say.

"You're not her, you know," he says after a beat or two of silence between us.

"My mom?" I chuckle sardonically. "Well, I'm half her."

"I'm half my dad, but that doesn't mean I'll someday turn into him. Even if I made the same choices."

"That's because we both work hard to not be like them."

"I don't work hard so I won't turn out like my dad," he says, turning his face to mine, his pace slowing as he does. "I work hard because I see the life he leads and I don't want that for myself."

"How's that different?"

Logan breathes out his nose, his chest falling as he does. "Because," he says, "there's a difference in working to not have the same life as someone, and choosing a completely different life because you're afraid you might turn out like them."

"I'm not doing that," I say, my response instant.

He gives me one of his signature Logan half smiles. The one that verges on a smirk.

"I'm not," I say emphatically and slightly annoyed. "I'm not scared, I'm . . ." I trail off as the voices in my head start arguing back in forth.

Do I do that? Do I purposefully keep my life the way it is because I don't want to be like my mom? Or is it because I'm afraid I'll become her? Like someday a switch will turn off—or on—and I'll be just like her.

"Wow, Logan," I say after I realize this might be too big for me to think about. Yes, this is definitely too much for me to contemplate right now as we walk along the Seine, the setting sun forming rays around the Notre Dame Cathedral not far in front of us.

"Wow, what?" he says, his face turned toward mine, his eyes squinting at me.

"I never pegged you for a deep guy," I say.

"I'm deep," he says, his voice a protest.

"And funny," I say flatly.

"That too," he says, not getting the sarcasm in my tone. Or at least pretending he doesn't.

"And a stalker," I say.

He laughs, this time a little more than his low and soft signature chuckle. A tingle shoots down my back, reminiscent of the time he kissed me, and I feel my cheeks warming at the thought.

"Well, you know what I have to say about stalkers," he says.

"I sure do."

CHAPTER 29

I had time to think about what Logan said. A lot of time, since I couldn't seem to get comfortable in my hotel bed. It felt like a whole different bed from the first night here. Like it had been switched out for a harder mattress. Or maybe it was my brain not being able to shut off.

I see what Logan's getting at, but I also don't see his point. So what if I've made some choices out of fear? They still got me where I am, didn't they?

Logan seems well rested when we meet downstairs for breakfast on our last day in Paris. Tomorrow we fly back home — back to reality. I'll finally be done with this trip and can get back to my life.

I should be ecstatic by that thought — going home and getting back to my life — but instead I feel an odd sense of disappointment. This trip was a bust, at least for the first half. But this part, well, it's been good. Great, even. I find I'm not as enthusiastic about being home as I should be. Or at least, as I think I should be.

JUST A NAME

"What's happening today?" Logan asks, pulling me out of my thoughts. He pours some milk into his coffee.

"First up, the Eiffel Tower," I say, trying to do my best impression of an announcer, which I fail miserably at.

He nods, his lips staying in that firm line of his. This is Logan's form of agreeing, I've found. He doesn't really have a say since he said I could plan the whole thing, and I'm not deviating from my plans. Not this time, or probably ever again. I've learned my lesson.

We leave the hotel and take an Uber to the tower. I had been doing my best to avert my eyes anytime I saw it since it's hard to travel around Paris and *not* see the Eiffel Tower—it's pretty much impossible, actually. Especially at night when it lights up. But I wanted the full effect when I saw it in person. I wanted to take it all in, so I tried to look away every time it came into view. Which was often.

It doesn't disappoint. It's grand and majestic and very . . . touristy. That part *is* a disappointment because in my research and planning, many people online had said it was less crowded in the morning. Even the Parc du Champ de Mars is much more crowded today. I'd read that most people usually don't show up there until afternoon, where they picnic in front of perfect views of the tower.

I also heard many complaints about the peddlers in the park selling touristy goods, so I had planned to skip this area altogether. But the Uber driver dropped us off on this side, so it couldn't be avoided.

"Look," Logan says, pointing up toward the tower.

I peer up and see someone in a black jumpsuit wearing a bright yellow helmet, and they look like they're floating in the air toward us. On closer inspection, I see that the person is on a line—someone is zip-lining off the Eiffel Tower.

Not long after the person gets to the end of the line, bobbing around as someone helps him or her up onto a makeshift platform about a hundred feet from us, I see another person coming down the line.

"Should we do it?" Logan asks, a smirk on his face because he already knows my answer.

"Hell, no," I say.

He chuckles, low and deep, a closed-mouth smile on his face, and I swear my ovaries quake at the sound. A laugh from Logan is so rare, I feel like I should write it in my diary.

Dear Diary,

Logan laughed today and it did weird things to my woman parts.

Sincerely, Holly.

We skip the ticket line since my planning-self had already purchased tickets online with a set time for us to go up to the top.

The wait for the lifts aren't so bad even with the crowds, so it's not long before we're on the one to the top. I want to start at the top first and then work my way down, ending on the first floor with the glass platform. I figured Logan and his thrill-seeking ways would want to see that. I want to see it too. See? I can be thrill-seeking when I want to be.

When it's controlled and not left to the whims of a wire or a parachute or an oxygen tank.

When we finally get to the top, I look out over the city. It's lovely—even through the grating they've put around the top floor. The fencing ruins all my pictures, so I make Logan take a selfie with me, and to his credit, he makes an effort to smile and not look constipated like he usually does. Then I put my phone back in the small black cross-body bag I have with me and resolve to take it all in, taking mental pictures.

Logan stands near me as we look out on the city, taking in the beauty that is Paris. There are a lot of people up here, but not enough to make it feel overly crowded. Despite the people, there isn't a lot of noise—at least the human variety. No loud talking or laughter. It makes me wonder if everyone is in awe of the view like I am. Like we all just want to take it in, this view below us. It's a peaceful feeling, even with the wind whipping and tossing my hair around.

"What do you think?" I ask Logan, who's also been quiet as he looks out over the city. But that's not rare for Logan.

I turn my head to find him scanning Paris below us, a bland expression on his face. So, his normal look.

"It's nice," he says.

"Nice?"

"Yeah, I . . . like it."

"Wow, Logan. Don't hold back. Tell me how you really feel," I say, a teasing tone in my voice.

This earns me a small smile — with teeth even. I feel tingles spread down my back and out through my arms and legs.

Dear Diary . . .

"Sorry," he says, his lips drifting back to that normal flat line. "I was just thinking."

"About?"

He lets out an exhale. "Work."

"Right," I say. The thought dawns on me that I haven't thought about work once since we've been up here. I don't know if I've thought about it today at all. That's . . . strange.

"Oh, yeah," I say turning my body toward him. "What happened with the AppLee presentation?" I'd totally forgotten about that until just now, and Logan hasn't mentioned it. Not even once. Which is odd, because it's kind of a big deal. The biggest deal for him and Nathan, actually.

He looks at me, his head cocked to the side. "I heard it went well," he says finally.

"You ... heard?" I repeat, removing my hand from his arm. Did something happen between him and Nathan? Has something been going on and I've just been dragging him around Paris, totally oblivious?

When he doesn't respond, I shake my head at him. "Well, you were there, weren't you?"

He looks at me, the corners of his mouth pulling up slightly. He reaches up and rubs the back of his neck. "I was . . . on a plane, actually."

"A flight? Where?" Something nibbles in the back of my mind and my brain flips through scenarios of why Logan would have been on a plane during what is probably the biggest opportunity of his career.

And then my eyes go wide, practically bugging out of my head as I realize what he's just said. Or rather, implied.

Here. He was on a flight here.

Well, not here exactly, since he flew to London. But . . . here.

"You missed AppLee . . . to fly to London . . . to me?" I ask, scrunching my eyes at him.

Logan doesn't say anything; he just gives me one quick head bob.

"Logan," I start, but then I stop myself because I'm not sure what to say. This feels almost like it's too much. Too much for him to do, too much for him to sacrifice, too much for me to accept.

"Wh-why? Why would you do that?" I ask.

He lets out a long breath and then he looks up, locking his eyes with mine. "Nathan handled it."

"But you were supposed to be there and now . . . you're here. Why?"

He blinks twice and then peers out at the city below. "I wanted to be here."

He wanted to be here. He risked the biggest opportunity of his career to be here with me. He flew to a different continent to make sure I was okay. He kissed me on the corner of Church Street. He paid for my freaking coffee for two whole years.

"Logan, I don't know what to say."

This is only because it feels like there so much I want to say, so much I want to ask him. So much I want him to say to me.

But all he does is turn his head to me, lifts one shoulder up and then drops it, and says, "You don't have to."

There should be more excitement as we work our way down the tower, stopping to take some pictures on the second floor, and then to the first floor to see the glass surface where we can see Paris sprawling beneath us. Instead, it feels almost awkward.

I keep peering over at Logan, to see his face. To see if I can read what he's thinking by his expression. But this is Logan, and I'm stupid for even trying. He just has that same bland look he always does.

I know that it's mostly me making this weird. I want to say something, do something to show him what this all means to me. Everything he's done. But I also don't know what this all means to me. It feels so massively huge that I can't begin to work it all out in my head.

Because of this, I find I'm not concentrating after we exit the tower and not paying full attention to where I'm going, so we end up exiting through the park where the zip line is.

Logan stops and looks up at it, watching someone zip down the line from the second floor of the tower, the crowd on the grass oohing and ahhing as they fly overhead.

JUST A NAME

As he looks up, once again I find myself searching his face. Searching for signs of . . . anything. Any facial expression I can garner information from. There's an expression there as he watches another person go down the zip line, one I'm not so familiar with. I'm not sure, but it's almost like longing. There's just something in his stance, something in the set of his jaw as he watches.

There is something I can do for him that would show him how much what he did for me means. Or at least sort of show him, since I don't exactly know what it all means to me.

I tap him on the shoulder. "You should do it," I say with a quick upward tip of my chin toward the second floor of the tower where the zip line starts.

"What?" he turns his face toward me. Then he shakes his head. "No. I'm good."

"Logan," I say, taking a step in front of him and pivoting around so I'm now facing him. "Just go do it."

"I don't want to," he says.

"Oh really? So that look of longing I just saw on your face, that's you not wanting to do this?" I point up to a person zipping over us, whooping and hollering as they go.

The corner of Logan's mouth lifts up ever so slightly. He folds his arms, rocking back onto his heels. "I wasn't longing," he says.

"Yes, you were."

He exhales out his nose, peering back up at the zip line. "I don't know," he says, a smirk slowly appearing on his lips as his face moves back to mine. "Is it on the itinerary?"

I roll my eyes. "No," I say. "But I can be flexible." I wink at him, which I don't think I've ever done before. I feel instantly silly for doing it.

"Okay," he says, his eyes holding steadily on mine. I smile brightly, elated that he's going to do this.

"Great," I say and begin searching the park for a place for me to sit while I wait. Preferably away from the peddlers. Which appears to be nearly impossible as I can see about a dozen only feet from where we are. Luckily, so far we haven't had to fight any off. Probably because Logan doesn't seem approachable.

Logan doesn't move from his spot. He stands there with his arms folded, looking at me. His eyes roaming my face as he does. "I'll go if you go," he says.

Just like that, any elation I had is gone. "What?" I search his face for a smirk, a half smile — anything that would tell me he's kidding.

"Come on," Logan prods, unfolding his arms and letting them hang by his sides.

I gape at him, a little taken aback by the fact that he's even saying this. "Logan. You and I both know that's not happening."

How many times? How many times had he seen me have the same conversation with Nathan — him wanting me to do something like this and me saying no? I think I'd have to have an extra hand or two to count it.

"Why not?"

"Because, it looks not safe. And I can't control how fast I go, and it doesn't look safe."

"You said safe twice."

"That's because it needed to be said twice."

His lips curl up into a grin and oh, dear heavens. It's not fair that his smile does crazy things to me.

"Have you ever zip lined before?" he asks.

I squint at him because I know he already knows the answer to this. "No," I say dryly.

"Then how do you know it's unsafe?" he asks.

"It just looks that way."

"Ever hear of anyone dying from it?"

"Well, no," I say, folding my arms. "But I'm sure I could Google it. And even if not, maybe I'd be the first."

He chuckles, low and quiet. Warmth spreads through me. I've made Logan smile and laugh today. More than once.

Dear Diary . . .

"See, I think you'd like it if you tried it," he says.

"Are you peer pressuring me?" I ask, putting my hands on my hips, jutting my right foot toward him.

"No," he says. "I'm only stating the facts."

"You don't know how I'd feel," I say. "I'd probably hate it."

"Okay, prove it. Try it, and if you hate it, I'll never ask you to do anything like this again."

"Logan," I say, chastising him with my tone.

"And if you do like it," he says and then looks down at the floor and kicks something with his shoe. Then his face moves back up to mine. "Then I get to kiss you."

My breath hitches at that. A quick intake of breath and my heart speeds up a bit.

"W-what . . . I . . . you . . . you can't just throw that out there," I stammer out, trying to keep my brain from traveling back to the last — and only — time Logan's lips have been on mine, which is not an easy thing to do. My mind wants to go there. As do all the butterflies currently multiplying in my stomach.

"Why not?"

"Because."

"Are you worried you'll like it?" he asks, that smirk back on his face.

I shake my head, telling my brain to stop reminding me of his hands on my face, his body pressed up to mine. *Must stop, must stop.*

"No," I say, and then I clear my throat and stand a little taller, trying not to show him his words affected me. Or at least pretend like they don't. "I'm pretty sure I'll hate it."

"Then what do you have to lose?"

"Uh, my life?"

"You won't lose your life, I promise." He takes a step closer.

I let out a breath looking up at another person zip lining above us. "How do you know?" I ask him. "I mean, with the way things have gone on this trip, it might be par for the course."

"Except for Paris," he says.

"*So far*, in Paris," I reply. "I never did do a background check on you."

Logan's lips pull up into a smile. "Come on," he prods.

"Uh-uh," I move my head slowly back and forth.

"Prove me wrong," he says.

I exhale out of my mouth, feeling my shoulders fall as I do.

"You're thinking about it." Logan's smile now morphs into a big, bright grin, his perfect white teeth sparkling in the sunlight. Like a toothpaste commercial. A toothpaste commercial that's trying to convince me to do this . . . and maybe succeeding. Dang it all.

"No, I'm not thinking about it," I say, trying to push away the spell that is Logan's grin.

"You are," he says with a single chin dip toward me. "You're twirling your hair. You do that when you're contemplating."

"I do not," I protest, even though I realize I *am* currently twirling my hair. *S*-word.

He reaches both hands up and places them on my shoulders, squaring my body fully toward his. It's feels like a strange thing for Logan to do. Not for him to be touching me—although that should feel weird, but it doesn't. But the way he's making me look at him, turning my shoulders so I'm forced to see him. That part feels out of character for him.

"What do you say?" he asks.

I reach up to grab some hair again, but then I stop myself. The earnest look in Logan's eyes, that smile that's melting into something less grand but even worse—he looks hopeful. Oh, dear heavens.

I swallow hard and peer up at another person zipping down the line, Logan's hands still on my shoulders. It doesn't appear that daunting from down here. Sure, it looks risky, but more of a controlled risk, if that's even a thing. Certainly not anything like traveling to another country with a stranger who ends up being a fraud. If I can do that and not end up at the bottom of a river, surely I can do this. Right?

"Fine," I say, setting my shoulders back. I try to seem confident, but as I say the word, my heart starts to pick up speed, nervous butterflies flutter around in my stomach.

"Fine?" Logan asks, his eyebrows shooting up.

"I'll do it," I say. I don't think he ever expected me to agree to this and that makes me kind of want to do it more.

I should get therapy.

He eyes me, dubiously. "Really?"

I cock my head to the side. "Yes, really. But if we keep standing here and you keep looking at me like that, I'm going to change my mind."

Without another word, Logan grabs me by the hand, and we head back to the tower.

CHAPTER 30

Holy crap. Logan may have been right.

I feel . . . well, I don't feel like puking as I fly through the air, my hands gripping the bar above me. Some of the onlookers in the park below are clapping and cheering me on. I'm wearing the most unflattering black jumpsuit, a bright yellow helmet on my head, and goggles on my eyes as I zip down a wire in a harness that's currently giving me a wedgie of epic proportions. I should hate it. I shouldn't like any part of this.

But I don't hate it. I don't hate it, a lot.

I almost didn't do it. I nearly called it off when I had to sign a waiver which had words on it like "injury," "disability," and — I kid you not — "death." But one of the guys running the whole thing talked me down. In his thick French accent, he promised that in his entire career, he's never seen anyone get hurt. He appeared all of nineteen, so I question how long his "career" has actually been, but I signed anyway.

Then when we were at the top—on the second floor of the Eiffel Tower, and even after I was all suited up, I briefly considered turning around and making a run for it—in the jumpsuit getup and all. It was that smile of Logan's that did me in. That stupid, mind-melting grin that you'd think would at some point start losing its luster. Especially the more time we spend together. But it hasn't. If anything, it's getting worse. It's very possible his smile might carry magical powers.

Now as I move down the line at a speed I'm fairly confident I don't want to know, the wind on my face, Paris below me, I think I might get why people do this. There's an energy pulsing through me, running through my veins, that I've never felt before. I like it. I don't feel out of control like I thought I would. I just feel exhilarated.

Before I know it, it's over and I'm at the end of the line, bobbing around as they pull me onto the platform and unhook me.

I feel like . . . well, still me. The me who just zip lined off the Eiffel Tower. My friends will never believe I did this.

I've only done it once, and I'm still feeling the adrenaline pumping through me, but I could probably do this again. I think. I don't know. All I do know is I liked it.

I take off my gear, and then stand to the side to wait for Logan. I watch him take off, not being able to see his facial expressions from so far away. As he gets closer I can make out the hint of a grin on his lips.

And then I remember our bargain. If I liked it, Logan gets to kiss me. I feel the adrenaline start to pulse through my veins again just as it was starting to taper off.

I have a few options and I need to decide quickly since he's getting closer and closer as each second passes.

First option: I could lie. I could say it was horrible and I never want to do it again. But I'm a terrible liar, and also I'm pretty sure I do want to do it again. I have half a mind to get right back in line now.

Another option would be to tell him the truth and then play it off like I forgot about the kissing part. Or tell him he's off the hook.

Or . . . or I could just let him kiss me.

This thought does all kinds of things to my body. Butter-flies in my stomach start reproducing rapidly and a tingle shoots down my back so quickly it borders on painful.

Before I can make up my mind, before I can make a solid decision, my time is up as Logan has reached the end of the zip line, the line bobbing up and down as he does. He's helped up to the platform by the people working on this end and once he's off the line, he starts getting out of his gear.

I decide, because I'm still not sure what I should do, that first I need to get off this platform. So I take the stairs down to the park and wait for Logan at the bottom.

Not even thirty seconds later, I see him walking down the stairs and the registering of relief on his face when he sees me there waiting at the bottom.

I must have a strange expression on my face because Logan asks, "Are you okay?" as he approaches me.

He eyes me with concern, his brows pulling downward, his mouth slightly open as he searches my face, looking for any signs that I may have been hurt. Like he did when he got to the hotel in London.

I shake my head as if to get myself out of a trance. I give him a smile, not sure what expression my face had taken on while I was weighing my options. "I'm fine," I say.

He doesn't seem convinced. He still looks worried — this man who's done so much for me. This man who I thought hated me, but I'm pretty confident he doesn't, and never did.

"Well?" he asks, after he's satisfied that I haven't broken anything.

"Well?" I echo.

He tilts his head slightly to the side. "You didn't die."

I move my head back and forth slowly. "I didn't die."

"I told you, you wouldn't," he says.

"You did say that."

"So then, did you like it?" he asks.

I don't answer. I take in a steadying breath and then I take a step toward him and, standing on my tiptoes, I grab his face between my hands and kiss him.

It's a quick kiss — a little longer than a peck. I let go of his face after I pull my lips away. My hands falling to my sides, I take a step back from him.

At first, he just stares at me, stunned. But then his lips slowly curve up until those straight white teeth of his can be seen in full view. "You liked it," he says.

I nod once. "I did."

Just as quickly as that grin appeared on his face, it falls. "That wasn't part of our deal."

My eyebrows shoot up. "Yes, it was," I say folding my arms in a pseudo-confident manner. "If I liked it, we kiss."

This was the deal; I know what he said.

Logan moves his head slowly back and forth, his eyes on me as he does. "The deal was *I* get to kiss you."

"Oh," I say breathlessly, unfolding my arms and letting them hang by my sides. That may have been what was said.

I start to nibble on my bottom lip, weighing my options. I could say my kiss counted, or I could let him kiss me again. With that intense gaze he has on me right now, and the echo of feeling his soft lips on mine, I'm kind of thinking the latter is the best option. I should let him kiss me again. It's only fair.

I wait for the voice in my head, the one that warns me that I'm making a bad choice — but it seems silent right now. In fact, the only voice I can hear is the one that's screaming, "Yes! Yes! Do that again!"

So when Logan takes a step toward me, a hand coming up to my face to cradle it, I don't move. When his face moves slowly down to mine, I close my eyes and tilt my head upward.

When I feel his lips on mine, soft and tender, I place my hands on his waist, pulling myself toward him. After only a brief moment of his lips on mine, he gently pulls away, leaving his hands on my face. I slowly open my eyes to find him looking at me. That intense gaze of his makes my insides feel gooey. What I'm feeling the most right now is wanted. Logan wants me. I don't know if it's just for right now, or if this is only the beginning, but I want to find out.

What I do know for sure is that I want more than the one kiss. Right now, I want all the kisses. I want him to kiss me the way he did on Church Street.

I lean in slightly, and this is enough for Logan to get the hint. He doesn't need any more coaxing than that as he crashes his lips onto mine and we go from zero to sixty in mere seconds. Gone are the chaste kisses we shared a moment ago—now his lips move over mine with such fire, such intensity, I melt into them, savoring every part of it. My hands move from his waist and wrap around his back and I pull myself against him. I want to be closer to him; I feel like I can't get close enough. I open my mouth wider to give him more access, more room to explore my mouth with his.

Once again, my mind is blank—void of all its normal distractions. I can only focus on his arms around me, his hands moving from my face to my back as he pulls me closer to him like he too feels we can't be close enough. All the while his lips are hot on mine, taking my breath away, making me feel like I never want this to end.

This must be how it feels to be present, to be in a moment. I think I finally get it.

I like this moment. I like it a lot.

CHAPTER 31

Logan: I'll be at the LJ today.

I'm home. Back in Orlando.

The rest of the day after the zip lining felt almost like something out of a fairytale with all the hand holding and stolen kisses as we took in all we could of Paris. I say almost, because it was with Logan. Fairytales aren't his thing. But I got to see a whole new side of him for the rest of the trip. I could be totally off base, but it felt like a side that only I was privy to. Gone was the awkward inability to touch me. This Logan kept a hand on me at all times, like he was afraid to let me go. And there was a lot of grinning. The toothy kind.

Even the flight back was idyllic, especially when I was able to move Logan next to me in first class. There just so happened to be a seat open next to me, since the person reserved for that seat is still back in London . . . or who knows where.

Now we're back in Orlando and Logan is at the Lava Java and I'm about to walk through the door of CT Anderson Bank and life is back to how it was before. Like old times. Only, it's different times now.

I'm not sure exactly what those different times are. Not where Logan and I are concerned, at least. We never had a discussion about what was going to happen when we got back. But after the flight, when we parted ways last night, Logan left me with a spine-tingling, mind-numbing kiss. And there was no finality in that kiss — it was more a promise of things yet to come.

And I like that notion. I like it a lot.

I have a lot of feelings for Logan. All of them the warm and fuzzy kind. Which, if I think about it, is so weird. I had half expected to wake up this morning — back in my own bed, back to my reality — and something would snap and I'd realize all the vacation warm fuzzies were left in Paris. But they weren't. They're still there, and maybe have grown with all the possibilities ahead of us.

What wasn't warm and fuzzy when I woke up this morning were my feelings about work. Which is a phenomenon I'm having a hard time wrapping my brain around. Maybe it's vacation brain and it's been so long since I've had a real vacation, I've forgotten how that feels.

Regardless, I have a serious case of the Mondays. But on a Thursday. I can't say I've ever felt this way about coming into work before. Like I don't want to be here. Like I'd rather be any place else than here.

JUST A NAME

The only thing that makes me feel somewhat excited about being here is to see Marie. I want her to see post-vacation Holly. I think she'll see a difference because *I* feel different. I can't pinpoint what it is exactly. I just feel lighter, happier, which is probably thanks to Logan and Paris. Had I come home after London, after everything went down with Nate, I would have probably been worse off.

I'm excited for her to see this new me and then I can start taking steps toward my future — toward the CCM position. The strange thing? The idea of the CCM position isn't giving me the excited butterflies in my stomach like they used to.

Maybe zip lining jumbled my brain. Or Logan's kisses did. Or a combination of the two.

There's no grand entrance as I make my way to my floor. Not that I expected there to be. It would have been cool to have a welcome back sign in my office somewhere. Tiffany's team did that for her one time when she was out for a week.

But there's nothing waiting for me when I get to my office and set my stuff down on my desk. I scan the room, with its boring decor and bland color palate. Such a contrast to the things I saw and did these past ten days. It kind of feels . . . stifling in here.

I leave the door to my office open, hoping maybe it's just being back in an office and not out in the world where there's so much to see that's got me feeling this way.

It's definitely vacation brain.

An hour later, though, as I've slogged through a ridiculous amount of emails, I'm not feeling that much better. I haven't even checked on my team yet. I'm actually surprised not one of them has come to my office to see if I'm back.

I decide to rip the Band-Aid off quickly and go see them. Maybe that will get me back into excited work mode, even though managing my team is probably my least favorite part of this job. Not probably. Definitely.

But who knows. Maybe absence has made my heart grow fonder for them, and vice versa. I'm sure it must have been hard being under Tiffany's thumb for the past ten days.

What I see when I enter my team's office, with the sunny yellow paint and the fluorescent overhead lighting, is not what I'm expecting.

They're all working. All of them. Every one of their heads are focusing on their screens, their headphones on, chatting away with what I can only assume are customers. This is not totally out of the realm of normalcy. I mean, it's happened before, but usually I can find at least one of them *not* doing their job. And most of them not doing their job right.

Sarah and Sara both give me small waves when they see me and then quickly focus on their work. I walk around the room observing this phenomenon in front of me.

I stop by Avery's desk and listen in on her call—she sounds … nice? Since when has Avery started using a nice voice with the customer?

JUST A NAME

I walk to the back of the room and . . . wait, what is this? Is Jim wearing a suit? He looks almost professional. I peer over at Brad and even he is looking businesslike with his moppy red hair tamed back with what might be some gel.

What's going on? I'm totally mouth-breathing, my jaw slackened by the scene before me.

As they all seem to be busy working, like some freaky fine-oiled-machine straight out of *The Twilight Zone*, I walk out of their office and leave them to it. Maybe this is all a big prank. Maybe they'll all pop out and say "surprise!" and Jim will have been wearing athletic shorts with that button-up and suit coat. And Brad's hair will go instantly back to its unruly ways.

"Yoo-hoo," I hear a high-pitched, sing-song voice from behind me, and I take a deep breath as I turn around.

"Hey, Tiffany," I say, trying to make my expression pleasant. I was secretly hoping I could avoid her today since I was pretty sure her presence would burst the bubble of happiness from my vacation.

I was not wrong.

"How was your trip, Miss World Traveler?" she asks, all cheesy and fake-like. She's wearing one of her signature suits today, her blond hair pulled back into a sleek ponytail.

"It was good," I say, trying not to scowl at her and her perfectly tailored everything.

Vacation did not cause my heart to grow fonder for Tiffany.

"Have you seen the complaints team yet?" she asks, a bright smile on her face, her eyes practically twinkling with glee.

"I was just in there," I say, with a thumb hitch in the direction of their office behind me.

"What did you think?" she asks, her eyes now dancing around.

"I, uh, I'm not sure what you're asking," I say, even though I have an inkling. And I don't like that inkling.

She smacks her lips. "Holly, you silly—what did you think about your team? They look good, don't they?"

I eye her through half-closed eyelids. "They look like they're doing their jobs."

"Right?" she says, all chirpy and happy-like. "And they're total champs at the PFC report." She pumps a fist in the air twice. Like a cheerleader.

I never liked cheerleaders.

"Good," I say.

"It just took some better training and a little motivation, and they grabbed right onto it," she says. "And now they're like little worker bees. You should be so proud."

There's the dig. I was waiting for it. Better training? Motivation? What is she talking about?

I pull my lips up into a smile—albeit a very fake one. I will not let her dig affect me. Sure, my team does look like they're, well, they're doing their jobs. But I doubt that had to do with Tiffany. It probably had to do with all the prep I did with them before I left. By the look of Tiffany's face, though, I'd say she thinks this was all on her.

Jim walks out of my team's office and sees us standing there. "Oh, hey," he says walking toward us, a small stack of papers in his hand. He has pants on. Real suit pants that match his suit coat. *S*-word.

"There's our Jim," Tiffany says like a proud mom. "Holly, would you look at Jim? That suit coat and tie just look fantastic on you," she says.

Jim preens. He tips his chin upward and sticks his chest out like he's some champion horse.

"I told Jim, here, that if you want to be treated like a professional, you need to dress like one. And now look at him." She beams at him and he beams back.

So much beaming.

"Well, thank you, Tiffany," he says. Then he looks at me. "How was your trip?"

"It was good," I say, feeling a little pride myself. Check out Jim taking an active interest in me. Put that in your pipe and smoke it, Tiffany.

He turns to Tiffany. "Hey, so can I get your signature on these?" he asks.

"Jim," I say, trying to get his attention.

"Yeah?"

"I can sign that for you," I say.

His eyes dart from me to Tiffany, the papers in his hand going from her to me and then back to her. "That's okay, Tiffany knows what these are," he says.

"It's the PFC report," I say, recognizing the front page.

"Yeah," he says, an expression of surprise on his face like I have no idea what that is. Like I never trained him on it in the first place.

"I've got it," Tiffany says, snatching the papers from Jim. "Don't you worry about that, Holly. You've got enough catching up to do."

She signs the papers and hands them back to Jim.

"Thanks, Tiffany," Jim says as he heads back to the complaints team's — *my* team's — office.

"It was good to see you, Holly. Let's catch up soon! I want to hear all about that vacation of yours," Tiffany says, her fake smile ramped up to a fever pitch.

I want to yell, "It'll be a cold day in hell before I tell you, and also I hate you!" but instead I just give her a curt nod.

"Come in," Marie says after I knock on her door.

I peek my head in and smile at her. It's good to see Marie. Her smile is broad, her blond, sleek bob perfectly coiffed as always. She tells me to come in and have a seat.

"You look fantastic," she says after I take a seat in one of the chairs opposite her desk.

"I feel pretty good," I say, feeling my lips pull up as I think about where I was just the day before yesterday — roaming around Paris, hand-in-hand with Logan. Unexpected butterflies prance around in my stomach.

"I told you that you needed a vacation," she says, pointing a manicured finger at me.

"And you were right," I say.

"I like being right," she says, giving me a wink, her hand landing flat on a pile of paperwork in front of her. "I want to hear all about it, but I have a meeting in five minutes, so you'll have to fill me in later."

"Sounds good," I say. Then tentatively I ask, "How did everything go while I was gone?"

She pauses for the briefest of seconds, something crosses her features that instantly gives me an uncertain feeling in the pit of my stomach.

"It went . . . well," Marie says, drawing out her words.

"That's good," I say, trying to keep my voice light and bright.

Marie leans forward, placing her elbows on her desk and intertwining her fingers. She exhales out her nose.

"Here's the deal," she says, my stomach sinking even more. No good news has ever started with "here's the deal."

"Okay," I say, trepidation in my tone.

"I don't have time right now to tell you everything, but Tiffany," she pauses for a moment, like she's trying to gather her words—the right words. "Well, she did a good job while you were gone."

I don't say anything, I just nod. I'm not sure if what she did with my team can be considered good. Okay fine, it might be good. But it also might be hypnosis. Or witchcraft.

"The executive team noticed," Marie says, her lips pulling downward.

I swallow. The executive team noticed. *All the cuss words.*

"So what does this mean?" I ask.

She purses her lips together for a moment. "I'm not sure yet," she says.

"So Mike's position — the CCM job — "

"Mike's given notice," Marie says cutting me off. "But nothing else is set in stone."

I place my hands flat on her desk, setting my shoulders. "Then I have work to do."

She dips her chin once. "That's my girl," she says, giving me a wink.

CHAPTER 32

The following Monday, I find myself walking across the street to the Lava Java to find Logan. I've been doubling down at work, trying to get caught up, and he's had a lot to catch up with as well, but we've found time to see each other a couple of times since getting back and we've been texting back and forth.

But today has been so frustrating that I needed to vent, and also see his handsome face, and maybe kiss him. But mostly I need to vent.

I walk past the counter, giving Denise the barista a quick wave, and then walk right over to Logan—who hasn't noticed my presence—where I proceed to poke him twice in the shoulder.

He pulls off his earphones as he peers up at me and he gives me an odd look. It's a half smile, half concerned expression, like he's happy to see me, but also not sure about it. Perhaps it's the look on my face right now that has him confused.

"That zip lining thing you made me do?" I say, without a greeting of any sort.

The half-smile that was there disappears and is now replaced by downturned lips and brows pulled inward. "Yeah?" he asks, his voice almost tentative.

"Well, it did something to my brain," I say. "I think it might have jumbled it around or something." I reach up and tap my head a few times with my fingers, possibly looking a bit psychotic, which might be the case.

"What's going on?" he asks, stretching the words out and scooting over in his booth, away from the crazy redhead currently hovering above him.

On second glance, I realize he's moved over for me to sit down.

Oh, well . . . okay, then.

I take a seat next to him, placing my hands in my lap. I look around. I've never sat here before, next to Logan. It's the perfect vantage spot in the café, with a view of the counter and the entrance. It's quiet in here right now, only the chatter of a couple of employees.

Logan nudges me with his elbow. Right. I came here for a reason.

"Something is wrong with me," I say, an unmistakable hint of blame in my voice. Because I do blame Logan for this.

He looks at me, waiting for me to explain. I start to forget why I came over here as I stare into those sea blue eyes of his and a feeling takes front and center—one of me grabbing him and making out with him, right here at the Lava Java.

But no, I need to focus because I'm frustrated and it's all Logan's fault.

"What's wrong?" he finally asks after I don't answer fast enough.

I let out a breath. "I can't do my job," I finally say.

He pulls his brows in even more. "You can't do your job?"

"I don't know what's wrong with me," I say, reaching up and grabbing some hair to twirl around my finger. "I thought maybe it was a vacation hangover or something, but then . . ." I trail off, thinking of how I woke up this morning after working through the weekend trying to catch up. Really, I slogged through the weekend, not enjoying any of it. Except for the part when I saw Logan on Saturday night.

I'd figured my feelings toward work would change by now, or at least I'd start to feel inklings of the old me — the me who gets up on Mondays ready for the week. I've never been a Monday-hater. But I didn't wake up feeling motivated in the slightest this morning. I just felt . . . blah. I went for a run, hoping to clear my head, but that didn't seem to help.

It also didn't help that when I finally got to work, the first thing I had to do was my Monday meeting with my team, and they did not seem happy to have me there. It was like it had been before I left. Back to their old ways. Jim was even back to wearing his ratty jeans and overly-worn polo and

Brad's hair looked like he'd stuck his finger in a socket. And the Sarahs hardly paid attention to anything.

It was when—toward the end of the meeting—Brad raised his hand to ask me if I could "get tips" from Tiffany regarding her management style, making me almost throw up in my mouth, that the thought occurred to me: Tiffany is a better manager than me.

This thought also made me almost throw up in my mouth.

I don't want to admit this, but it might be true. I mean, in ten days she whipped my team into shape. I haven't been able to accomplish that in the two years I've been their manager. What does that say about me? I can see the CCM job slipping through my fingers and being snatched up by Tiffany's perfectly manicured ones.

Then I had another thought. If I do—by some miracle—snag this promotion, I won't be managing my team anymore—instead I'll be managing an entire floor of people. Possibly more Jims, and Sarahs, and Brads. It would be a lot more drama, more people to make sure they're doing their jobs, more employees to be in charge of. Is this what I really want?

I tell Logan all this and he just sits there watching me intently.

"So I think that zip lining thing you made me do—I think it messed with my brain." It's the only explanation.

One corner of Logan's lip pulls up ever so slightly. "I doubt it," he says.

I huff out my nose. "Then how do you explain it? This . . . this . . ." I trail off, tapping the side of my head with my fingers again.

He looks at me, his eyes searching my face. "It didn't jumble your brain," he says. "I think it made you realize things."

"Realize things?"

"Sure," he says. "Like the fact that you find me irresistible."

This makes me snort out a laugh. "Is there alcohol in that drink?" I point to the coffee cup on the table near us.

He puts one arm over the back of the booth and rests his other hand on the table, his body angled toward me like he's surrounding me. I could scoot just a few inches toward him, and maybe he'd wrap those arms around me.

Oh, man, maybe I do find Logan irresistible. I almost laugh at the strangeness of that thought.

"Maybe," he says, his voice low and rough sounding — it does maddening things to my insides when he talks like this. "Maybe getting away from here and trying something different made you realize there's a whole world out there. And you've been stuck in yours."

"Oh, look at you, Mr. Psychoanalyzer," I say, my tone dripping with sarcasm.

This makes both corners of Logan's mouth turn up.

"Did you miss your work while you were gone?" he asks.

I pause for a second, taking in his question. "Yes," I say pseudo-confidently.

He angles his head to the side, a disbelieving expression on his face. I twist my lips back and forth and I try to think of a time while I was gone that I missed work. That I missed being back here. And I can't think of one. In fact, in Paris, when I was with this man I'm sitting with right now, I kept forgetting I had a job at all.

"Well, maybe I didn't miss it," I say.

"So it might not have been the zip lining then," he says.

I swallow. "I'm tired, Logan," I finally say, leaning my head back against the booth. I feel his hand — the one he had rested behind me — move so that his fingers could caress my hair.

"So what do you want to do?"

I turn my head toward him. "What do you mean?"

"What is it that you want to do?"

I let out a breath, feeling safe and happy sitting right here letting Logan play with my hair. Can that be my answer? Just stay here?

"I don't know," I say finally. "Obviously, I'll get to work and keep pushing forward."

"You don't have to," he says.

"What?"

"If you don't like it — and it sounds like you haven't in a while — maybe it's not what you really want."

"So, what, I just quit?"

He lifts his shoulders in a brief shrug. "Why not?"

I let out a sardonic laugh. "I can't quit."

"Sure you can. No one's making you stay."

"I'm making me," I say, sitting up, and I immediately regret it as the hair caressing stops. "I've worked too hard for this."

He ponders this for a moment. "It's okay to work hard at something and not have it turn out how you expected it."

"Says the super-successful app designer," I say, holding a hand out toward him, palm up.

And then before I forget, I ask him, "Did you find out about AppLee?" I've been carrying a weight around regarding that and all Logan sacrificed for me. I don't want him to regret coming to Paris. I can't help but wonder if he will, given the stakes.

He shakes his head. "We haven't heard yet. But it doesn't matter."

"Yes, it does," I say.

"There'll be other AppLees."

"How can you say that?"

"Because," he says. "I know there will be."

Therein lies the problem for me. I don't know that there will be more promotions on the horizon if I don't get this one. I don't know what I'll do if the job goes to someone else — or heaven forbid, Tiffany.

"And," he says, "it doesn't matter, because I made my choice."

I look up at him, his face serious, his eyes full of . . . I don't know what, but something not very Logan-like.

"I hear you say that," I say, turning my eyes away from him and focusing on the table in front of us. "But I worry you'll regret it."

"Do you regret it? Going to Paris?"

The thought did cross my mind Sunday morning as I was trudging my way through my work hardly taking breaks to eat since I've been back. The thought that maybe if I would have just left and not let Logan talk me into going to Paris, or maybe if I hadn't gone at all, none of this would be happening.

But even as I had those thoughts, they were quickly pushed away. I don't regret any part of Paris. I don't even regret London with Nate because all of it got me to Paris. Funny how life works like that.

"I don't," I say, pulling my lips up into a smile. "And I hope you get AppLee so you won't either."

He shakes his head, the corners of his mouth turned up thoughtfully. "It won't matter," he says. "I won't regret it."

I snuffle and look away from him. Out toward the entrance of the coffee shop. "You can't know that."

The hand that was on the table moves to the side of my jaw, lightly touching it as he nudges my head to move toward him, to see his face. I let him, and he leaves his fingers there, running a thumb over my cheek.

"I won't regret it," he says.

"You don't know that."

He huffs a frustrated breath out his nose. "I'm in love with you, Holly."

Say what? My eyes go wide at his confession.

"I think I fell in love with you the moment Nathan first introduced me to you."

"I . . . you . . . but . . ." I stammer out, my breath picking up speed, my heart beating practically out of my chest.

His fingers that were caressing my face move slowly, inching their way behind my ear and weaving into my hair. Logan leans into me, bringing his lips to mine in a soft kiss that makes me tingle all over. I reach up and lightly wrap my hand around his forearm.

"No regrets," he says after he pulls his lips from mine. Then he leans in and kisses me again.

"I'm totally lost right now," Quinn says after I've filled in my friends on the events of my life for the past two weeks.

The gang's all here—Quinn, Bree, Alex, and Thomas. I haven't been able to see them, or my dad, since I got back, since I was doubling my efforts at work, trying to prove myself.

I told them everything that happened before the Mugshot Mondays incident—giving Thomas a small but firm lecture on the importance of never pulling a stunt like that again, which, to his credit, he did look somewhat ashamed about. Then I told them everything that happened after. After confronting Nate, and after Logan showed up.

"You zip lined off the Eiffel Tower," Alex says, repeating the last thing I told them, disbelief in his voice.

"I did," I say, feeling quite proud of myself as I tell them this. If for nothing else, the shock value has made it worth it. And they're definitely shocked.

Thomas reaches over and pokes me in the arm like he thinks I'm not real. Like maybe I'm an apparition.

"And then what happened?" Bree asks. She's the member of the group who's the least shocked by this. I think she's still having a hard time getting over the fact that I ditched hottie Nate.

"Then . . ." I trail off, thinking of that kiss with Logan. The one right after the zip lining. The one that made me forget about everything and just be in that moment with him. That was, until we got some catcalling from people in the park. That was sort of embarrassing.

"You're blushing," Quinn says, letting her jaw hang down, her voice accusatory.

Of all my friends, I wish I could have talked to Quinn before we got here. About the trip, about everything. But she only got back from fat camp—or whatever that was—last night, and this was the first time either of us had a moment to talk.

"So, you and Logan . . ." Bree trails off, her eyes going wide.

"Oh, my gosh, this is agonizing," Thomas says, leaning his head back dramatically. "I actually can't remember a time *before* you started telling us about this trip."

"Shut up, Thomas," Quinn says, waving his words away with her hand.

"Did you make out with Logan or not?" Thomas asks.

I try to stifle a smile, but it's no use. They can all see the truth written on my face.

"You did!" Quinn yells loudly, which gets us looks from the surrounding tables.

"And are you like a thing now?" Thomas asks, frustration in his voice.

I nibble on my bottom lip.

"You are!" Quinn yells, possibly even louder this time.

"You're so freaking loud," Thomas says to Quinn. And she gives him a finger — the middle one.

"It's all new, you guys," I say, keeping my voice low. So new that I didn't bring him with me tonight. I knew I needed to let my friends get the crazy out before I invited Logan to hang out at Hester's with us again.

"Oh, my gosh," Quinn says. "Look at you. You're like . . . glowing. I'd like to take some credit for all this." She gives me a crap-eating smile.

I give her one back. "Yes, you do get *all* the credit for Nate."

"That was Jerry's fault, not mine," she says.

"But it was your idea."

"Yes, but it all worked out and that's what you should thank me for." She sticks her tongue out at me.

"You're lucky it did," I say.

"Hey, you saved me, and I can't thank you enough for that," she reaches her arm around me and gives me a quick, tight, side hug.

The whole trip did work in Quinn's favor — the news station seems to be off her back over the viral video and are thrilled with the ratings the whole trip brought in. They never mentioned on air anything about Nate or what happened there. As far as the viewers know, we had a great time and that was that.

"So what about work?" Alex asks. "Word around the office is that Mike is leaving and it's between you and Tiffany for the job."

I nod my head. "Yep, that's the word."

"You don't seem very excited," Quinn says.

I sigh. "I am," I say disdainfully.

"You should quit that stupid job," Thomas says.

"What are you talking about?" Quinn asks.

"It's so boring," he says while inspecting his fingernails.

"How would you know?" I ask. Even though that thought has been going through my mind as I worked through the weekend and all today.

"It's just so . . . blah," he says. He looks around the table. "Like I'm a lawyer, Quinn's a news reporter—"

"And internet famous," Bree pipes in, which gets her a dirty look from Quinn.

He points a finger at Bree, "that too. And Alex is a . . . wait, what do you do Alex?"

"Marketing," says Alex, his voice monotone.

"Right, Alex does marketing. And our dear Bree, here, serves food to the stars," he says with a palm out toward Bree.

Bree nods her head because this is true. She's served all kinds of celebrities, and partied with some of them.

"And what do you do?" Thomas says, tilting his head as he looks at me. "You work in a call center." He says this like it pains him.

"She manages a call center," Quinn says, trying to make it sound better, but it doesn't help.

I stop myself from piping in and specifying that I only manage a small part of the call center, because that would not help my plight.

"Sorry to bore you," I say to Thomas.

"Well, I'm only pointing out the obvious," he says. "I mean, there are other jobs out there, Hols."

These are the words that Logan said after he kissed me soundly in the booth at the Lava Java.

There are other jobs out there.

This thought has been spinning around in my head, playing on repeat. The most annoying earworm ever.

"So tell me, oh wise Thomas, what could I do that would make you more proud?" I say, my voice mocking.

"I don't know," he says on an exhale. "We could use someone in the group who can bake stuff." He scans the group and everyone nods, since not one of us can cook or bake.

"Hard pass," I say.

"You'll figure it out," Thomas says.

I laugh out my nose. "I'm not leaving my job," I say. "Definitely not for your reasoning."

"Have it your way," he says, adding an eye roll for emphasis.

CHAPTER 33

The following Monday, the funk I'm in doesn't get better. It actually gets much, much worse.

The lack of motivation isn't improving at all. I've now found myself daydreaming at work. Me. Daydreaming. I've never been one to fantasize like that, but I can't help myself. I picture myself in Paris with Logan. Walking hand-in-hand through the Louvre. Taking a picture of him next to his twin—the Mona Lisa. He didn't find it funny when I did that, but I sure did.

Maybe it's because I need to go to a happy place when I'm with my team—with whom my relationship hasn't improved. In fact, if and when they do another manager assessment, I doubt it will be any better than last time. It might even be worse.

A little voice in my head keeps chirping over and over, asking me what all this was for. If nothing at work changed—the reason I took the vacation in the first place, well, the biggest reason—then where did it go wrong? Why do I feel worse off in my career now that I'm back? Rather than refreshed, excited, renewed, ready to tackle whatever is put before me? What did I learn from all of this?

The answer is on my mind as I take the stairs up one floor to Marie's office. I've asked to meet with her this afternoon.

"Hello," I say, after knocking and hearing her tell me to come in.

"Have a seat," she says, pointing to the chair across from her desk.

"How are you?" I ask as I sit down. I give her a smile, looking at her over the pale desk that separates us.

"I'm good," she says. "You?"

I smile what feels like might be a sad smile. "I've been better."

She leans an elbow on the arm of her chair, resting her chin on a closed fist. "You're different since you've been back," she says.

I nod once. "I know. I think I have a serious case of vacation brain," I say.

She chuckles at that. "I think it goes deeper than that."

I look out the window of her office, watching the planted palm trees swaying in the wind. "I think you're right."

"So tell me," she says.

I exhale loudly, my shoulders coming up as I do. I turn my face away from the window and look at this woman sitting across from me—Marie, who has been such a great boss and has taken me under her wing and guided me like a pseudo mom, in a way.

"I don't think I want the CCM job," I say. It's the first time I've said it out loud—actually admitted it to anyone, and it doesn't feel wrong. It feels a lot like zipping down that line in Paris. It feels freeing to say those words out loud.

She nods her head. I half expected her to try to talk me out of it, but then I realize this is Marie, and she's always had my best interest at heart.

"I think," she stops herself, pursing her lips together as if she's not sure how she wants to say what needs to be said. She places her hands in her lap. "I think that's a wise choice. Not because I don't think you can do it—I have full faith in you, Holly, I always have. But because I think you can do better."

I close my eyes for a second, the feeling of tears starting to pool at the bottom of my eyelids taking over.

I can do better.

"So now what?" she asks when I open my eyes and try to blink away the tears.

I lift my shoulders and then drop them. "I have no idea," I say.

She breathes out through her teeth. "Now that," she says, shaking her head slowly back and forth. "That sounds like a lot of fun."

I don't go back to my office after my meeting with Marie. I walk straight over to the Lava Java. But when I get to the corner, I see Logan is just walking out, his computer bag over his shoulder, a hand in the pocket of his dark denim jeans.

"Hey," I say, waving a hand at him to get his attention.

He lifts his chin once when he sees me and starts walking toward me.

"Are you leaving?" I ask.

"Yeah," he says.

I lick my lips, feeling slightly unsure of myself. "Want some company?"

He lifts his eyebrows. "Sure," he says. "But don't you have work?"

I smile at this man — this man who means so much to me, more than I ever thought he would. "I think . . . I think I may have just quit my job." I expect a sick feeling to fill my stomach when I say this, but instead I feel lighter, breezier, maybe even happier.

Logan's lips pull into that smile of his, teeth and dimples and all. The very one that does wonders to my insides.

"So, now what?" he asks.

"I don't know," I say, throwing my hands up in the air, palms toward the bright blue Orlando sky.

He pulls his hand out of his pocket, grabbing me by the waist as he pulls me into him, his lips landing on mine so quickly, so soundly — right here on the corner of Church Street.

Right now, in this moment, not knowing isn't so bad. I kind of like it. A lot.

EPILOGUE

Logan

There's too much distraction in this coffee shop. Too much chatter at the counter, too much whirling, fizzing, and grinding from the coffee machines. All this noise didn't used to bother me.

Or maybe it's *her*.

Holly. Sitting across the booth from me, staring at her laptop, her finger twisting some of her red hair as her other hand moves a wireless mouse.

She's the one distracting me. And I don't have time for distractions. Too much to do. She might have to go somewhere else. Even though that's the last thing I want.

I don't want her to be anywhere else but with me. That's all I've wanted since the day I met her—since the day Nathan introduced us at that bar in Winter Park. The one I haven't been able to go back to since.

Remembering how it felt to see her on his arm, this woman that I knew right away was not meant for my best friend, still makes me sick. I'd never bought into love-at-first-sight or any of that crap. Not until that day. And I had to watch all of it—feel all of it—for two years.

She doesn't know all that, though. I'll tell her someday. I'll tell her how I used to avoid hanging out with the two of them. How I couldn't have a conversation with her because I was afraid I'd give too much away.

There's a lot of things Holly doesn't know right now. Like where she'll work next. Or what her future holds. She doesn't like that—not knowing. She also doesn't know that we're getting married. Not right now, but someday. Because this is it for me. Holly is it. I won't ever want anyone else. I'd ask her to marry me right now if I didn't think she'd run straight out the door of the Lava Java.

"Why are you staring at me like a creeper?" she asks, not even looking up from her laptop.

"I'm not," I say, keeping my face from responding like it wants to. I've learned to have a pretty good poker face after having to watch her and Nathan together.

"Yes, you are," she says, still not looking up.

I reach up and scratch the side of my neck. "It's because you have something on your face and I was trying to figure out how to tell you."

Her green eyes shoot up to mine, her hand coming up to cover her mouth and nose. But she drops the hand away and her shoulders slouch when she sees the smirk on my face.

"Jerk," she says, her lips pulling up into half of a smile.

The side of my mouth pulls up in return and then I make my eyes move back to my laptop. My screen has gone to sleep. She really is a distraction.

This isn't the first time my screen has timed out since we've been sitting here. I've stolen glances as we've sat across from each other, each working on our own computers. Well, like I've said, she's been doing most of the working. I need to be working. I've got loads to do for the Applee purchase that we found out about last week. Holly has been less distracted than me. At least it seems that way. But she's also determined to find something for work. Or to start something. Whatever it is, she'll do it right.

Her friends keep asking how Nathan is dealing with all of this—me and Holly. I tell them he's fine with it. They don't believe me. I don't know how to make them see that it's Nathan. Cool, calm, rarely-lets-anything-bother-him Nathan. He knows how to compartmentalize like no one I've ever known. It's a talent. And he's really fine with it all. He's happy for me. He even helped me find the plane ticket to go to London to find her. I knew that's how he'd be. Because I know Nathan. So there was no fighting, no drama. Her friends aren't buying it. I don't really care what they think, as long as Holly is with me.

Without permission, my eyes travel back to her face. Maybe I *am* a creeper. This time, though, Holly's eyes lock with mine. She gives me a sly grin and I hear the sound of a flip-flop falling on the cold tile floor. Then I feel her foot on my lower calf, her toes slowly making their way up to my knee. Her smile morphs into something more devious, and I have to take in a steadying breath.

"You're going to have to leave," I say, keeping my poker face on, my voice flat.

"Why?" She asks, a smirk forming on her lips.

"Because you're a distraction."

"Am I? Well, too bad."

I pull my eyebrows down. "Too bad?"

"Yep. I'm here," she says, her face turning more serious. "And I'm not going anywhere."

My lips pull up into a smile—the full one that I know she likes. The one she might even love.

I can get used to distractions.

THE END

ABOUT THE AUTHOR

By day, Becky Monson is a mother to three young children, and a wife. By night, she escapes with reading books and writing. An award-winning author, Becky uses humor and true-life experiences to bring her characters to life. She loves all things chick-lit (movies, books, etc.), and wishes she had a British accent. She has recently given up Diet Coke for the fiftieth time and is hopeful this time will last... but it probably won't.

Other Books by Becky
Thirty-Two Going on Spinster
Thirty-Three Going on Girlfriend
Thirty-Four Going on Bride
Speak Now or Forever Hold Your Peace
Taking a Chance
Once Again in Christmas Falls